QUEEN TAKES ROSE

A WICKED VILLAINS NOVEL

KATEE ROBERT

TRINKETS AND TALES LLC

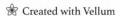 Created with Vellum

ALSO BY KATEE ROBERT

CONTENT WARNING

This book contains depiction of the death of a comatose parent (mother). This may be triggering for some readers.

1

AURORA

Everyone talks about hope like it's a silver bullet. As if it's enough to keep a person putting one foot in front of the other even in the most impossible situations. As if hope alone can see a person through anything.

Once upon a time, I even believed it.

Back when I was young and foolish and, even though the world had kicked me in the teeth time and time again, I somehow kept the stars in my eyes. I was so sure that if I could just believe hard enough, that if I could hold on to *hope*, one day my mother would wake up.

I didn't realize that hope could sour, could slowly go dark and begin to poison every bit of me. I couldn't have known that I'd learn to hate through virtue of that faltering light.

The woman in the hospital bed is my mother, but she might as well be a stranger. Even before a fight for dominance put her in a coma, she was more fantasy than reality to me. Nothing more than a promise of a relationship *later*, when I was older, when I could handle myself without being a liability. I just had to be a good girl and obey my grand-mother and eventually my mother would send for me.

Another hope, dashed to pieces at my feet.

Twenty years later, and it's finally time to admit that she's never waking up. It's time to make the decision I've put off for far too long. It's time to finally let her go.

"Aurora."

I suck in a breath and turn to Allecto. She's the only other person who knows everything there is to know about my bargain with Hades, knows all the dirty little details of how I got to this place. Of who's to blame. "I'm fine."

"No, you're really not." She states it as fact, without a bit of pity. I appreciate that bluntness. Allecto won't coddle me or tell me pretty lies. It's one of the reasons she's my best friend. "You don't have to do this now."

"Yes, I do. I only have two weeks left in my contract with Hades. If she hasn't woken up now, she's not going to." I almost sound like I accept it as truth. As if I didn't spend the entire night pacing my apartment and debating whether this is really the right call. But that's cowardice talking. Facts are facts, and the *fact* is that if my mother were going to wake up, she would have done it years and years ago.

Allecto huffs out a breath and crosses her impressive arms over her chest. She's wearing her normal street clothes outfit of jeans and a pale-gray T-shirt that sets off her dark-brown skin, and she's got her long, black braids fastened back from her face. "You know as well as I do that Hades will continue to pay this bill as long as you ask him to. He's not going to cut her off, not after all this time."

She's likely right, but I can't ask him to do that. I won't. "It's time."

She opens her mouth like she's going to keep arguing

but finally gives a sharp nod. "Do you want me to get the doctor?"

"Yes, please." No reason to wait. No reason to give myself time to lose my nerve.

I wait for her to leave and turn back to the hospital bed. The machines that breathe for my mother make soft sounds that grind against my nerves. I've always hated hospitals, and this long-term care facility might pretty itself up, but it's a hospital where people go to die. Today, my mother joins their number.

Truth be told, she died within a week of the injury that put her in a coma. At least according to the doctors.

My grandmother used to always tell me how much I reminded her of my mom. We have the same light-brown skin and delicate features, but it's hard to see the similarities right now. She looks like a shadow of the woman she used to be. A ghost still retaining flesh, whose spirit has long since fled.

I close my eyes and try to breathe past the burning in my throat. "I'm sorry, Mom. I'm sorry that I'm giving up." I take a ragged inhale. "I can't fix what happened, but I'll make sure she pays."

She. *Malone.*

The woman whose bid for power took *everything* from me.

The door opens, and I wipe hastily at my eyes. Neither the doctor nor Allecto comment on it. Dr. Volsce has been in this facility nearly as long as my mother has. He takes my hands, expression carefully neutral but somehow sympathetic at the same time. "Are you ready?"

No. I'll never be ready.

"Yes."

He doesn't ask me if I'm sure, for which I'm grateful. He simply gives my hands a squeeze and nods. "Okay."

Things move quickly after that. Two nurses appear and begin fiddling with the machines. Allecto and I end up near the foot of the bed, and she throws an arm around my shoulders, holding me tightly as, one by one, the machines go silent.

The seconds tick by, filled with the roaring in my head. It's over. It's truly, finally, over. I hate that there's an element of relief, hate that I've been grieving this woman for two-thirds of my life but somehow there's still plenty left in the well. I'm shaking, but Allecto holds me steady. She doesn't offer meaningless kind words or even look at me. She simply stands as a rock at my side, providing me with the strength I don't have right now.

I feel like I blink and we're in the car, heading back to the Underworld. "There are arrangements—"

"We'll take care of it." She glances at me. "Give yourself the day. Hell, give yourself the week, the month. As long as you need."

If only it were that easy. My emotions are a tangled mess inside me, grief and anger and loss and helplessness. For so long, the shining star I've held aloft is hope that my mother would one day come back to me, that she'd open her eyes and we could finally be a family. A silly, childish dream.

My dreams for the future never extended beyond that point.

I lean back against the seat and watch the city blocks cruise by. I was born in Carver City, and I've lived here the entire time. First with my grandmother, then I moved into the Underworld and beneath Hades's wing at twenty-one. I've never traveled, barely moved beyond the center of the city that compromises Hades's territory. It's never felt claustrophobic before, but now I can't quite draw a full breath. "I have to get out of here."

"Are you about to be sick in my car?"

I close my eyes. "No."

Allecto is silent for a long moment. "You mean get out of the city."

"Yes."

"It might be good for you."

That surprises me enough that I look at her. "What?"

She shrugs. "I know you've been happy here, but fuck, Aurora, you're thirty. Even with Hades taking his percentage of your income in repayment, you have more than enough money to travel the world for a decade or two without worrying about finances. Why not do it?"

She's right. I like my indulgences—pretty clothes and the best beauty supplies money can buy—but even with those expenses, I have a rather large savings account. Nearly ten years working as the premier submissive in the Underworld will do that for a person.

I tentatively consider the thought of traveling. It's not unappealing, though my stomach twists nervously at the thought of being alone. Truly alone in a way I never have in life up to this point. There was always someone there. My grandmother. Then my found family in the Underworld: Allecto and Meg and Hercules and even Hades. My patrons, Gaeton and Hook and Ursa. Even a few boyfriends and girlfriends over the years, though those relationships didn't last. "I'll think about it."

"Think fast. You have two weeks left in your contract." She pulls into the parking garage beneath the Underworld and nods at the white guy manning the booth. He's new enough that I haven't memorized his name, but the intense way he looks at us says that he's serious about his job. Good.

After what happened with Tink's personal items not too long ago, Hades has upped security throughout the building to ensure no one gets in that he doesn't want there.

It's not until Allecto's parked and we've climbed out of the car that I really stop and think about what the deadline means. "Do you think he's going to kick me out?"

She laughs. "Fuck no."

"He kicked Tink out." I follow her into the elevator and lean against the wall. "There's no reason he won't do the same to me."

"I can think of several." She rolls her eyes. "One: Tink might have been damn good at her job, but she didn't really love working here. She was using it to hide. Two: not only do you genuinely love your job, but you bring in a truly absurd amount of money. He'll keep you on as long as you want to be here, trust me." She slants me a look. "Three: Hades has a soft spot for you."

"He does not."

"You know better." Allecto snorts. "I'm not going to say he sees you as a daughter, because that'd be weird as shit, but he's protective of you in a way that he isn't of most people who work here. Just trust me on this."

I want to, but my ability to be optimistic died with my decision to pull the plug on my mother. There's nothing left but a strange, dark sensation in my chest. I should feel more, shouldn't I? I should be crying and wailing and unable to function.

Instead, all I feel is empty.

The elevator doors open on the floor that houses the private residences of people who live here. There aren't many these days. Me, Allecto, Tisiphone. Technically Hercules and Meg have their own rooms, but they're rarely used since they spend most of their nights with Hades.

I start toward my room, but Hercules appears at the end of the hall, looking harried. "There you are."

"Here I am." My voice sounds decidedly normal, which is a small revelation. At least the vines full of thorns embedded in my chest are invisible to anyone else.

"Hades would like to see you."

I take a step forward before Allecto catches my shoulder. "The old man can wait. Give yourself a little time to catch your breath."

She's probably right, but I'm not in the mood to wait. No matter what Hades has to say, it will offer a distraction from the memory of the silent hospital room we just left. "It's fine." I inject some sunshine into my tone because Hercules looks worried. "I'll go see him now."

The elevator is the closest way up, but I don't trust Allecto not to follow me into it and then demand to be present for whatever Hades has to say. She doesn't normally meddle in Underworld affairs unless it's directly related to security, but one look at her face shows a worry she can't quite hide. "I'm fine."

"The more you say that, the less I believe you."

Hercules looks between us. "What's going on?"

"Nothing. Nothing at all." I slip past Hercules before Allecto can keep arguing. She curses but doesn't try to chase me down, probably because she knows Hercules *will* demand answers until someone tells him what's happening. Explaining what I've done today means explaining how I've had a mother in a coma for two decades, which means explaining the terms of my bargain.

I know Hercules. He won't understand.

I take the stairs up to the floor that houses the main club and Hades's public office, and then I pause on the landing for several long minutes while I put my armor back in place.

Soft spot or no, it doesn't do to meet with Hades while bleeding from an emotional wound. He won't be able to help himself. He'll poke at it until I spill all my messy emotions all over both of us.

When I'm reasonably sure that I can walk into the office without breaking down, I leave the stairwell. The hall is empty, which is a small blessing, and I stride to Hades's office and let myself in.

A quick glance around the room shows that it's the exact same as it's always been. Hades has a private office, but this is the space where he prefers to handle any club business that arises. The room is done in shades of gray, and careful lighting always leaves the man behind the desk bathed in shadow. It's very dramatic, but I'd never be fool enough to say as much to Hades.

He's the only one in the room.

I clear my throat, fighting down a flutter of nerves. "You called for me?"

"Sit."

As I make the short trip across the office to sink into a chair across from him, the empty feeling in my chest yawns wider. I clasp my hands in my lap tightly enough to grind my bones together and try to keep my voice even. Hades doesn't immediately speak, which only heightens the sudden concern that I'm right and Allecto is full of shit. "Are you going to kick me out the same way you kicked out Tink?"

Even with the shadows, I can see Hades's surprise. "You and Tink are hardly the same, Aurora."

A sentiment I've heard more times than I can count, especially since I took over her position. If Tink weren't one of my closest friends, it might make me hate her. As it is, she gave me large shoes to fill when she left. I try to still my sudden shaking. "With respect, that's not an answer."

He gives a nearly soundless sigh and leans forward to prop his elbows on his desk. It brings his features into the light. Hades is an attractive, older white guy with salt-and-pepper hair and black square glasses that frame his dark eyes. He's handsome in a scary kind of way, but he's never been anything but kind to me.

Not that he'd label it as such. The man has a reputation to uphold, after all, and if I ever pointed out that he got the raw end of our bargain, he'd deny it. Hades doesn't do *charity*, but in my case, there's no other way to describe it. What other man would give an astronomical amount to a thirteen-year-old girl and then send her away with a command to return when she's twenty-one?

I tested him to see if he'd come looking for me. Letting a week and then a month slip by after my birthday. He never showed to enforce the command. In fact, he seemed surprised when I finally arrived at the Underworld.

So, yes, I suppose Allecto is right in a way; Tink and I are nothing alike, and neither were our bargains.

I clasp my hands in my lap. "Then what is this about?"

"You're more than welcome to remain in the Underworld once your bargain with me expires. This is your home as long as you choose to stay, and once your time is officially up, the negotiated percentage that I take out of your wages will be halved." His lips quirk. "But I'd be remiss if I didn't point out that half of Carver City would happily welcome you into their homes."

Into their homes, and into their beds.

But not in a permanent way. I've been here long enough to watch them find their true loves, one by one. They might enjoy scening with me from time to time, but I'll always be on the outside looking into those relationships. No invitation to their homes would be permanent. I'm not naïve enough to believe otherwise.

There was a time when that knowledge wouldn't bother me. I'm not sure it *does* bother me, or if I'm just feeling particularly sensitive right now. "Is that what you called me in here to say?"

"No." He sits back, once again bathed in shadows. "I called you here to convey an offer to contract out for the next two weeks."

I raise my brows. Hades is notoriously reluctant to allow this kind of assignation. Both he and Allecto are control freaks when it comes to security in the Underworld, and he can't guarantee the safety of his people outside it. Most everyone in Carver City is too smart to cross a line, even without constant security surveillance in place, but Hades takes no risks with his people. "I'm surprised you're even considering it."

"Yes, well, I don't have much of a choice. The request came from a territory leader."

The gaping, empty feeling in my chest roars, and I know the answer even before I put the question to voice. "Which one?"

He holds my gaze. "Malone."

"*Malone?*" I suspected it had to be her, I still can't keep the shock from my voice, from my face, from my very being. It's finally happening? *Finally*, after all this time?

"Yes, it surprised me, too." Hades watches me closely. "I'm inclined to say no, but Malone doesn't demand much and it runs the risk of alienating her. However, considering your history with her, it's a terrible idea."

Hades is the only one besides Allecto who knows who my mother really is. Who's responsible for putting her in that coma to begin with. He's right. I should say no.

If he knew where I'd just come from, he wouldn't have even given me the option. He would have rejected the offer instantly.

But as I sit here, staring at my hands, darkness rushes into that void inside me. A screaming that demands action, demands revenge. Malone is careful and particular, and in my nine years of working here, I have only truly interacted with her once, years ago when we scened together. If I say yes to this, I will be close to her for the next two weeks. I'll be close enough to strike, to do something to hurt her as much as she's hurt me. "I accept."

"Aurora."

"Hades." I can't quite soften my tone into playfulness. I never talk back to Hades. Never. Partly because I owe him so much, and mostly because of the sheer dominance he exhibits without seeming to try. He's got himself bottled up right now, but the man can send me to my knees with a single look. Not today. I feel like nothing can touch me today. "I need to do this."

"You really don't."

"This is why I came to you to begin with!" I stop short and make an effort to modulate my tone. "Do not take this chance from me."

He looks like he's torn between yelling at me and coming around the desk to wrap me in a tight hug. "Malone will eat you up and spit you out. She will *harm* you."

I shove to my feet. "There is nothing she'll do that hasn't already been done to me a hundred times over during my years here." I laugh harshly. "You know me, Hades. I like *everything*. Pain and humiliation and degradation. Soft words and gentle touches and kindness. It all gets me off. Malone can't harm me."

"Aurora." Hades stands slowly. I don't know how he manages it, but it feels like his power unfurls through the room. "I would have thought age would make you less reckless."

The desire to apologize bubbles up inside me, but I shove it down. I am not weak, and I am not a fool. All those years ago, I came to the Underworld with two goals: to keep my mother alive and to get revenge. I've managed the first. Now it's time for the second. "I'm not reckless."

"You are the very definition of reckless." He sighs. "But

you're an adult who knows her own mind. I can keep you from Malone now, but the moment the bargain is done, I suspect you'll be taking that contract."

I will. Now that she's finally made a move on me, I refuse to miss this opportunity. "Better to let me do this while I'm still yours." I'm being cruel, but I can't help it. If I do something to Malone, Hades might bear the price of it alongside me, but he's more than capable of navigating the situation. He'll be fine.

He takes off his glasses and pinches the bridge of his nose. "I dislike you attempting to manipulate me."

"I'm just speaking the truth."

"You are willing to say anything to convince me to agree to this. Don't deny it." He cuts me a sharp look. "But you do have a point."

I press my lips together. Pushing him now won't guarantee victory, and it might just backfire. So I force myself still and wait while he thinks about it.

Finally, Hades shakes his head. "I'll allow it."

Relief makes me a little dizzy. There's no guarantee that Malone's offer would stand in another few weeks once I'm free of Hades's bargain. I won't get another chance like this, to get close enough to her to strike. "When do I start?"

"Tomorrow."

∼

"You goddamn *fool*."

I don't look over as Allecto storms into the gym. I just increase the speed on my treadmill, feet pounding in time with my racing heart. "I'll talk to you when I'm done."

"The fuck you will. You'll talk to me now." She stalks to

the treadmill and reaches past me to slap the bright-red *Stop* button.

I stumble as the track suddenly stops moving. "Hey!"

"What the hell are you doing, Aurora?" She's practically vibrating with anger. "Why the *fuck* did Hercules just tell me that you're about to go spend two weeks with *Malone*?"

"Because I'm going to spend two weeks with Malone." I try to say it calmly, rationally, but it comes out spiked. "She offered. It's an opportunity I can't miss."

"An opportunity." She looks like she wants to strangle me. "An opportunity to do *what*?"

I could hedge, but the truth is that if anyone will understand, it's Allecto. "Kill her."

My friend stares at me for several long beats as if waiting for the rest of the joke. She finally shakes her head slowly. "No. Absolutely not. Your mother just died. You aren't in your right mind."

"My mother died twenty years ago. That wasn't her."

"Don't try to twist logic with me now, not when the entire reason you bargained so much of your life away with Hades was to save her."

Something cracks inside me. I didn't save her. No one could save her. It didn't matter what I did, how high I reached for assistance. My mother was lost to me the moment she entered that fight with Malone. I look at Allecto, trying to make her understand. "I have to do this."

"No, you don't." She glances at the door as if she's going to charge up to Hades's office and tell him everything. "She's going to kill you."

I grab her arm, holding her in place. "She won't get a chance to."

"Yes, Aurora, she will. Malone is one of the deadliest people in Carver City, full stop. She's ruthless and ambitious, and she cuts down people who cross her without a second thought. If you move against her and fail, she'll kill you. If you somehow manage to succeed, her people will kill you. There is no outcome where this ends happily."

"That's fine. I don't believe in happily ever after. Not anymore."

Allecto sighs and steps onto the treadmill to take my shoulders. "I can't say I know how you feel right now, and I'm shit at comfort, but this is not the right course. You are not a killer." When I start to protest, she speaks right over me. "She is going to twist you up, break you down, and you're going to end up hating yourself because you'll start to care and won't be able to take her out."

"I will *not* start to care about Malone."

Allecto snorts. "Aurora, you *already* care about her. You've been eye-fucking her for years."

I try to jerk back, but she tightens her grip on my shoulders, keeping me in place. "I have not."

"You sure as fuck have." She shakes her head. "You fall in love with everyone you sleep with. And she's *Malone.* You're already fucked, and you're too stubborn to realize it."

I poke her in the chest. "I do not fall in love with everyone I sleep with."

"Prove it." Allecto releases me and glares. "Gaeton."

"He's my friend, of course I love him." He's a brutal giant of a man with a surprisingly gentle heart, and we've been scening for years.

"Isabelle."

My skin goes hot, and I try to fight down my reaction. "She's different." Who wouldn't fall at least a little in love with a woman like that, so shiny and new to kink and embracing it full-heartedly with her two men? The fact that one of them is Gaeton only makes playing with her more enjoyable.

Allecto holds my gaze and starts ticking up her fingers with each name. "Meg. Hook. Jafar. Ursa. Alaric. Stop me when I find one that you haven't been at least infatuated with."

"Stop it." I glare. "There is nothing wrong with caring about people."

"Don't get pissed now because I'm right." She drops her hand. "And that's not even getting into those jackasses that you dated. Finn. Hazel. Oliver." The last of her fingers go down.

"You're supposed to fall in love with the people you date."

"Uh huh." Allecto snorts. "And look how well that worked out. I was cleaning up the heartbreak tears for *weeks* after those relationships went down in flames."

"Heartbreak after a breakup is also a normal thing."

"You will fall for her, you will hate yourself for doing it, and then you won't be able to go through with it."

I hate how her words feel like daggers aimed right at the heart of me. "You are such a bitch sometimes."

"Ooh, fierce words from the asshole who's planning murder." She shakes her head. "Killing Malone won't fix anything. It's only going to compound that horrible mess of emotions you're refusing to address. It won't bring your mother back or make time go in reverse."

"*Enough*." I shake my head as if I can dispel her words. It's never that easy. Allecto knows me well enough to know exactly the right thing to say to have her words set up residence in my head. "That's enough. It's my choice and I've made it."

"Aurora." Some of the fierceness bleeds out of Allecto's

tone. "If you really want her dead, I'll take care of it. It won't fix anything, but at least then you'd be safe."

I stare. Now it's my turn to wait for the joke to land, but I should know better by now. Allecto doesn't joke about things like this. She sure as hell wouldn't choose to start now, with this topic. "What?"

"It'll be a mess. She's a strong leader, and her territory is stable, and the ripples will affect the rest of the city, but if you need this done, I'll do it for you."

For a moment, I actually consider it. Allecto's good, and she can likely do exactly what she's offering. One moment Malone will be moving through this world, the next she will be a memory. Just like my mother.

I take a slow breath and finally shake my head. "No. I can't ask that of you."

"You aren't asking; I'm offering."

I shake my head again. "It has to be me."

Allecto scrubs her hands over her face. "Fine. But don't you dare beat yourself up when you change your mind. There are people capable of murder, and you're even one of them when you get heated, but an assassination is a totally different animal."

It's irritating that she doubts me. "I'm more than capable of doing this."

"Sure. Capable." She turns for the door. "That's not what I said, though, is it?"

She's gone before I can come up with a response. I don't care what Allecto says or how many theories she has about me developing feelings for the people I have sex with; none of that has to mean anything. Malone isn't just anyone. She's the enemy.

I huff out a breath and turn back to get the treadmill going again. As I take up the steady pounding rhythm of running, my traitorous mind flickers to the single scene I had with Malone all those years ago. I agreed to it out of some perverse desire to understand the woman who hurt my mother. I didn't expect Malone to systematically dismantle all my defenses and shatter me to pieces. The woman is the single best Dominant in Carver City. I'd know —I've been with them all at this point.

It doesn't matter.

I've already agreed to this assignation, and I'm going through with it.

I'm going to kill Malone.

3

MALONE

I've never had a problem taking what I want. The world respects power and power alone, and that's particularly true in *my* world. In the past, it's been a simple matter of seeing something and going through the necessary steps to acquire whatever it is—*who*ever it is.

As I sit in the chair across from Hades's desk, it's with the uncomfortable knowledge that I don't know what he'll say in response to my request to contract Aurora out. The old man has a soft spot for the girl, and has ever since she came to work in the Underworld nine years ago. It's not exactly a fatherly love, not with the games we all play, but he cares about her. It colors his perspective, ensures that he won't be able to make this decision based on possible gains or compensation. He's making it emotionally.

Because of that, I can't guarantee what his answer will be.

After all, I didn't expect him to make me wait a full twenty-four hours for a response, and yet here we are.

Hades steeples his hands in front of his face. He doesn't

bother with a greeting. We both know why I'm here. "There are conditions."

Something like giddiness courses through me. He's going to say yes. I keep my expression cold and unmoving through the ease of long practice. "I expected as much."

"Aurora is too reckless to put hard limits in place, so I will do it for her."

That surprises me enough to raise my eyebrows. "You don't trust her to know her own mind after nearly a decade in the Underworld? Hades, you're getting soft."

"Violate the terms of this contract and see how soft I am." The quiet menace in his voice has me going still. Hades might be an old dog, but he's still got claws and teeth. There's a reason why all the territory leaders, me included, respect his territory as neutral space. My mother taught me never to walk onto a battlefield unless I was sure I could win. I'm not entirely sure I could win a conflict with Hades, and because of that I'm forced to play these polite games.

"What are your conditions?"

"No blood play. Nothing that could scar." He considers me. "No breath play or water play."

I'm not exactly surprised, but it's interesting that he feels the need to vocalize this list. "Those are the rules of the club."

"And you won't be in the club, so it requires stating explicitly. If you harm Aurora, I will destroy you."

This is a fault line I could exploit if I so wished. Everyone looks at Hades and assumes the way to hurt him is to hurt one of his lovers—Megaera or Hercules. Very few people look deeper to realize that, no matter his cold attitude, he takes the protection of his people seriously. Especially Aurora.

He's not the only one in Carver City that feels that way. If I harmed the girl, most of the territory leaders would turn on me. Even Ursa might, and she's been my closest friend for years.

I lean back and cross my legs. "I have no intention of damaging your little princess, Hades. I just want to play with her."

"Why now?"

I shrug, feigning nonchalance. "Now's as good a time as any. Word has it that her bargain with you is almost expired. It's my last chance to enjoy her." *Enjoy her.* Such simple words that don't come close to describing the fire in my blood whenever I'm around that pretty submissive. It's been years since that single scene we shared, and I can barely be in the same room as her without wanting to wind her colorful hair around my fist and drive her to her knees. To make her cry and beg and orgasm. She ignites all my worst impulses, tempts me to forgo the control I value so highly.

If I were less stubborn, I'd let her go. Nothing good can come of having Aurora in my home for two weeks, but I have to risk it if there's even a chance I can purge this burning desire from my veins. Moreover, a small, secret part of me wants to indulge in this selfish thing.

It's been so long since I wanted something that I couldn't take simply by the nature of who I am. Twenty years. Two decades of having everything I could possibly dream of at my fingertips.

Hades shakes his head. "The contract starts tonight. In one week's time, I will either send one of my people to check in with Aurora, or you can bring her here. If I'm not satisfied at that point, you will forfeit the remainder of the time with her."

"So protective," I murmur. "Do you think I'm going to cut her into little pieces? Surely you know better."

He holds my gaze. "I wouldn't put anything past you, Malone. Anything. Better that you understand the consequences before agreeing."

His determination to think the worst of me might sting if I hadn't spent half my life curating a reputation that I am not one to be fucked with. Fear accomplishes as much, if not more, than violence does. Make a few examples of people and suddenly you have much less conflict on your hands. Another lesson from my mother. If only my sister had taken that particular rule to heart, she wouldn't be dealing with the shitshow going on in Sabine Valley right now.

I push the thought away. There's no point in worrying about my nieces and little brother. There's nothing I can do to assist the situation while I'm here in Carver City, and trying to interfere will only make things worse. It doesn't mean the knowledge sits comfortably, though.

Not that any of that matters right *now*. It's simply time to stop denying myself Aurora. I wave a lazy hand in his direction. "I agree. She'll be returned to you in the same condition she's delivered."

His jaw clenches, but he manages to resist the urge to threaten me again. "Do you have specifications for what she should pack?"

"That won't be needed." Two weeks ago, when I finally decided to do this, I made all the necessary preparations. "Aside from anything personal she needs to stay overnight, I have everything taken care of."

He stares at me a long moment. "Very well. Wait here." He rises and moves around the desk, striding to the door.

It takes everything I have not to turn to keep him in my line of sight. The man is a predator, and offering him my back goes against all my training. I resist. It's a power play, and getting out of my chair as much as admits that I don't trust him not to knife me in the back. That I'm afraid of him. Unacceptable.

The door opens and closes, but I don't relax. This office undoubtedly had cameras set up, and as tempting as it is to rifle through the desk, everyone knows that this is only Hades's public office. He's too smart to keep anything damning here where anyone could come sniffing and find it.

Instead, I fall back into an old habit of my childhood. The first lesson my mother taught me was patience, and there's little more torturous than a child being forced to sit for long hours without any entertainment. It took me weeks before I realized that there *was* a point to the exercises. An observant person can tell a wealth of information simply from categorizing the room they are in.

The monotone black and gray paintings lining the walls are from an artist who goes by the moniker *Death*, something that no doubt amuses Hades. The black desk and gray furniture are all top-of-the-line and deceptively sturdy despite their elegant lines. There's plenty of kink play that goes on in this room, and knowing what I do of Hades and Megaera's tastes, it makes sense that they wouldn't want to break the furniture every time someone gets rowdy. The bookshelves behind the couch are filled, but the black and gray and white spines aren't creased, which further confirms that this room is for show, not for traditional office use.

The door behind me opens, and this time two sets of footsteps approach. Hades doesn't round his desk again. He simply leans against it and crosses his arms. "Aurora has agreed to the contract." His gaze flicks over my shoulder. "Behave."

"Don't I always?" Aurora's sweet tone ignites something

in my chest. Something I spent the first half of my life stifling and the latter half molding into something useful. Ambition is one hell of a drug, and there aren't many mountains left to climb in Carver City. I'm at the top. No one challenges me, no one dares stand in my way when I want something.

Except this woman.

I rise slowly and turn to face her. The sight of Aurora is always a kick in the chest. She's a gorgeous Black woman with a petite frame and light-brown skin. Over the years, her hair has run the range of every wild color in existence, though she seems to favor pink and blue the most. Tonight, it's a deep indigo that's nearly black in this light. She's wearing a blood-red lace teddy that does little to hide her body. Another change. Up until a few months ago, she only ever wore white.

Such a small difference shouldn't incite my curiosity, but something's altered within her since she took over the second-in-command position beneath Megaera. She'll never be as sarcastic or fierce as Tink was in the same position, but she's managed to avoid being steamrolled by the Dominants that frequent the club.

She's also barefoot.

I raise an eyebrow at Hades but don't comment on it. His lips quirk a little, but his eyes stay cold. "Her overnight bag is at the front desk with Adem. You may pick it up when you exit."

"Good. We're leaving now."

Aurora's head jerks up, her large brown eyes wide. "You're not going to play in the club first?"

I stalk to her and tap her pretty lips. "When I want you to speak, I'll say so. Tell me your safe word."

"Thorn," she whispers.

"Good. Let's go." I flash a look at Hades over my shoulder. It shouldn't please me to find his expression stormy with displeasure, but I've won this round and we both know it. "See you in two weeks, Hades."

"Remember what I said."

"Of course." I take three steps past Aurora and snap my fingers, pointing to spot about a foot behind me.

She obeys the silent command, moving to follow with her head bowed and her hands laced in front of her. I don't look back again, but I keep half my attention on her footsteps behind me as we head through the door and down the hall, bypassing the lounge where patrons come to chat and drink before indulging in the wide variety of offerings available in the Underworld. I recognize plenty of people at the bar and sitting in the booths tucked against the walls on either side of the room, but I'm not in the mood to chat.

I've waited years to get my hands on Aurora again. Years of denial and thwarted desire. I might go out of my mind if I wait another hour.

I collect her small bag from Adem, and Hades's concern is mirrored in the Black man's dark eyes. He opens his mouth but decides against whatever he was about to say. Good.

Aurora follows me into the elevator and resumes her position on my left as it takes us down to the parking garage. Her body practically vibrates with the desire to ask questions, but she's too well trained to do anything but obey. For now. No doubt she'll find that backbone she's gained in the past year sometime soon, but I'm enjoying this moment of submission without stipulation.

The elevator opens, and I don't pause to think too hard

about my motivations before I turn and scoop Aurora up into my arms. She squeaks a little and goes tense but doesn't argue as I stride into the parking garage. I inhale slowly, catching the faint scent of vanilla, likely from her lotion or something like that. It's too faint to be a perfume.

It makes my mouth water.

I find my head of security, Sara, leaning against the trunk of my town car. They look at me and raise their eyebrows. I'd informed them of my plans; Sara doesn't like me to bring unknowns into my penthouse until they've run all the necessary background checks. They don't like Aurora in particular, because she's a ghost. There's no record of her before she showed up in the Underworld as a submissive nine years ago. No birth certificate. No school records. Nothing. It raises Sara's hackles, but they know better than to challenge me on this sort of thing when I set my mind to it. When push comes to shove, I'm just as capable of protecting myself as Sara is, and they know it.

They move to the back door and open it, holding it steady as I set Aurora onto the seat. "Scoot." I wait for her to obey before I glance at Sara. "Take us home."

"Short trip."

"I got what I came for." *Whom* I came for.

Sara waits for me to slide into the backseat and then shuts the door. A few seconds later, they climb into the front seat and we're off. It's only when we pass the boundary between Hades's territory and mine that I allow myself to relax a little. I didn't honestly think he'd change his mind, but Hades isn't quite rational when it comes to Aurora. I couldn't afford to rule anything out.

It's happening.

She's mine for two weeks, and mine alone.

I twist in the seat to find her sitting sweetly beside me

with her hands clasped and her head bowed. The urge to touch her is almost more than I can deny, but I shove it down deep. There's plenty of time for that later. For now, it's important to establish how this will go. "Take off your panties, Aurora. Now."

4

AURORA

How many identical orders have I been issued over the years? Quiet commands. Loud ones. Sweet. Cutting. None of them affected me the way Malone's idle sentence does. *Take off your panties, Aurora.* She sounds almost disinterested, as if commenting on the weather. In the darkness of the back of the car, I can't quite see her expression. Not that it would matter; I've never seen anything but ice in Malone's eyes. Even the single time she brought me to orgasm, she didn't thaw in the least.

I try to hold on to my anger, my hate, but it feels so fucking good to submit. To set aside all the messy emotions that have been clinging to me like spiderwebs for the past two days. When I submit, it all ceases to exist.

I have to obey if I want her to let her guard down.

The plan feels flimsy at best, but I refuse to admit that Allecto might have been right. She wasn't. I have this under control. Truly, I do.

I lift my hips and slide my panties down my legs. The temptation rises to do more, to spread my legs or let a strap of my teddy fall, but I manage to restrain myself. To give perfect obedience. There will be a time to press Malone later. Right now, I can be a good little submissive.

"Make yourself come." Again, a cold command in a disinterested tone.

I'm almost ashamed by how wet I am. That this woman, this *enemy* manages to turn me on despite the hate burning strong in my chest. I pull my teddy up and stroke my pussy. Malone doesn't even watch. She's looking out the window as if this is a normal car ride and I'm not fingering myself less than a foot from her.

Even in the shadows of the backseat, lit only by the lights of buildings we pass, she's gorgeous enough to steal my breath. Malone is a white woman with the kind of pale skin that makes me think she's never seen the sun. I know she's forty-one from the file Meg keeps on her in the Underworld, but looking at her, she could easily be a decade younger. Her short white-blond hair is styled back from her face as always, and she's wearing one of my favorite outfits of hers. Red-bottom black heels, black cigarette pants with a white blouse that's left unbuttoned halfway down her chest. I have the most unacceptable desire to drag my mouth over that V of exposed skin. To unbutton the shirt farther until I'm kneeling between her thighs.

Will she still act as unaffected once I get my tongue in her pussy?

Part of me hopes so.

There are as many flavors of submissive as there are of Dominants. Everyone has the thing that twists them up in knots in the most delicious way possible. I like a little bit of everything, but this? This disinterest mixed up with lust and my desire for approval? I thrive off attention, and being deprived it is the most delicious of cuts. I have to bite down a moan of sheer lust. I *hate* how easily she cranks me up while appearing to do absolutely nothing at all. It feels particularly dirty to circle my clit like this in the backseat while her driver is witnessing the whole thing.

For all my kink experience, I haven't played outside the Underworld until now. Or at least not in anything resembling public. Even the few relationships I've had were ones where *they* came to *me*. Partly because Allecto is paranoid as hell. Partly because the draw of the Underworld as almost as intense as the draw I provided; something I didn't realize in each of the relationships until far too late. These days, I barely leave the building unless I'm going to visit my mom...

Except I'll never be able to do that again.

The reminder of *why* I'm here is a bucket of cold water in the face of my desire. I slow my movements, loathing myself for the small part of me that keeps enjoying this moment despite everything the woman beside me has done.

"Is there a problem?" Malone's icy voice sends chills down my spine that are entirely too pleasant.

Yes, but I'm not about to admit the extent of it. I close my eyes and strive to keep my mask in place. How can I want to attack her and also beg for more pleasure? Those two feelings shouldn't exist at the same time. It's wrong for me to want her, isn't it? I've spent so much time believing that there's nothing that happens between consenting adults that should result in shame, but here I am...feeling shame.

I lift my hand from my clit. "I'm not really in the mood to come."

She taps her fingers on her knee. "I see."

She moves so quickly, I barely have a chance to flinch. Malone hooks my leg and yanks. After how she carried me through the parking garage—something I refuse to even think about—I shouldn't be surprised by how strong she is despite her slim frame. She easily flips me onto my stomach and tows me back onto her lap, shifting slightly to ensure I don't ram into the door.

I tense, expecting her to spank me or something harsh, but she just wraps her fingers around my upper thigh, gripping me tightly and holding me in place. Her knuckles are barely an inch away from my pussy, and somehow that distance is just as hot as if she shoved two fingers into me. She smooths her free hand over my ass, pushing my lace teddy up and baring me from the waist down.

"There seems to be some misunderstanding of how this works." She traces a single finger down my spine, stopping at the small of my back. "Your flouncing and bratty attitude will not provoke the response you want. It's best you learn that now. If you don't obey my commands, you will be punished." She taps my spine lightly with her nail. "Punishments are not to be enjoyed, Aurora."

I should keep my mouth shut, but this woman manages to rile me like no other. I squeeze my eyes shut and fist my hands against the leather seat. "Then maybe you shouldn't have contracted a submissive who gets off on being punished, *Malone*."

Her quiet laugh raises the small hairs on the back of my neck. "I am not like your regular playmates." She lifts her voice. "Sara, I need to make a stop on the way home. I feel like a drink."

"Will do."

The car slows and turns. Malone doesn't release me, doesn't touch me more, just holds me in place with my bare ass on display. Humiliation and shame heat my cheeks. She slapped me down as easily as she would a fly. I hate that it turns me on. This would be so much easier if she didn't affect me, if I could just endure this without wanting to rub against her leg like a horny teenager.

We finally stop, and she gives my ass a light slap. "Up."

This time, I obey without arguing. She nudges me back into my seat and reaches over my chest to pull my seat belt on. The click feels obscenely loud in the quiet of the car. Malone's breath brushes my ear. "Sit here silently and wait for me. Sara will remain in the car with you. Don't try to talk to them; they won't indulge any of your disobedience." She lifts her voice. "Isn't that right, Sara?"

"Yes, boss." Sara sounds amused, but it's hard to tell for sure because I can only see the back of their dark hair on the other side of the headrest.

Malone opens the car door and climbs out. I sit there in shock and watch her walk into the building we're parking in front of. She...left me? I glance at Sara, but they don't seem interested in counteracting the command to not talk to each other. It's just as well. What would I even say? That doesn't stop me from wanting to do it out of spite. "How long am I supposed to wait?"

No answer.

I huff out a breath and slump back against the seat. My pussy is throbbing in time with my heartbeat, and I have the imprint of Malone's hand wrapped around my upper thigh. Lust and anger create a heady mix inside me, and I reach down to stroke myself. Fuck her if she thinks she can leave me on the edge like that.

"Wouldn't do that if I were you."

I glare at the back of Sara's head. "Or what? She left me in here."

They laugh lightly. "Do what you want, kid. Just saying it won't work out like you're hoping."

I manage to wait another five minutes. My desire and fury increase with each second that ticks by. She *left* me in the car like a dog so she could go have a drink. Maybe I'll appreciate the simplicity of this punishment later, but right now all I can do is clench my fists and glare out the window.

Punishments are not to be enjoyed, Aurora. Her cool voice filters through my flurry of thoughts, which only twines me tighter. Being bratty *never* results in something like this with other Dominants. Scenes follow a predictable pattern; they let me rile them up, and then they punish me, and we all enjoy ourselves immensely. I have never been set aside like a child in time out and left for... I check the clock in the dashboard I can see around Sara's broad shoulders. Twenty fucking minutes.

I almost ignore Sara's warning and masturbate out of spite. Almost. But just when my frayed patience has worn itself away completely, I catch sight of Malone walking out of the bar. She strides like she's on a runway, and if I didn't know better, I'd think she was putting on a show for me. But that's not how this woman works. She strides everywhere she goes, a predator that send people scurrying out of her wake even in the Underworld, where power is the rule rather than the exception.

It only makes her more breathtakingly attractive, and that unwelcome feeling of awe reaches me even through my irritation. She opens the door and slides easily into the backseat. She doesn't even look at me. "That was refreshing. Let's go."

"Mmhmm." Sara sounds like they're fighting down a laugh.

Malone ignores me the remaining fifteen minutes it takes to get to her building. I'm familiar with the location even if I've never been here before. Meg has files on every single power player in Carver City, and extra detailed information on the territory leaders in particular. I've spent more time studying Malone's file than anyone else's. I know she has a staff of fifty security people, though she keeps a smaller team in charge of her personal residence. She's CEO of a company that employs hundreds of people. The company has great healthcare, and all full-time workers get paid vacation as well as paid parental leave for up to three months. The employee turnover rate is practically nonexistent, from the mail room to the COO. As irritating as it is to acknowledge, she seems like a good boss. And the same policies are enacted with her people for the less than legal parts of her business.

In my darkest moments, I wondered if my mother had anything similar set up for her people when she was in charge. I have next to no information about the years she ruled this territory. My grandmother refused to speak of it, and it wasn't as if I could go in and ask people who had actually been there. I considered it, of course, but ultimately chose not to. Even Hades's immaculate records are sparse when it comes to her.

The parking garage looks like every other one I've been in. Malone barely waits for the car to stop before she opens the door and motions me to follow with an imperial flick of her fingers. I start to climb out of the car, but Malone once against scoops me into her arms.

I've been carried a lot. Some Doms really like this sort of thing, but I didn't think Malone was one of them. She's only a few inches taller than me, but her strong arms band around me and I have absolutely no fear that she's going to drop me.

That doesn't mean I like this.

"Put me down."

"You're speaking out of turn again." She doesn't glance down, just eats up the distance between the car and the elevator with that stride of hers, completely unchanged despite the fact that I'm in her arms. She waits for Sara to push the button to call the elevator. "At this rate, I won't let you come the entire two weeks you're with me."

I want to pretend she's bluffing, but I'm not that naive. Malone is more than capable of following through on that mildly delivered threat. For the first time in a very long time, I have to fight to lower my eyes and inject some submission into my tone. "I'm sorry."

"No, you're not." She steps into the elevator.

Sara follows and presses the button for the highest floor and the one below it. We rise in silence. I expect Malone to set me down, but she shows no interest in doing so. The doors open on the second-highest floor, and Sara steps out. They turn back and level a severe look at me. "Don't try anything. If you do, once she's done fucking you up, I'll fuck you up."

This isn't an idle threat, either. I press my lips together and nod. As if I'm not planning to do exactly that the first chance I get. As if the very reason I took this assignation wasn't to get close enough to slip a knife between Malone's ribs.

It's not going to be easy. I knew that even before Allecto made her doubts known. Malone is a fucking *Amazon* from Sabine Valley. The name isn't the only thing they share with their ancient Greek counterparts. They're a matriarchal warrior society built of clans, and Malone was part of the ruling family. She's a formidable enemy in every sense of the word.

She is a warrior by both the literal and corporate definition. It's going to take everything I have in order to succeed in taking her out. And patience. Lots and lots of patience.

And then we're rising again. This time when the doors open, we're not looking at a corporate-type hallway. There's a nondescript white room with a single door in it. Malone walks into the room and looks up at the camera positioned against the ceiling. A few seconds later, the lock clicks open, and she pushes through the door.

The apartment is decorated exactly like I imagined it would be. Clean lines. Minimalist decorating. Elegant furniture. Color scheme that leans white and gray with a few pops of silver and crimson to keep things from being soulless.

She sets me on my feet. "Get rid of that hideous thing."

I look down at my teddy. "I like it."

"You look like a sorority girl playing dress-up. Take it off."

I almost argue, but the memory of the car has me reaching for the hem of the teddy and pulling it over my head without complaint. Malone takes it from my hand and strides deeper into the house. "Follow."

I grit my teeth and obey. I round the corner in time to see her stuff the nightgown in the trash can in the kitchen. She keeps going before I can take a moment to study the room, stalking down the hallway and opening a door.

It leads to a room outfitted in high-end kink gear. There's a spanking bench, a contraption meant to suspend someone on, and a hook attached to the ceiling in the middle of the room. From the hook dangles a spreader bar with cuffs on either end.

Malone positions me below it and then moves to a ring on the wall where it's tied off, lowering it until it's just within reach. Without a word, she walks back and fastens my hands on either side of the bar. It spreads me wide, leaving me unable to cover myself.

Malone steps back. "Now. Let's see what I've claimed."

5

There are certain expectations that come with being the leader of a territory. Carver City is nothing like Sabine Valley—too carefully refined, too polite, too kind—but that truth remains the same. I am a law unto myself within my territory, and as long as I don't push too hard at my neighbors' borders, they're unlikely to start something. The factions here don't need feasts and curated times a year to keep blood from shedding, aren't always on the brink of a new war.

It's made me soft.

There was a time when I wouldn't hesitate to take what I wanted. It's how I got this territory to begin with. When I arrived in the city, I took a month to analyze every territory's strengths and weaknesses before choosing one for myself. The southern chunk of the city was ruled by a woman who really *was* soft. Too lax. Too lazy. Too willing to let her people do whatever they pleased. A few weeks of undermining her and one brutal fight, and the territory became mine.

But since then?

I haven't had to fight for anything, aside from squashing a handful of squabbles and power grabs over the years.

Claiming this woman glaring at me with large dark eyes will be a battle. It doesn't matter that I have no intention of keeping Aurora. She's an itch I haven't been able to scratch, a thorn in my paw for years. If I can just purge this woman from my system, then I can go back to my carefully ordered life. I've worked hard to create balance, and my heady desire for Aurora disrupts that balance.

She's beautiful. She possesses the kind of perfect features that everyone recognizes as the standard to be strained toward: high cheekbones, full lips, big eyes, and flawless light-brown skin. Her body is just more of the same perfection. She's short and built soft. Not quite curvy, but she's got a figure that says she doesn't spend too much time worrying about achieving a model-thin look. I like it. A lot. Her breasts are high and tipped with brown nipples that have shiny silver barbells through them, and her waist draws my eye down to hips just made to be grabbed.

There's a reason she's the favorite of everyone who's ever come into the Underworld, and her face and body are only half of the equation. The rest is the sunny disposition she shines at everyone...except me.

Ever since that first scene right after she started working in the Underworld, Aurora's never been anything but coldly polite when she's forced to interact with me. It shouldn't bother me. I don't want the girl, and no matter what the other fools in this city seem to think, she's not one for keeping.

Now she's mine for two full weeks. The thought fills me with a vicious delight, a feeling akin to my younger years, when I'd step into the ritual combat ring on Lammas.

I can't think about Lammas now. Can't think about what

my sister has allowed to happen. There's nothing *I* can do, and the helplessness I'm not used to feeling is why I contracted Aurora in the first place. She's a distraction to keep me from doing something unforgivable.

She's practically quivering from a combination of anger and anticipation. I've allowed my thoughts to wander long enough. It's time to get down to business. I cross to her and catch her chin with my fingers, digging my nails in just enough to make her flinch. "You have the terrible habit of trying to top from the bottom."

"I don't," she grits out.

"If I want you to speak, I'll ask you a question. You most certainly do top from the bottom." I've spent far too many hours watching her play in public, studying her interactions with the other Dominants. They indulge her new bratty behavior. They flat-out indulge her. "You have them all wrapped around your pretty finger. Does it get boring? Never having to wonder what will happen next because you already know?"

She blinks up at me. I'm only a few inches taller than her, but the heels give me extra height. Aurora licks her lips. "You *would* like to pretend you're special, wouldn't you? Just because you've spent years watching me doesn't mean you *know* me, Malone."

"Such a mouth on you," I murmur. I can't quite resist dragging my thumb over her full bottom lip. "You won't provoke me into doing what you want."

"If you say so."

The challenge she presents thrills me to my very soul. It's been so long since I had to work for something, for someone. When you're queen—or what passes for it in my territory—people are all too willing to offer you everything you could ever dream of. It's enough to tempt a person to flirt with war just to alleviate the boredom.

Yes, Aurora will do nicely.

"Your safe word."

"Thorn." She practically snarls it.

I permit myself a cold smile. "For your insolence, you won't be permitted to orgasm tonight. Please me well during this scene and I'll lift the ban in the morning. Keep up this bratty behavior and I'll extend it." At her shock, I almost laugh. "It's really simple, Aurora. Be a good girl, obey, and you'll be rewarded."

She stares. "You'd really deny me for the next two weeks, wouldn't you?"

I don't want to. The desire to bring Aurora to orgasm, over and over again, is like a sickness in my blood. I crave this woman in a way that made me wary enough to avoid her for years. But if I give an inch on this battlefield, she'll take a mile.

"Yes."

She gives another of those aggravated breaths that thrill a dark part of me. "In that case..." She smiles, as bright as a sunny morning. "I bow to your every will, Mistress."

The smile is a lie, just like the submission is a lie. Oh, she's submissive. There's no doubting *that*. But Aurora spent years playing the sweet, biddable girl. The persona she's settled into since taking over as Megaera's second-in-command is closer to the truth, but it's still an act. She's been wearing a mask since she started working at the Underworld, and I want to know what lies beneath it.

I leave her standing there and walk to where I store my toys in a massive antique wardrobe. I take my time considering my choices. As if I haven't played this scene out a dozen times in my mind before contacting Hades.

Anticipation is half the battle. It softens the submissive, primes them to be in the right headspace for what comes next. I bypass the rainbow of strap-ons hanging in a precise row and snag a silver chain with three clasps on it. I run it over my fingers as I walk back to Aurora, letting her get a good look at it.

I press my free hand to the small of her back to keep her from retreating and bend down to take one nipple into my mouth. Her shocked gasp pleases me as much as the fact that I finally, *finally*, have my mouth on her again. This time, she isn't in control like she was at the virginity auction awhile back, sliding her fingers into my mouth in front of a room full of people and retreating before I was anywhere near satisfied.

This isn't required, not really, not when she has her nipples pierced now. I don't care. I want to taste her, so I do it. First one breast and then the other. I could spend hours playing with her breasts, but I ignore the temptation and force myself to move to the next step. I fasten the nipple clamps, one after another. "Too tight?"

"It's fine," she snarls.

"Mmm." The thin chain pulls at the clamps, weighing them down a little, adding to the sensation. I sink to my knees and give her an arch look. "Spread your thighs."

She considers disobeying. I can see the conflict written across her pretty features, the desire to submit coming up against her perverse need to fight me every step of the way. Desire wins out, like I suspected it would. Slowly, oh, so slowly, she spreads her thighs.

Like many of the submissives in the Underworld, she's chosen to go completely bare down here. Her clit doesn't technically need the same treatment I gave her nipples, not when she's so blatantly turned on that she's practically dripping down her thighs. This woman might act like she loathes me, but she's getting off on what I'm doing all the same.

I part her pussy. She's so fucking soft, so hot and wet, I almost forego my plans for the night and just spend the next few hours tonguing her until I'm satisfied. "The lady protests, but her pussy likes me just fine." I fasten the clamp around her clit before she can come up with a response.

As I suspected, the picture she creates is perfect. The chain shakes a little with every breath she takes, glinting prettily. I push to my feet and move back to the wardrobe. Two weeks is a small eternity yet nowhere near long enough to get through everything I want to play out with her.

For our first night, I want to make an impression, but I don't want to do anything that will bruise her enough to hamper future scenes. With that in mind, I pick a flogger on the lighter end of the scale.

I stride back to her and give her breasts a light flick with it. She jerks back and then moans when the chain pulls at both nipples and her clit. I consider her. "I know you like pain. Will you come from that alone?" I motion to the chain and clamps.

Her expression takes on a mutinous cast, but she finally says, "Possibly, Mistress."

Oh, I like it when she calls me Mistress. I like it a lot. Far too much to comment on. "If you get close, tell me."

She glares. "Yes, Mistress."

"Your words are correct. Your attitude isn't." I shake my head slowly, as if I'm not thrilled down to my very core at the challenge. "Don't disappoint me." Without another word, I move to her back. I don't give her a chance to brace for the first strike. I started a mental timer the moment I cuffed her hands over her head. Even with her feet touching the ground, there's only so long a person should be bound like that. Aurora's stubborn. I honestly don't know if I can break through the first barrier of her attitude before it's time to end the scene.

I'm going to try.

I get a good rhythm going, working across her back in uneven pacing so she can't anticipate where the next strike will come from. Before too long, she's whimpering and her hands are grasping at air above the cuffs. By the time my arm begins to ache, she's arching back into every strike. I consider continuing, but ultimately there simply isn't enough time. She may see tonight as a single scene, but I know better. This entire fourteen days is a scene, and it must be played out to perfection.

I drop the flogger on the floor by her feet and circle around to her front. She's a little wide around the eyes, her breath coming in gasps, but she's not completely checked out the way some subs get from being flogged. "What a little pain slut you are." Before she has a chance to reply, I reach out and unfasten the first nipple clamp.

Aurora cries out, her back arching beautifully as blood rushes back into the deprived nipple. Before I can remind myself that this isn't part of the plan, I dip down and suck her into my mouth, soothing her with my tongue, playing with her piercing. I wait until her whimpers have gained a molten edge before repeating the process with the other nipple.

By the time I sink to my knees in front of her, she's trembling. I glance up at her face. "Remember, Aurora. Do not, under any circumstances, orgasm. Do you understand me?"

"Yes, Mistress," she whispers. For the first time since agreeing to this contract, she doesn't sound bratty. As if she

can't decide if she's dreading what comes next...or antici-
pating it.

I unfasten the clamp around her clit and, as she shrieks,
I lean forward and taste her. *Gods*, she's so wet, I have to
smother my own moan. I hitch one of her legs up over my
shoulder so I can get better access to her and stroke her clit
with my tongue. Once. Twice. A third time.

"Stop!"

I meet her gaze without taking my mouth off her pussy
and raise my eyebrows. She bites her bottom lip. "I'm close."

I give her one last lick, gathering up as much of her taste
as I can, before I lift my head. "Good girl."

"Malone... Mistress..." She keeps nibbling on her
bottom lip. "You aren't really going to leave me like this, are
you?"

I drop the chain and rise to my feet. "Yes. I am." I clasp
her chin again and use my thumb to tug her lip from
between her teeth. "And if you hadn't been such a little brat
in the car, you'd be coming all over my mouth right now.
Again." Stroke. "And again." Stroke.

"Just obey," I say softly. "Surely it's not too much to ask of
you. You deny us both when you throw tantrums."

A single tear escapes. "I hate you."

"Maybe." I release her and shrug. "But you don't hate
what I do to you." I reach up and undo the cuffs around her
wrist one at a time, pausing to rub the circulation back into
her hands. The cuffs themselves weren't overly tight, but I
towed the line of how long she should have them above her
head. "Do you have circulation problems?" Something I
should have asked before starting this.

"No," she whispers, staring at where I gently massage
her hand. "I'm okay."

"In that case, you're more than capable of cleaning up

after yourself." I drop her hand and head for the door. I pause just before leaving the room. "Clean the toys and put them away, then come to the door at the end of the hallway. Don't tarry."

I'm smiling as I walk out the door.

Yes, things are coming along perfectly.

My legs barely hold me up as I watch the door close behind Malone. At this point, any other Dominant would have wrapped me up for some cuddles to bring me down. I don't know why I expected the same of her. Maybe that's how she treats other submissives. Of course it wouldn't apply to me.

I don't *want* it to apply to me. Letting her beat me, fucking her, all of that can be waved away in the name of getting close to her. I don't want to *get close* to her. It feels good to be held as my adrenaline drops off after a scene, to feel like I'm being treasured by my Dominant.

But Malone isn't mine. She never will be.

I have been in her care for a few short hours. Surely I'm not in danger of forgetting that already? No. Of course not. I'm simply playing the game.

I gather up the chain and flogger and pad to the wardrobe. The whole room is immaculate, and the wardrobe itself is perfectly organized, right down to the rainbow of strap-ons that Malone is known for. Each is a different size and shape, and I stare at them for a long time, my buzzing brain wondering which one she'll use on me.

If she'll use one on me.

She's edging me so hard right now, I feel a little dizzy from the denied orgasm. I was *so close*. Remembering the feeling of looking down my body and seeing her mouth on my pussy... I shiver. For a moment there, I was sure she'd throw caution to the wind and push me over the edge.

I find some cleaning solution in the top drawer and methodically clean the clamps. Most of the Dominants I play with don't bother to order this kind of thing, but when I finally wore Hades down into agreeing to let me work as a submissive, cleaning up after scenes was one of my responsibilities while I trained. It's tedious work, but soothing in its own way. Putting everything to order and all that.

I hang the flogger on the empty hook and carefully replace the chain in the drawer she pulled it out of. I haven't stopped shaking. My body is finally realizing that there is no orgasm waiting in the wings and the endorphin crash is about to knock me on my ass.

It's tempting to disobey her order to come to that room. She's already said I'm not orgasming tonight, so whatever she has planned is more torment. I probably shouldn't get a thrill from that, but I am who I am.

Even my enemy can make me wet.

I take a deep breath and leave the playroom. The wood floors are cool beneath my bare feet, and it reminds me of her carrying me so I wouldn't walk in the parking garages. Every other thing she's done has been almost cruel, but that? It was almost kind. Protective.

It's just Dominant instincts. That's the only explanation that makes sense. No Dominant worth their salt would let their submissive potentially walk on something that might hurt them. Dealing out that hurt is the Dominant's role, and they do nothing without reason. Letting it happen by accident is an insult.

Malone might be a monster in a number of ways, but from the whispers of the other submissives in the Underworld, she's an excellent Domme. Even my one experience with her, while several years out of date, supports that fact.

I still didn't anticipate her scooping me up and holding me close for that handful of moments.

I reach the door at the end of the hallway and open it. I'm not sure what I expected, but this must be Malone's bedroom. The bed is large and covered with a deep-burgundy comforter and more pillows than one person has any right to own. A thick rug spreads almost the breadth of the room, and the pair of doorways on the opposite wall must lead to a closet and bathroom.

Malone has changed. She's wearing loose, gray silk pajamas that somehow manage to look elegant instead of sloppy. She crosses her arms over her chest and surveys me. "Come along."

Again, the urge to dig in my heels arises, and again I stomp it down. I have two weeks to pull this off. Rushing now, when I'm shaky and tired, is a mistake.

I follow her into the bathroom and stop short when I realize the large, claw-foot bathtub is filled with steaming water. "So a little drowning to finish the night off?"

Malone arches a perfectly shaped brow. "That is the last time I'll allow you to speak out of turn, Aurora. Don't test me."

Somehow, I'd forgotten that little rule. I don't know what it is about this woman, but being around her is like being a submissive again for the first time. I feel awkward and bumbling, and it makes me want to strike out. To scream and throw things and maybe set something on fire.

Or maybe it's just Malone herself. Yes, that makes sense. I only feel like this because I hate her, and I can't remember ever submitting to someone I didn't enjoy in at least one way.

The knowledge propels me closer. Malone takes my hand as I step into the tub, guiding me down. She grabs a stool and brings it around to sit behind me. Before I have a chance to figure out how to deal with my hair, she sweeps it off my back and twists it up on top of my head. "All the way."

I sink into the water. It's nearly too hot to be comfortable, but I sigh in pleasure all the same as heat works its way into my body. Now that I've stopped moving, I finally register how exhausted I am.

The last forty-eight hours have been some of the longest in my life. First in dealing with the decision about my mother, and then agonizing over accepting this assignment. Despite what I told Allecto, I'm still not sure finally pulling the plug was the right thing to do. But it felt like the *only* thing I could do.

Malone's fingers drift over my temples. "You change your hair a lot." When I don't say anything, she softly chuckles. "This is a conversation, Aurora. You may speak while you're in the tub."

I don't miss the qualifier. She's far stricter than a lot of people I've worked with in the past, and it's going to take some getting used to...at least until this is over. In the meantime, the bath feels good, and her light stroking feels even better.

How fucked up am I that I'm accepting comfort from the woman I have every intention of killing? I close my eyes and push the question away. Did she ask me something? Oh yeah, my hair "I get bored."

"I've seen you in nearly every color of the rainbow at this point, but you seem to gravitate toward pink the most often."

"I like it." It's such a girly color, and it draws the eye of people when I walk through a room. I like the attention. I like that it sets me apart a little in a room full of beautiful people. There's also the added bonus that I can tell a lot from a person by how they react to pink hair, in particular. It's like it short-circuits something in people's brains, especially men. If they curl their lip when they see my pink hair, I know immediately that I won't agree to scene with them. It's a nice way to filter out assholes.

"The indigo is nice." She moves down the back of my neck, finding a knot there and working it with her fingers. It feels good-bad, a hurt that is almost like a release. I have a private theory that all good massage therapists are sadists, and this feeling only reinforces that belief. "You carry a lot of tension in your neck."

Maybe it's the warm bath or her competent hands, but I forget myself for a moment. Forget who I'm talking to. "Why the massage and bath? A quick cuddle with a blanket would have gotten the post-scene job done." That's the standard procedure in the Underworld. Obviously, I know that every Dominant-submissive combo has their own preferences, but this is outside my realm of expectations and for some reason, it's throwing me for a loop.

"Because I want to." An answer that isn't an answer at all.

She keeps up that idle massage until I feel almost drunk. I have the distant thought that maybe falling asleep in the tub wouldn't be such a bad thing, but before I can follow through on that ridiculous thought, Malone's touch is gone.

I open my eyes in time to see her reach into the water and open the drain. She grabs a ridiculously fluffy towel and gives me a long look. "Can you stand without falling over?"

"Of course." I'm not sure if I'm lying or not, but I'm not about to admit it. I climb carefully to my feet and step out of the tub. She instantly engulfs me in the towel. I start to take it from her, but another severe look has me dropping my hands.

She dries me off just like she seems to do everything. Competently. If I didn't have so much experience in submission and scening, I'd mistake this for actual intimacy. It's not. It's simply aftercare and a Domme ensuring her submissive coasts back to reality carefully. Not that I'm *hers*. Not really. But for the next two weeks, I might as well be.

Exhaustion weighs down my thoughts, making them sticky and confusing. This is why I didn't want aftercare from this woman. It muddies the waters, even for me, an experienced submissive. Tomorrow, they'll be clear again, and I'll reinforce my plans.

Tonight, I just feel like crying.

She doesn't comment on the shining in my eyes, which is the smallest of favors. Once I'm dried to her satisfaction, she folds the towel and hangs it back in its place. I've reached the satisfied numbness of a post-scene drop, so I simply stand there and wait for her to tell me what she wants. What little energy I had to fight this disappeared with the water from my body.

When she pulls out a bottle of the exact same brand of lotion I use, I raise my brows. Someone did their homework, though I can't begin to guess *how*. I'm particular about lotion, and I'm extra particular about scent. This is the only one I've found that doesn't make me sticky but also has a subtle enough scent that it doesn't irritate me.

Even through my daze, I start a little when she begins rubbing lotion into my skin. She moves slowly, as if learning my body. It feels too intimate, too... I don't even know. "You don't have to do that."

"You should know by now that I don't do anything I don't want to do." She doesn't look up as she massages lotion into my stomach. "Be silent, and be still."

There's no point in arguing. I'm too tired and worn down to bother. It's easier to simply submit as she slowly works her way over my body, taking extra time and care to ensure she doesn't miss an inch. Aftercare. That's all it is. Simply thorough aftercare.

But despite the strange floating feeling in my head, I don't miss the way pink tinges her cheeks. She wants me. She might not *want* to want me any more than I want to want her, but she does.

Before I can think better of it, I catch her wrist. "Malone. Mistress."

Her brows wing up. "I'm listening."

Why am I doing this? Just another manipulation. That's all. I refuse to think too closely about how flimsy that excuse is. "Surely *you* aren't going to go without orgasm tonight just because I am." I lick my lips. "Let me help."

She laughs, a low, wicked chuckle that sends heat zinging through my body. "Access to my pussy is a privilege you haven't earned, Aurora. You don't get to mouth off and then get your way." She considers me for a long moment. "But since you've managed to behave for the last few hours, I suppose you may watch." She turns and snaps her fingers. "Come along."

I pad after her into her room. She moves to the bed and points to a spot near the bottom corner. "Kneel here."

I refuse to think too closely at my eagerness to obey. I

simply climb up onto the bed and kneel where she indicated. She disappears for a moment into her closet and comes back with a piece of clothing. "Put this on." When I frown, she sighs. "I prefer my home cold. It helps me think. While you will be naked when I want you to be naked, you won't sleep well if you're freezing."

I blink. "Thank you?"

"It's not too late to change my mind about allowing you to watch." She tosses the nightgown at me. I quickly pull it over my head. It's similar to what she's wearing, but instead of being a shirt, the button-down will reach my calves when I stand.

"Thank you." I manage to inject some sincerity into my tone this time. The truth is that it is cold in this place.

And the horrible truth is that I *do* want to watch.

Malone slides out of her pants and climbs onto the bed, moving to position herself in the center. She crooks a finger. "Closer." I follow her direction until I'm kneeling between her spread legs. She unbuttons the bottom few buttons of her shirt and parts the fabric, baring herself from the waist down.

Her pussy is pretty and pink and so wet, I can see her glistening from my position. My mouth waters, and I can't help a flicker of regret that I don't get to touch her tonight. Taste her. She reaches between her thighs and strokes her clit. I watch, enraptured, as Malone winds herself up. Her lean thighs tense, and her heels dig into the mattress on either side of me. I want to unbutton the shirt the rest of the way, to her see body framed by the slick, gray silk. To follow the lines of her collarbones and breasts and the curve of her hip with my mouth, to replace her fingers with my tongue until she comes all over my face.

Need pulses through me in a heady rush. I spend so

much of my time cold and empty. I hide it with smiles and sunshine, but the truth is that a part of me died when my mother went into a coma. The rest of me died yesterday with her.

Few things chase away the dull ache in my chest. Alcohol and sex. I'm too wary of the temptation alcohol offers, so I don't drink much. But sex? Getting sweaty and slick with another person or three? It's an addiction I welcome with open arms.

I just want to forget all the hurt and grief, to set it aside for a few hours. I'll pick it back up in the morning. I always do. Is it too much to ask to dive deep into lust when the feelings become too much to bear?

I shouldn't want to do it with this woman. Anyone but her. Except I can't deny the pull Malone exerts, like her own particular brand of gravity. She touches me and I'm in danger of forgetting everything. A danger, yes, but a gift that I desperately crave. I reach out but stop short before I make contact. "Malone. Please."

Her fingers slow, and for a moment, I think she might be swayed. But those green eyes stay cold even as her lips curve. She lifts her hand. "That's about enough of that."

"Wait. What?"

She sits up. "I told you before, Aurora. You might be able to simper and smile your way through disobedience and bad behavior with other Dominants, but that's not how I operate." She buttons her shirt with quick, efficient movements, removing herself from my line of sight. "Off the bed."

One look at her face has the wicked thing inside me flaring to life. I want to push her, but that little lick of fear over what she might do has me climbing off the bed like an obedient little submissive. I'm not cowed, not exactly. But there is push and pull in any good scene. I know where

Malone's line is now. Throwing myself against it will just mean she continues to punish me, and she's already proven that her punishments actually *are* unenjoyable.

I want the pleasure. More than that, I want her to think I'm cowed and obedient so she lets down her guard.

I'll only have one shot at this.

I have to make it count.

She almost got me.

There was a moment there, where Aurora watched me with hungry eyes, that I almost threw my rules out the window and commanded her to finish what I started. *Almost*. But almost doesn't mean a single damn thing unless I want it to. I maintained my plan, which is all that matters.

I set her up in the mostly unused guest room. "If you disobey the order not to come during the night—"

"I'll be punished." She climbs onto the bed in a flash of long, lean legs and stretches out. "Yes, Mistress. I'll be a good little submissive and keep my hands off my pussy."

I shouldn't enjoy her mouthiness, her obvious anger. A person doesn't get to be where I am if they embrace chaos in any form, and so I adhere to order in every aspect of my life. Work. Territory squabbles. Kink. All of it. I prefer to play with submissives who are obedient, though I made an exception for Tink back when she still worked in the Underworld. But Tink was all bark and no bite. When push came to shove, she hit her knees and happily did everything I asked of her.

Aurora is not like that at all.

"You have them all fooled." I don't mean to speak, but seeing her pull on her sunshine mask irritates me for some reason. "They see the sweet, biddable Aurora because that's what you want them to see. They have no idea that you're a vat of gasoline just waiting for the right match strike to set you aflame. One wrong move and you burn down all of Carver City."

Aurora pulls the covers up to her chest and smooths down the fabric. She finally says, "There wasn't a question in there."

"Because it's not a question." I shouldn't indulge this conversation. I shouldn't have even started it. But I can't quite seem to relay the message to my body to leave the room. "How long have you been a submissive for the Underworld?" I know the answer, but I want to hear her say it.

"Nine years."

It seems to defy belief. By thirty, I was nearly ten years into running this territory. I was a thousand times harder than Aurora is, even with her spikes and fiery temper. For all that the Underworld exposes her to all manner of vices, I can't help feeling like she's been sheltered this entire time. I push the thought away and focus on the subject at hand. "In all those years, you've only slipped once."

Her eyes flash. "What are you talking about?"

"Everyone else seems content to forget that you were willing to literally burn Hook's home to the ground when you thought Tink was in danger." I smooth a hand down my hip. "One blink of your big eyes, and they're half sure they imagined that fierceness."

She blinks those big eyes at me right now. "How did you even hear about that?"

"Come now, Aurora. You know better. I hear everything of value that happens in the territories that border mine." I've been around long enough to remember what *that* territory was like under Peter's rule. I had no interest in dealing with him as a neighbor again. Hook might have a misguided honorable streak a mile wide that occasionally makes him inconvenient, but he's not a malicious fool. If Peter had taken back the territory, I would have been forced to make a move to crush him. Not that I'm interested in explaining that to Aurora.

She considers me. "Even Ursa's?"

"Of course. Neither of us is so sentimental as to let friendship get in the way of business." The friendship is genuine, but we're both smart enough to understand that it's beneficial to both our territories for us to work together on occasion. Between the two of us, we hold nearly half the city. Striving for more is just greedy and runs the risk of hampering our ability to lead. "The only way to maintain power is to expect a knife in the back at every turn. A good territory leader knows that."

She shuts down. I didn't even realize she had opened herself up a little until she's withdrawing from me. I can practically see the shutters closing over her eyes, shielding her thoughts. Aurora finally looks away. "I've very tired. If that's all?"

I don't want to leave this room, to end this conversation. The realization has me turning and walking away from her. These two weeks are about getting this woman out of my system, not about indulging in small talk. "I have work in the morning. Be quiet and entertain yourself until the afternoon."

"Yes, Mistress." There's a snarky little lilt to her words, but I choose not to call her on it. Not when it means staying in this room a second longer.

I close the door softly behind me. There's too much broiling energy inside me for me to sleep, so I stride down the hall to the entrance. It takes exactly two minutes to put on shoes and ride the elevator down to the floor that houses my security team. Sara meets me the second the doors open. They raise their eyebrows but fall into step next to me as I head for their office.

I don't speak until we've closed the door. "Report."

If anything, their eyebrows rise higher. Sara has the bearing of former military, but they've been in private security since graduating college. When I left Sabine Valley, I poached them and brought them with me. Because of that history, because of all our years together, I trust Sara with more than my life. I am good, but even I don't know everything. An excellent head of security has to be comfortable enough to speak up in order to keep me safe and enact the things I require. Someone easily cowed would have been run out long before now.

Sara props a hip on the desk. "There's nothing to report. Everything is running as it should. The only new development is upstairs sleeping in your guest room."

Aside from the landing outside the elevator and the emergency exit leading to stairs down, I don't have cameras in my private residence. Just like I trust Sara to handle small things that arise without bothering me with it, they trust me to handle anyone I allow into my home. "I have it under control."

"No one says you don't." They consider me. "Did you need to spar?"

Yes. Undoubtedly. The scene didn't provide the release

kink usually brings me. Instead, Aurora's presence in my building, in my home, is a buzzing beneath my skin. I've never been one to waffle about things once I decide on a course, but I can't settle on a route with this woman. I want to ice her out. I want to drag her by her hair to my bed and make her come so many times, she loses the ability to speak any word beyond my name.

I hold Sara's gaze. "I'm fine for tonight. Maybe tomorrow."

They nod. "As always, the offer stands."

I don't know what I'm doing down here. I run a hand through my hair. "When's the last time *you* slept?"

"Luna is taking over in ten minutes." It's not really an answer, which is answer enough.

Neither Sara nor I have ever been that good at getting a full night's rest. Another thing we share in common. Luna is a Sabine Valley transplant as well, just like the rest of my personal security team. There's nothing wrong with the people we've hired in Carver City, but old habits die hard. No matter how long I'm in this place, the only people I really trust are fellow Amazons. We're a varied people with different goals and personalities, but the loyalty to our queen—to my sister—is the thread that holds us together.

Maybe *that's* what's bugging me. It's not Aurora at all. She's a symptom of the problem, not the issue itself. Yes, that must be it. "I don't like what happened at Lammas." While Carver City has Hades and the Underworld to provide neutral territory to handle disputes and small power struggles, Sabine Valley takes a different route. Its roots go back farther, to darker places. Four times a year, during the pagan feasts, all three factions gather and deal with things in a way that's designed to avoid bloodshed and an all-out war. Lammas is for ritual battle, a time to safely settle disputes and grudges between various people so they don't fester into true conflict.

The faction leaders, in their arrogance, made a bargain this Lammas that they can't take back. Now two of my nieces and my youngest brother are trapped in handfasts with men they didn't choose for themselves, playing a role in revenge for an act my sister committed.

I press my fingers to my eyes. "I should—"

"No."

Reluctantly, I drop my hands. "You don't even know what I was going to say."

Sara gives me a sympathetic look. "I figure it's a fifty-fifty chance that you were going to say we should just sneak into Sabine Valley and assassinate the Paine brothers or that we should go back there and whoop your sister's ass for letting this happen. Neither is an option."

"Honestly, I was considering doing both."

They shake their head. "My response stands. The laws are there for a reason. You can't just ignore them because you don't like the outcome. Especially since we've spent two decades in Carver City. You'll always be an Amazon, but you're an outsider now. We all are."

"I know." It's the price I've paid for my ambition. I could have stayed in Sabine Valley and taken over as CEO of one of my mother's many corporations. But I would never lead there, would never be queen—or what passes for it. "It doesn't mean I like it."

"None of us like it." Sara crosses their arms over their chest. "Maybe you should call your sister."

Something I've been avoiding ever since I heard the news. What is there to say? To coldly detail how she's failed, how disappointed our mother would be? Even after all these years, there's no way Aisling hasn't shared the same recriminations for herself. No matter what else is true, she's a good leader. Most of the time. "Perhaps tomorrow."

"Yes, maybe." Sara's tone says they know I won't do it.

I glance at the clock. It's late—or early, depending on how one looks at it. Avoiding going back up to my penthouse any longer is a delay reeking of cowardice. I chose this. I am the one in charge. Fleeing the space because Aurora occupies it is unacceptable.

Tomorrow. Things will be clearer tomorrow.

I glance at Sara. "Get some rest tonight."

"Only if you do."

That draws forth a small smile. "Consider it a bargain."

We walk back to the elevator, and Sara clears their throat. "This might be out of line."

"When has that stopped you?"

"A valid point." They grin. "Stop thinking so much and playing out scenarios with that girl. You want her. You already effectively have her for the next two weeks. *Take* her and work out some of this stress."

Deceptively simple advice. Easy to agree to. More difficult to pull off. "I'll consider it."

"Sure you will."

I step into the elevator. "Sleep."

"I will." Sara turns and walks back down the hall as the elevator doors close.

I'm in danger of becoming a nag in order to avoid my own thoughts. How unforgivable. Sara and I have the history to let it slide, but I don't have that same history with everyone I interact with. I have to lock it down, to push these uncomfortable thoughts away. It's never been an issue controlling that before, but now they bubble up inside me.

It's not even a choice to pause outside the door of the guest room. My body has taken over, even as my mind details the ways this is ridiculous. I can't seem to help myself. My hand falls to the doorknob, and I turn it, silently stepping into the room.

Aurora sleeps the way I imagine a child sleeps. All tangled sheets and trusting abandon. She must have gotten out of bed when I left, because her hair is covered by a silk wrap in a pretty floral print. She's only half beneath the covers, one long leg exposed, leading my gaze up to where her nightshirt has rucked up around her hips. It's just an extra few inches of skin, but it feels like seeing her like this is sharing a secret with me.

A secret I most assuredly do not deserve.

I back out of the room as silently as I entered and shut the door behind me. What am I doing? Topping her, dominating her, fucking her. All those are reasonable courses of action. Standing over her bed and watching her sleep? Wanting to touch her, to stroke my fingers over her skin simply because? Unacceptable.

I stride back to my bedroom. This is ridiculous. Tomorrow, things will make more sense. I simply need some sleep to get my perspective back.

Yes, tomorrow will be better.

8

I sleep late. Or maybe it's not late at all. Working in the Underworld for so many years has turned me into a nocturnal creature. I'm rarely up before noon most days. It takes me several long seconds before I remember where I am and why I'm here. Malone's.

Two weeks of kink. Revenge. Murder.

Damn it, I didn't mean to fall asleep. I fully intended to wait for her go to bed and then take a look around the penthouse to see what I could find. I stare at the ceiling, and I can almost hear Allecto's voice in my head. *You call that a plan?*

"It's better than nothing." I feel so unmoored. It's not just that I have nothing to do until this afternoon. For so long, the possibility of my mother someday waking up was what kept me going each day. But as the years ticked into decades, that hope became more fairy tale than reality. The truth is that the doctors were right when, three years in, they told us there was no possibility of her waking up.

I didn't take that answer as truth then.

Now, lying in the guest bedroom of my enemy, I can't

help wondering where I'd be if I'd just...let her go. If I'd grieved her back then, at thirteen, instead of making the trek to the Underworld and throwing myself at Hades's mercy. If I'd allowed myself to admit that she might be my mother, but she was barely more than a stranger to me, and the fantasy future I'd painted in my head was exactly that— fantasy. Would I have moved away from Carver City after high school? Maybe met a nice person and fallen in love? Had a couple kids and a white picket fence?

I don't know. When I try to picture what that life might look like, it's as flimsy as mist.

Frustrated with myself, I sit up and look around the space that is mine for the next two weeks. The guest room is a replica of Malone's, though on a smaller scale. The color scheme is all gray and black with those same pops of red I've seen in the rest of the penthouse. Even the bathroom follows it: classy gray tile interspersed with a delicate, red-rose tile. Black marble counters. A large, white claw-foot tub. Deep-red towels.

I shower and decide to explore the closet. I'm not sure if she wants me wandering the place naked, but I'd feel better if I had some kind of clothing on while I'm snooping.

I stop short in the doorway, shock rooting my feet to the floor. This is... She... The closet is half full. Does someone else stay here? As far as I—or people at the Underworld— know, Malone is single and doesn't even have a normal fuck buddy. Certainly, no one close enough to keep clothing at her place.

But when I finally manage to walk the rest of the way into the closet, I find the clothing is a wide variety of lingerie in pink, black, and red. There are some dresses and even a suit, but it's primarily sexy stuff designed to seduce.

It's all in my size.

Coincidence. It must be. Except I don't really believe that, do I? Last night, she said she had everything she needed for the next two weeks. I assumed she meant toys and the like, but Malone is the type to prepare for any eventuality. She planned this, must have planned this for some time, because I recognize several of the pieces as ones designed by Tink and, these days, the waiting period for her stuff right now is measured by months.

I run my fingers over the lines of the suit, feeling conflicted. The pieces are gorgeous and, yes, probably things I would have chosen for myself. The fact that Malone not only knows my size—or at least did the homework to find it out—but my style... I don't like it.

I'm not exactly surprised she did this if I think about it logically, but there's nothing logical about the fluttering in my chest. Panic. It must be panic. All I've wanted for as long as I can remember is revenge for what Malone did to my mother. She could have taken over the territory without that one-on-one fight. She practically already had at that point. My mother might have been ruthless and occasionally cruel, but she wasn't a warrior. Malone *had* to know that, and she didn't care. She simply wanted to remove an obstacle, and she never once considered who that obstacle might be to other people. Mother, daughter, loved one.

I want to make her pay.

Standing here in this closet full of evidence of how many moves she thinks ahead, I start to shake. Maybe Allecto really was right. I'm never going to be able to pull this off if I'm just reacting. That whole thing about playing checkers while your opponent is playing chess. I can't take the woman in a fair fight. I've had years to examine her legal business in an attempt to find fault to exploit. There is none.

On the criminal side of things, her people love and fear her in equal measure. There's no turning that tide.

It makes me want to shatter something.

I reach for the first piece of lingerie, a black lace body-suit, intent on shredding it to ribbons, but stop myself before my fingers make contact. This isn't the best option. I've come too far to let my chaotic impulses get the best of me. There's a way forward; I just have to find it. I've never been so close to actually making progress before. I just need to be patient for a little while longer.

In the end, I don't change out of the nightshirt I slept in. A quick check in the mirror shows that I look a bit rumpled and pretty low-key sexy. That'll work.

As satisfied as I'm going to be, I head out of the room. The penthouse is eerily silent, or maybe that's just my nerves threatening to get the best of me. I make a round quickly, walking through room after room to ensure I'm alone. Empty. All of them, empty. Good. There will be time to look in more detail later; I need to take advantage of this opportunity while Malone's gone. With that in mind, I make my way back to the hallway with my room, the playroom, and Malone's room. I consider the trio of doors. I highly doubt that she's left anything useful out where I can find it, but it can't hurt to check.

I take a step toward her bedroom and that's when I hear it. A low yowling sound that raises the small hairs on the back of my neck. I turn slowly to find a white long-haired cat standing in the middle of the hallway behind me, its back arched and hair standing on end. It hisses.

It's a gorgeous creature, but there's no denying it'll try to take a bite out of me if I approach. Figures. "She *would* have a feral fucking cat."

"Rogue is simply a creature of habit. He doesn't like change."

I let out a surprised shriek and spin around. I'm distantly aware of the cat fleeing, but the majority of my attention is all on Malone. She's wearing a black suit with a white silk shirt that's *just* shy of being too sexy for corporate work. And she's barefoot.

I don't know why *that* detail sticks in my brain and derails every thought in my head, but I can't quite drag my gaze from her pretty red-painted toes. She was barefoot last night, but somehow it didn't register the same way it does while she's in business clothing. "You have a cat."

"Yes."

"Where is your cat stuff? Cats have stuff, right? Like a litter box or whatever?"

"There's a specially made cupboard in the laundry room." Malone snaps her fingers, and I'm obeying without making a decision to move my body, walking to her side. She pivots easily and leads the way into her bedroom. "This way."

I manage to stay silent despite the questions swirling through me. When she said she had work, I just assumed she'd left the apartment. That was careless of me. If she catches me snooping, I'm not sure what she'll do. I'm still under Hades's protection right now, so I doubt she'd toss me out a window, but there are a number of less lethal ways she could punish me. I have to be better than this. To be better than *her*.

A laptop and phone are sitting on the low table in front of the chairs arranged in a small sitting area. Malone stops in front of the one she was obviously using and turns to me. "I'm sitting in on a meeting with a new team giving their first report. My presence is more to lend additional heft to their manager, so it will be tedious."

I manage to clamp my mouth shut before I press her for more information. She hasn't asked a question, and she's already proven to be a Domme who won't put up with her submissive edging past the lines. Not that I'm *hers*, but the label applies for the next thirteen days.

She lifts an elegant brow. "Well? You're wasting time." When I still hesitate, Malone sighs. "With your experience, I didn't think I'd have to spell it out for you." She motions to the front of her slacks. "Keep me entertained, Aurora."

Oh.

Oh.

I hit my knees, the soft rug cushioning me, and go for the front of her slacks. Even as I tell myself this is solely for the scene, I know I'm a goddamn liar. I want my mouth on her again, want to taste her, want to feel her come all over my face. I unfasten her pants and ease them down her legs, taking a little longer than strictly necessary. She's built lean, but Malone is *strong*. Her legs show the same strength as her arms, muscle readily apparent with each move she makes. She steps out of the pants and waits while I fold them neatly before she sinks onto the chair and casually throws a leg over one of the arms. "Be quiet."

"Yes, Mistress." I move to kneel in the space she created for me. I should...

But there's no room for *should*, not when she's so pretty and pink and right there waiting for me. I dip my head down and kiss one inner thigh and then the other, easing my way up her legs. Malone makes an impatient noise but doesn't stop me. Instead, I hear her picking up her phone.

When she speaks, it's coldly professional. "Yes, I'm here.

Bring on the team and do what you need to do. You're taking lead on this one, Marshall."

I slide my hands up her hips, pushing her shirt higher. She reaches down without looking and stops me before it reaches much past her navel. A severe look tells me that this is all the territory I have to work with. I bite down on the disappointment I have no business feeling. Why should I be annoyed that I don't get access to her breasts when her pussy is right here and waiting?

Maybe I'm just annoyed at everything Malone does.

Or, more accurately, I'm annoyed at myself for wanting her despite everything she's done. And I do want her. I'm honest enough with myself to admit that. I dip down and kiss her pussy, doing what I always do—channeling my frustration and anger into lust. It's so much easier to manage this way, to smile and orgasm and cry out the emotions I'm not comfortable showing to the world. When I'm in a scene, no one expects me to display perfect control. The carefully orchestrated shattering is the point.

I want Malone to shatter. I want to be the one to cause it.

She tastes exactly like I remember, a truth that should have been blurred by time and many partners, but it's there all the same. Every moment of that night is seared into my memory. I'm not the same person I was then, but it doesn't change the way one lick takes me back.

That night I was sure she saw into the very heart of me. Saw all my scars and trauma. Saw my desires. Saw *everything*. She pulled it out piece by piece, breaking me down until I was an exposed nerve for her to strum at her leisure.

I could have survived that. Other Dominants have brought me close to that point over the years, though no one quite so skillfully. No, it was how she held me afterward that fucked with my head. It's the only time in nearly ten years of knowing her that she wasn't icy and distant. She felt warm and soft and all too human.

She felt like mine.

I shove the memory away and focus on the task at hand. Malone says something about annual review reports, and her voice isn't even breathy. She could be sitting at a desk in the middle of a crowded office, rather than in her bedroom with my mouth on her pussy. I look up at her and push two fingers into her. She doesn't bother to so much as glance at me. She simply reaches down, grabs a fistful of my hair, and guides me back to her clit.

What a magnificent bitch.

As irritating as I find her control, it feels like she threw a gauntlet at my feet that I'm only too happy to pick up. I toy with her clit as I carefully explore her with my fingers, looking for her G-spot. It doesn't take long to find it, and her legs go tense as I stroke my fingertips against it.

Got you. I keep up that motion as I focus on her clit. There may be time for teasing and playing later, but I'm on a mission right now. I want her to come and crack that perfect iciness she presents to the world. I want her hot and fiery and on the edge of control. I want to be the one to cause it.

Her fingers tense in my hair, so I keep doing that motion with my tongue, teasing her higher and higher. I look up her body to find her cheeks have gone pink and her lips are parted. She's not making a single sound, but the evidence of how close she is to orgasm is written in her expression, in her legs tensing on either side of my face, on her harsh grip in my hair.

She moves the phone away from her face and hits the mute button. "Stop playing around and make me come."

It's so tempting to reach between my thighs with my free hand, but I already know she won't grant permission. She might even stop me from making *her* come, which is something I desperately want to avoid. I suck her clit into my mouth and work her with my tongue, and she moans a little and orgasms hard, clamping around my fingers.

Malone's grip in my hair softens, and she trails her fingers down my temple. Her expression isn't exactly warm, but it's not as distant as normal. "Don't stop. This call will go on a while yet."

I lick my lips, tasting her there. "Yes, Mistress."

What am I going to do about Aurora?

Half my instincts want to continue to put her in her place, to prove that she doesn't have the same pull on me that she seems to on every other Dominant she comes across. The rest of me wants to stop fucking around and take what's mine for the next two weeks.

The rest of the call is as uneventful as I expect it to be. Marshall has things well in hand, he just needs a little confidence to fully step into his new position while working with a team he's unfamiliar with. He's got all the necessary skills and experience, but he's still a bit green. He'll figure it out.

I hang up and set my phone aside. That was the last obligation of the day. I purposefully lightened my schedule during this time because I didn't want to be distracted—not from work, not from play. There are still things that can't be shifted around, so that's what I'll spend my mornings doing. Aurora is a nocturnal creature like all the other Underworld residents, so it works well.

I dig my hand into her hair again, enjoying the way the

indigo tresses feel against my palm, and pull her off me. "That's enough."

"But—" She catches herself quickly, losing some of the bliss that's filtered into her expression over the last twenty minutes. If I let her, she'll retreat from me again. It's the smart thing to do, to allow that distance, but I find myself reluctant to let it happen. "Come here." I guide her up even as I lean down.

I shouldn't do it. It's a mistake, and I already know it's a mistake, but I can't seem to help myself. I kiss Aurora. Her lips part in shock, and I use the opportunity to trace her bottom lip with my tongue. She has some of the most perfect lips I've ever seen, shaped as if a sculptor molded the ideal mouth. Something I've tried and failed not to notice over the years.

Aurora's hands land on my thighs, and then she's kissing me back. Here, she's just as fierce as I know she can be, subtly fighting me for control. For dominance. A heady feeling rises in me, a flicker of something I've worked hard to keep locked down. This woman makes me want to fight and stab and scream. To annihilate everything in my immediate vicinity until she has no choice but to admit that she's mine.

That's enough.

It takes every ounce of my fraying control to break the kiss. Even then, I only gain an inch between our lips; our panting breath mingling in that tiny space a reminder of how easy it would be to just keep kissing her. To throw out any plan of scening or dominance and submission and simply sink into this woman until the hours tick away and we lose all track of time and ourselves.

It can't happen. Losing control, *any* kind of control, is unacceptable. That's what happened to my sister and now look at the situation back home. Two nieces and our brother in danger. The trust of our people wavering. An old enemy threatening everything our family has spent generations working toward. Aurora is hardly the Paine brothers, but there are thousands of people in my territory who depend on my keeping the status quo. Allowing myself to become wrapped up in her might not endanger everything I've worked so hard for, but I don't know that for sure.

Because I can't guarantee it to be true, I create more space between us. It's not quite the boon I need it to be. Not when Aurora is clutching my thighs as if she's fighting the pull of me as much as I'm fighting the pull of her. Her eyes are a little too wide, and her lips are parted with each harsh breath that escapes.

I don't make a conscious decision to reach down and begin unbuttoning her nightshirt. My body simply takes over. With each button, a larger slice of her light-brown skin is revealed. The curves of her breasts, the smooth skin of her stomach, and finally her pussy. I sit back and study her. A stalling technique to keep myself from falling on her like a starving creature. It barely works.

"Why did you say yes, Aurora?"

She blinks those big brown eyes at me. "What?"

"You dislike me intensely. You have for years. Why say yes to this assignation?" I don't know if I care. She agreed and that paved the way to the outcome I desire. But the way she hesitates now has curiosity flaring in response. "Answer the question."

She meets my gaze for a long moment before pointedly dropping her gaze. "I was angry for a long time after that scene with you when I first started. I want you to want me, and then I will walk away and leave *you* wanting something you can no longer have."

Shock and something like admiration course through me. "Do you think your pussy is so amazing that I'll never get over fucking you?"

She flashes a look at me, and there's no evidence of the innocent woman she's played for nearly a decade. No, it's all fire and fury and no small amount of lust. "I am more than my pussy, Malone. There's a reason every single Dominant in the Underworld favors me; the same reason you've avoided me for nearly a decade."

The statement is an arrow of truth I have no defense against, spearing through my carefully placed defenses. She's not wrong. No matter what I've told myself—or pointedly not told myself—I've never treated another submissive the way I've treated Aurora. Still, I lean forward until our faces are almost within kissing distance. "Do you think to make me fall in love with you?"

"You wouldn't be the first."

That surprises a laugh out of me. "No, I suppose I wouldn't be." I sit back. "But it will never happen, so put whatever petty revenge schemes you're considering out of your head. This is two weeks of simple lust. Nothing more."

"Yes, Mistress," she answers sweetly.

Why the hell am I irritated by how easily she agrees with me? I push the nightshirt off her shoulders and snap my fingers. "Up."

Aurora rises gracefully to stand naked before me. The woman really is a work of art, all long lines and soft curves and the pretty bars piercing her brown nipples. I palm her breasts and coast my thumbs over the jewelry, enjoying the way she inhales sharply. "How long have you had these?"

"A few months."

I know that, of course. I clocked her the second she got them done, flaunting the new additions with a carefully crafted underbust corset and sheer bra. "Have you changed out the jewelry?"

"No... Not yet."

"Mmm." I lean forward to suck first one nipple and then the other. She shouldn't taste so damn sweet everywhere I put my mouth, but nothing about Aurora follows the rules. No matter what she pretends.

She starts to reach for me, but I grab her wrists and guide them to the small of her back without stopping what I'm doing. I use one hand to press them there and skate my other down her stomach to cup her pussy. She jerks but widens her stance to allow me better access. I expect her to be turned on, but something about finding her soaked, about knowing that she got this ramped up because she was eating me out, frays my control even more.

I need—

Damn it, what am I doing?

I jerk back, barely managing to recover and catch her shoulders when she sways. "The playroom. Now." Confining our scenes to that room is the only way to go. Honestly, I should have simply taken out an exclusive contract with her in the Underworld and gone there every night instead of bringing her into my home. That's the smart, logical thing to do.

But a deep, wild part of me wants her here, available to me at all times. Surrounded by my things. Possessed by me completely.

I pull my pants back on and follow her into the playroom. Distance. I just need a bit of distance. "You've pleased me."

Aurora stops in the middle of the room and bows her head, the very picture of an obedient submissive. In her way, she's frantically trying to put more distance between us, too. Again, that irrational irritation rises.

I stalk to the far corner of the room and snap my fingers. I don't need to look to know Aurora follows. I motion at the sex machine. It's a custom piece that was built by a friend of a friend, a leather bench-like creation designed to be knelt on. Once the submissive is fastened in place, the portion holding the knees and shins stays immobile while the center part rocks. It's meant to create a delicious grinding motion with the dildo, and the curved section at the front rubs against the clit with every stroke. "Climb on."

Aurora hesitates. "Is this a reward or a punishment?"

I could leave her in suspense, but I'm not kind enough to do that. "A little of both." I grab a bottle of lube and spread it over the dildo. "Now, Aurora."

She moves slowly, perching one knee in place. I fist the dildo and hold her hip with my other hand, guiding it into her. Her hiss of surprise brings me more joy that I have right to. She wiggles a little as I move around the machine, fastening her legs in place with padded leather buckles. I double-check the restraints. "Too tight?"

"No, Mistress." Her voice has already gone a little breathy.

I take her hips and guide her to rock a bit. "And this?"

"It feels perfect."

I catch her chin. "Tell me your safe word, Aurora."

"Thorn." She licks her lips.

"Good girl." I force myself to release her. "You may come as many times as you like."

Her eyes go wide. She's experienced enough to know this really *is* both a punishment and a reward. How many times will she orgasm before it's too much? Will I stop the machine before she reaches that point? I can see the anticipation and trepidation curling through her, and she looks down at the device.

"One last thing." I retrieve a pair of cuffs and fasten her hands behind her and then clip the cuffs to the hook at the back of the seat. It's not a tight enough connection to bend her uncomfortably, but it will keep her completely at the machine's mercy.

I move to the overstuffed chair a few feet away and sink into it. A click of the remote, and the machine begins to rock slowly. Aurora makes a muffled sound of surprise, her gaze flying to me. I smile and pick up the book I left on the side table this morning for solely this purpose. It's one I've reread many times, its spine cracked and bent, and I open it and begin to read.

Or at least I try.

The first time Aurora comes, her breath hissing out, her curse choked, I lose all concentration. She's just as beautiful like this as she is in every other instance, and I can't help but watch from the corner of my eye. I slow the machine to give her a second to recover and then change the mode to a different pattern, winding her up again.

A reward and a punishment. As many orgasms as she can take, but she's deprived of my touch, my attention. A special kind of torture for a little brat like Aurora.

By the fourth time she comes, her skin has a sheen of sweat, and there are tear tracks down her pretty face. "Mistress, *please*."

I make a show of putting my book aside and focusing on her. "Please, what?" She clamps her mouth shut as if she didn't mean to let those words loose. I raise my brows. "If there's nothing else..." I click the remote, increasing the tempo.

"Oh, gods." Aurora's breath sobs out. "Please don't make me come like this again."

There it is.

I have to concentrate to rise slowly, to not rush to her side and do exactly what I've been fantasizing about for far too long. She broke first. It's important to not give over any power in response.

I sift my fingers through her hair and give it a tug. "What do you need? Speak plainly."

She doesn't want to. I can see it written across her face. But the seat keeps rocking against her clit, grinding that cock inside her, and she shudders. "Touch me. I need..." She gulps. "I need you. Please, Malone."

My name on her lips in that agonized tone of voice completely unravels me. I turn the machine off and unstrap her in quick movements. I unfasten the cuffs from the seat but leave them on her wrists. Her legs won't work properly after being in the position for so long, so I lift her and carry her to the chair I just occupied. "Your arms."

"They're fine. I can stay cuffed like this for a long time."

I should check for myself, but I'm too focused on what comes next. I set her on the chair and sink to my knees between her spread thighs. Her pussy is drenched and swollen from the machine, from coming so many times. I lick my lips. "Next time you come, you do it while screaming my name."

10

AURORA

The first drag of Malone's tongue is agony and heaven, all at the same time. If I could string two thoughts together, I'd be terrified right now. She's done it again. I am dismantled, a person fractured into a million pieces. The only thing that matters is the way she touches me, what comes next.

My shoulders ache from being cuffed in this position for an extended period of time, but I don't care. Not with the sight of Malone kneeling between my legs, her elegant hands gripping my thighs to keep me positioned where she wants me.

She's so *strong*. Physically. Mentally. She makes me want to crash against her walls again and again, until she breaks... Or I do. I almost welcome the shattering.

Liar.

I *crave* the shattering.

This is a woman who can outlast me. One who holds herself apart no matter how close she is, no matter what kind of scene we're participating in. I can't reach her, and a twisted part of me worships her for it. No other Dominant has been so distant, has made me want them so much. I hate it. I need it.

She parts my pussy with her thumbs and exhales against my clit. "Remember what I said."

Next time I come, it had better be screaming her name. I swallow hard, and my voice emerges in a croak. "I remember."

"Good girl." She closes the last little bit of distance between us and strokes my clit in the exact motion I need to get off. How the hell does she know my body so well already? I don't understand. It's something I'll poke at later, when I'm not on the verge of losing it.

I whimper, but I can't move with her holding me down like this. The knowledge only drives my need higher. I'm so over-sensitized, pleasure blends into pain and back again. Too much. Not enough. Both at the same time. "Malone, *please*."

She hesitates for the barest second and something shifts in her. The careful restraint is gone. She goes after my pussy like she needs this just as much as I do. Her fingers dig into my thighs, forcing my legs wider, forcing me to give her everything.

My body turns weightless for one heartbeat, and then I crash back down to earth, a comet happily free-falling into its inevitable destruction. I think I scream. I can't be sure. All I can feel is her mouth on me. All I can taste is her name on my lips. "*Malone.*"

She presses her forehead to my stomach, and I'm dazed enough to wonder if I'm imagining the way her breathing is harsh against my skin. Surely she's not actually as affected as I am. *She* isn't faltering in her path. I shouldn't be, either.

I hate how weak I am when she touches me.

She finally sits back and runs her hands up my hips and sides, tugging me forward so my weight is no longer on my arms. Malone closes the distance between us as she reaches for the cuffs, bringing us nearly chest to chest. Her mouth is wet from my desire, and her green eyes look more like green flames.

I really, really want to kiss her.

A click and my wrists are free. She guides my arms forward and carefully massages my shoulders. "Pain?"

"No." I hardly sound like myself. "I've been cuffed like that longer with no problem."

"Not with me." She moves down my arms, touching me as if she can divine every single ache and twinge. She ends her examination at my wrists, bracketing them with her hands. "And here?"

"I'm fine." I try to pull away, but she tightens her grip, holding me in place.

Malone traces her thumbs over my inner wrists, her expression going contemplative. "What is it that you want, Aurora?"

I almost blurt out the truth. Sex and endorphins and the aftermath of too many orgasms, and the words nearly spill from my lips at that tiny prompting. I manage to lock myself down at last moment, manage to shove everything down deep. It takes more effort than it should to dredge up my sunny smile. "What more could I want than what I already have?"

Her perfect brows lower, and she squeezes my wrists once, a warning. "You want to be a plaything for the rich and powerful? Always the bridesmaid, never the bride, constantly watching your patrons find love and relationships and their forever people while you are constantly left in the rearview mirror." She laughs, pretty and cruel.

"Don't lie to me. You have too much fire to be content with that."

She's not wrong, but I bristle all the same. "You don't know me."

"I know enough." She releases me and pushes to her feet. "Then again, I suppose I could be wrong. You might be nothing more interesting than a toy to be played with and then discarded."

It stings. Good lord, it stings. How dare she pull out a layer of pain I very carefully don't think about? "I have friends and people who care about me."

"Yes." Malone snags a small towel from a hook on the wardrobe and wipes her mouth. "And when they're done having fun with you, they go home with the people they love and leave you in the shadows."

Against all reason, my throat feels thick, and my eyes start to burn. "I've had relationships. Real ones."

Something goes flinty in her eyes. "I'm aware." She leans down until our faces are even, until I can't escape her gaze. "And how did those relationships go? Every single one of them."

"That's none of your business." I shouldn't have even brought them up. I wouldn't have if I was thinking clearly.

"I'll tell you how they went." She's unrelenting, her cruelty quiet and cutting deep. "They saw what they wanted to see, what *you* wanted them to see. The surface shit. They liked the idea that they could have pretty, submissive, sunshine Aurora whenever they wanted. The darling of the Underworld. How long did it take for reality to creep in? How long until they started to resent you for the very thing that drew them in the first place?"

My eyes are burning, but I refuse to break her gaze.

"Choosing the wrong partner doesn't mean I'm not worthy of love."

"You're correct." She tosses the towel into a metal basket near the door. "But it brings me back to my original question: What is it that you really want?"

I swallow hard. "I don't know you or trust you enough to answer that question." A last ditch effort to drive her off. If she persists, I'm not certain I can keep my secrets buried. A terrifying thought. I need time and space to get my armor back into place before we go another round. At this rate, the entire two weeks won't end in my revenge being enacted; they'll end with Malone taking my future the same way she took my past.

She considers me for a long moment before nodding. "I suppose that's fair." She grabs a thick blanket and starts to wrap it around me, but I move first, trying to stand so I can grab it from her hands.

My legs don't hold me. My knees buckle, and I start to crumple.

Malone catches me before I hit the ground. Her expression is downright forbidding as she scoops me into her arms. "What the hell are you doing?"

"I don't need aftercare."

"Aurora."

"Yes?"

"Shut the fuck up."

I blink. Have I ever heard her sound so heated before? I don't think so. She sinks onto the chair I just vacated with me in her lap and wraps the blanket around me. Malone looks... Well, she looks furious. She glares down at me like she wants to throttle me, and not in a sexy way. "Listen to me closely. You are not in charge of this situation, and you are certainly not in charge of me. You do not get to decide what's best for you, because *I* already know what you need."

I can't give her that power, Dominant or no. "But—"

She covers my mouth with her hand. It's a gentle touch, but it shuts me up all the same. Malone glares. "Let me put this another way. What would Hades or Meg—or *you*—do to a submissive that attempts to refuse aftercare they obviously need?"

I really, really don't want to answer that, but it's clear that she requires a response. Finally, I wrap my hand around her wrist and nudge her away from my mouth. I lick my lips. "I'd —we'd—tell them that aftercare is a vital part of the process, for both Dominant and submissive, and their instincts aren't functioning at one hundred percent after a scene."

She stares at me for a long moment. "Do you think you're exempt from that?"

"I—"

But she talks right over me. "Are you so superhuman that you don't need aftercare, Aurora? You're too experienced to believe that lie." She pauses, the breathless moment before the sword falls. "Are you that frightened of me?"

"I'm not scared of you." I speak too quickly, giving myself away.

"Mmm." Malone settles back into the chair and pulls me with her, tucking my head against her shoulder. I want to fight the closeness, but fighting it is as much as admitting that she's right about me being scared of her. A neat little trap, which no doubt she's fully aware of.

We sit like that for a long time. Long enough for the sweat to cool on my body and the shakes from adrenaline letdown to come and go. Long enough for sleepiness to set in. I fight it. It's enough that I've submitted to this care; I'm not going to nap on top of her, too. No matter how tempting the idea, how good it feels to be curled in her lap. Malone is all sharp edges, but somehow she feels just right with her arms wrapped around me.

She finally sighs and releases me. "I have some things to do. Find something to eat. We'll continue this later."

I refuse to categorize the weight in my chest as I climb off her on shaking legs and head for the door. I can't look back. It feels like she's shattered my very foundations, but the reprieve will be enough to build them back up again. It has to be.

I bypass the kitchen to head to the room that's mine for the next two weeks. A quick shower gets my head back on straight. The apartment is echoing and empty as I pad to the kitchen and make myself a light snack. Malone's fridge is stocked up to the brim, which fascinates me despite myself. She seems like the type of person to cut down on any unnecessary tasks, which would include meal-making. Easier to delegate that task to someone else. Maybe she has someone come in and cook for her, though she seems territorial enough that that's a reach.

After I eat, I do another careful search of the apartment. There's nothing more to find, and Malone's locked her bedroom door. I might be able to pick the lock, but I have a feeling she'd know if I was there, so I hold off. Getting impatient right now would be a mistake.

Still...

I'm bored.

In the Underworld, my days and nights are filled to the brim with tasks and scenes and various duties that come with being Meg's second-in-command. The only time I'm not running from one thing to the next or checking things off my list is when I'm sleeping. I don't know *how* to be idle.

Not to mention my body is still riled up from what Malone and I did earlier. I'm not going to be able to calm down until I work off some of this energy.

With that in mind, I dig through my closet of new clothes and find a drawer full of workout clothing. I raise my brows a bit as I eye the selections. Malone is a woman of particular taste, all right. After some consideration, I pull on a pair of shorts that fit me like a second skin and a bra with more straps than strictly necessary, both in black. There are even running shoes in exactly my size. The whole thing would be eerie if I didn't recognize that this is just how Malone works; preparing for any eventuality.

I don't want to admire that about her. I sure as hell don't want to be able to draw lines between her preparedness and her success as a leader. She's gorgeous and savvy and ruthless and *evil*, and the latter is the most important thing for me to remember.

I head for the elevator and, after some consideration, push the button Sara did the other night. That must be the security floor, or staff floor, and someone there will be able to point me in the direction of the gym. Malone didn't tell me I was confined to the apartment, so I don't see why I can't explore the *tiniest* bit.

The elevator doors open to a floor that looks just like so many businesses around town. It's white on white on white, a stylish front desk sitting in the center with a white, shaded pane of glass behind it, mostly shielding the rest of the room from my gaze. There are spaces on either side to walk past, but one look at the woman manning the desk and I know better than to try without permission.

I smile brightly and head for her. She's a curvy Black

woman with a shaved head and bright-purple lipstick. She's also got the cold eyes of a killer. I stop just short of touching the desk. "Hi, I'm Aurora. I was hoping you could point me in the direction of the gym."

She eyes me for a long moment. "Down one more level."

I wait for some kind of warning not to go farther, but she just stares at me as if she can read my mind. No doubt this place has security cameras in every conceivable location, though I didn't clock any in Malone's apartment. I don't know if that's incredibly reckless of her or simply an indication that she doesn't need her security team in order to protect herself. Somehow, I can't help thinking it's the latter.

I keep my smile in place as I back into the elevator and wave. "Thanks!"

On the next floor down, I find a tall white woman waiting. She jerks her chin at me. "This way."

I was barely in that elevator for twenty seconds after talking to the woman upstairs. Allecto would be hard-pressed to match a time response like this to adapt to someone's movements. I follow the woman through a door and down a long hallway. She motions to a few of the doors we pass, rattling off what they lead to. Pool. Sauna. Locker room. Racquetball court. At the end, there are three doors. She glances at me. "Weight room, general fitness, or sparring?"

I had fully intended to jump on a treadmill and run for a bit, but the option of sparring perks me up. *You shouldn't.* I shouldn't...but I want to. "I have no one to spar with."

The woman gives a slow smile. "Not yet." She leads the way through the third door and into a large room with thick, blue mats and an honest-to-god boxing ring. She catches my look, and her grin widens. "Most of us like to have this sort of thing in our regular lineup."

"I see." Except I'm not seeing anything but the pair of people moving around the middle mat, almost too fast to follow. I recognize the tall Maori person with their long, black hair braided back and tattoos covering both arms. Sara.

The other is Malone.

11

MALONE

I catch sight of Ivy walking through the door, Aurora behind her, and almost get Sara's massive fist to my face for my distraction. I throw myself back, but even then I can feel the air displacement from their strike. Sara really isn't capable of pulling their punches, which is part of the reason I prefer sparring with them. It keeps me sharp.

Or it would if Aurora hadn't just walked into this room.

I go on the defensive, moving around the mat, dodging Sara's attacks, so I can get a look at Aurora. Foolish. In a real fight, it'd likely mean my death. Knowing that doesn't stop me. She's wearing a cute little outfit that shows off her body, and I recognize it as one of the ones I purchased for her before this assignation started. Why is she *here?*

I duck under Sara's next attack and come up quickly, using all my strength to drive my fist into their stomach. Sara's breath releases in an agonized groan, but it's not enough to put them on the floor. No, they're made of tougher stuff than that.

"We have guests."

Sara nods, but they curse a bit under their breath. "I almost had you."

"Yes, you did." There are many reasons why Sara is my second-in-command; their deadliness in a number of arenas ranks high on that list.

I stride to where Aurora and Ivy stand and accept a towel from Ivy to wipe my face. "What are you doing here?"

Aurora is looking at me like she simultaneously wants to knock me on my ass and devour me whole. "You're fast."

"That's not an answer."

She shrugs. "I have too much pent-up energy. I need to run it off somehow."

"Then obviously I haven't done my job correctly," I murmur.

She looks away. "She said there would be people to spar with." She jerks her thumb at Ivy. "I don't see anyone else."

"Shift change was two hours ago. Most of them have finished up and gone home." Why am I telling her this? I should send her back to the penthouse, or at least to another room. I suspect I'm not going to be able to concentrate properly with her here, and that's a recipe for a black eye when sparring with Sara. I have absolutely no intention of walking around with a marked face because I was distracted when I shouldn't have been. "Go find somewhere else to run off that energy." I motion to Ivy.

"Do you only spar with Sara?"

I stop short. "What?"

Aurora finally looks at me, a stubborn set to her expression. "Do you only spar with Sara?"

"Aurora," I say her name slowly. "I know you're a masochist, but this is not a scene and I have no desire to harm you."

"Malone." She matches my tone and yanks a hair tie off

her wrist to pull her hair back. "Maybe *I'm* the one who will hurt *you*."

Who *is* this woman? I've spent far too long studying her, to the point where it borders on inappropriate. Distraction does not begin to describe Aurora. She's a blazing light in any room she walks into. I wouldn't be who I am if I didn't have the desire to bottle it up and keep it for myself. But this? I don't have the information to respond appropriately to this. I've only ever seen her in the club.

It never really occurred to me that she'd have hobbies outside the Underworld. Or that it would matter. After all, we become our truest selves in that place. All the polite masks are removed and there's only base need. No right way, no shame, no rules but consent. I *know* Aurora right down to her core.

But I also know next to nothing about her on a surface level.

"Clear the room." I speak without looking away from her.

Sara sighs. "Try not to break her." They nudge Ivy with their shoulder as they walk past, which prompts her to pick her jaw off the floor and follow Sara from the room.

I wait for the door to close behind them to motion Aurora onto the mat. "I'm not capable of going easy."

"I don't expect you to." She rolls her shoulders and, after some consideration, kicks off her shoes and socks.

I try to view her through the lens of an opponent, but it's like my brain skips every time I look at her. All I can see are her graceful movements, the curious tilt of her head, how fucking *breakable* she is. No matter what she believes, it was never my intention to shatter Aurora. I'm not sure I can do this without harming her. "Aurora—"

"Are you ready?"

"Yes." I answer without thinking, still trying to find the right words to let her down gently without harming her pride.

She comes at me like a whirlwind. One moment, she's several feet away, and the next she's too close, delivering a punishing kick to my thigh and following it up with a right hook I barely dodge. Fuck, she's quick. And well-trained.

I move out of the way before she kicks the same spot on my thigh. A few more hits there and the leg will buckle. Damn. I shove my hesitations away and feint a few times, testing out her response time. Fast. So fucking fast. "You've done this before."

"Many, many times." Aurora knocks my hand away, but I'm expecting it, and I come in with my other fist, forcing her to block me to avoid a hit to her face.

I retreat, still studying her. Now that I know what I'm looking at, I realize I recognize the way she moves. Smooth and dangerous and intent on her mission. Not like Aurora at all. No, she looks like... "Allecto."

Aurora grins. "We're good friends."

I know that, of course. In the last year or so, it's been impossible to miss the strange sort of friendship that's cropped up with Aurora and several other women in the Underworld. Maybe it was always there, but they're out in the open with it now.

Allecto is one of the few people in Carver City that gives me pause. She could be an Amazon for how superior she is to everyone around her in every way. She's smart, capable, and famously brutal with the people who cross Hades. I always assumed her friendship with Aurora was one where she took on a dominant role and looked after the younger woman like a protective older sister.

If they've trained enough to make Aurora this skilled, they're closer to equals than I could have imagined.

Which means Aurora is a threat in a way I didn't anticipate.

I'm thinking too hard. It slows my reaction time, which is the only excuse I have for Aurora sneaking past my guard and clipping my chin. It's a glancing blow, but it snaps me into the present. I step back a few times, putting myself out of her range, and touch the spot. "Are you angry at me, Aurora?"

A fine sheen of sweat glistens on her skin. She clenches and unclenches her fists. "Why would I be angry at you, Mistress?"

Answering with a question is its own kind of confirmation. The knowledge creates a strange feeling in my stomach. No matter what else has happened, I've inundated her with orgasms this afternoon. She shouldn't want anyone touching her pussy for a few hours yet, no matter how insatiable she is. Surely she's not still angry that I pushed the issue with aftercare?

Aurora takes advantage of my distraction. She comes at me in a concentrated effort, alternating kicks and punches until I'm scrambling to keep any of the hits from landing. The little asshole feints with her leg, aiming for the same spot now aching from that first kick, and when I move to block, she punches me in the face.

I'm on her before I make the conscious decision to move, bearing her to the ground. She tries to roll us, but I'm stronger, and I have as much experience grappling as I do with the rest of it. I straddle her hips and hook her thighs with my feet, pinning her lower body to the mat. She tries to hit me again, but I easily catch her wrists and shove them down, holding her in place.

My leg hurts, but it has nothing on the throbbing in my face. I move my jaw carefully, but everything seems to be functioning as it should. "You didn't pull your punch."

"Oops." She doesn't sound the least bit sorry.

It should piss me off, but the feeling surging through me isn't anger. It's admiration. Admiration and a heavy dose of lust. This delicate flower has more thorns than I could have imagined. Instead of turning me off, it makes her that much more interesting. I stare down at her. "I should have expected this." I'm the one who pointed out how dangerous she is, how ready to do violence when incited.

"Sounds like a *you* problem."

I sit back a little, careful to keep her wrists in place. "Can you shoot? Use weapons beyond fire?"

Aurora's gorgeous face takes on a stubborn set. "Want to grab some guns and find out?"

That surprises a laugh out of me. "So you can shoot me? I don't think so." But it also answers my question in a round-about way. "What was Allecto preparing you for?"

Aurora narrows her eyes. "Who says she was preparing me for anything? Maybe it has nothing to do with her at all."

I'm making assumptions again, something she's proven time and time again that I can't afford to do. I trace her inner wrists with my thumbs and am gratified to see her breath catch. "I have you pinned. To the victor goes the spoils."

"Am I the spoils of war now?" The way she says it is all wrong. She might like the way I touch her, but she is *furious*. Far angrier than this loss warrants, especially since she landed such well-placed blows.

I contemplate her for several long moments, but she offers me nothing. I don't know the source of her rage, which means I can't work with it. Surely it's not... I take a breath. "Are you angry because it took eight years for me to circle back to you?"

"Yes. Next question."

No, she answered too easily. It's the truth, yes, but not the full truth. Gods, this woman is a puzzle I only have half the pieces to. If I have one vice, curiosity claims the honor. Aurora's layers are what draw me to her, and realizing they go deeper than I expect is like a gift just for me.

I settle myself more firmly on top of her. "We'll add sparring to our schedule."

"Pass."

I ignore that and nod to myself. "A bet, if you will. Winner gets a favor."

She opens her mouth but seems to reconsider whatever she was about to say. Aurora frowns up at me. "What kind of favor?"

Got you.

"Whatever you like, within reason." I allow myself a satisfied smile. "Today, I win."

"Give me a rematch now that the terms are set."

I chuckle. "I don't think so."

She licks her lips. "What do you want?"

I should demand answers, information to sate my curiosity. This woman has secrets upon secrets, and I want to hack my way through her barriers to get to them. "A kiss."

She blinks. "A kiss?"

"Yes." I lean down, pressing myself to her. Gods, she's something else. Soft and strong and straining to kick my ass. But the anger has faded from her eyes, and she's watching my mouth as if craving a taste. I'm only too happy to close the distance and touch my lips to hers. She tenses, as if she expected me to plunder her mouth. Another time, I might—

I *will*. Right now, I intend to enjoy my prize to the fullest extent.

I nip her bottom lip and trace the spot with my tongue, deepening the kiss when she gasps a little. Pretty Aurora. She's a revelation. It doesn't seem to matter how many times she's experienced something, how many people she's kissed. She reacts like this is the first time, like it's a shock. Or maybe I'm projecting. There's something about this woman that brings a fierceness to the fore. I want to conquer her, to brand our shared experience all over her hot little body. The desire is inconvenient, but if I could get rid of it, I would have done it by now. That's what these two weeks are about: purging her from my system.

She kisses me back. I shift, settling on top of her and pressing my thigh between her legs. Aurora instantly digs her heels into the mat and arches up to rub herself against me. Wicked little thing.

I don't mean to lace my fingers through hers. It seems the most natural thing in the world to go from gripping her wrists to pressing palm to palm. The shock is almost enough to jolt me out of this moment, but then she makes a delicious little whimpering sound, and I push away my misgivings in favor of drawing that sound from her again.

She rocks against me, and I press my thigh more firmly to her, giving her the friction she obviously needs. She kisses me like she needs me more than she needs air. It doesn't matter that this is pure chemistry. That it doesn't mean anything. I sink into the feeling of Aurora with everything I have.

Fuck, but if I were a different person, I might decide to keep her.

T hey say love and hate are different sides of the same coin. So are lust and anger. Malone has turned my fury into an inferno that I'm terrified will burn me down to nothing but ash. She's kissing me. Something I refuse to admit that I can't get enough of. More, her entire body is pressed against me, and it feels like I've been starved for touch until this moment. Like the one thing I'm missing in my life is the slow slide of her soft skin against mine.

She's holding me down, but it feels like we're clutching each other, like we exist in a space outside the simple rules of gravity. I can't help rubbing myself against her leg as her tongue strokes mine. It must be the endorphins still raging from the sparring session because I'm so turned on, I can barely think straight.

I *can't* think straight.

I am pure need and raging emotions. I can't tell which way is up, don't care about anything but the press of Malone's body against mine. She's wearing a similar outfit— shorts and a sports bra—and I wish it was less. I want all of her against all of me with a ferocity that leaves me breathless. I knew I wanted her, of course, but I never bargained for how much. She overwhelms me.

Malone shifts, pressing my hands more firmly to the mat, and uses her thigh to spread my legs wider. She releases my mouth long enough to nip my neck, sending a delicious frisson of desire through me. "Make yourself come. Use me."

She kisses me again before I can respond, but what is there to say? I want this. Her command just makes it easier to take what I need. I grind on her leg like a horny teenager, chasing the pleasure sparking through my body.

Gods, the woman can kiss.

Malone maintains control, even in this. It's perfect and precise and hot enough to set me aflame. She kisses me like she's memorizing me. I shouldn't like it as much as I do. I shouldn't like it *at all*.

My orgasm overwhelms me between one breath and the next. I moan, and she drinks the sound. I could almost swear that she shivers in response, but it must be my imagination. Malone's too distant to ever react to something as simple as a little grinding orgasm.

Finally, a small eternity later, she lifts her head and looks down at me. "Do you have something else you want to do to finish your workout?"

I blink. What is she...

My mind clicks into place sluggishly, pleasure making it hard to focus. "Um." I lick my lips, tasting her there. "I was going to go for a run."

"Good." She sits back and pulls me up with her. Only then does she release my hands. I can feel the imprint of her there, too, but that's no surprise. I can feel her all over my body. Somehow it never registered with the aftercare or her carrying me, but having her body against mine is more intoxicating than any alcohol. I want more, and I want it now. I start to reach for her, but she lightly slaps my hand. "Go finish your workout, Aurora."

Shock eliminates my verbal breaks. "But what about you?"

"What about me?"

"I came." I motion vaguely at her hips. "You didn't."

Her smile is more like the Malone I'm used to, sharp and icy. "You'll make it up to me later. Finish your workout," she repeats. "Then go upstairs and get ready. Cocktail attire, no bra or panties. We leave at seven." She turns, and I can't help but watch her walk away. She's so fucking flawless, it's almost offensive. Her workout gear shows off her muscle definition with every step, a visual indication of the strength I've felt time and time again. Maybe if she was just strong, she wouldn't have such an effect on me, but Malone is so much more than brute strength. She's an elegant kind of violence in a beautiful package. The perfect predator, anyone with a hint of intelligence recognizes it the moment she walks into a space.

She seems to take all the air of out of the room with her when she leaves. I press my hands to my chest, my heart racing so hard, I can feel my pulse through my palms. What was *that?*

I hadn't meant to show my hand, but the temper I normally have no problem locking down slips its leash more and more the longer I'm around Malone. I want to blame it on being close to my end goal of putting Malone six feet under, on seeing an opportunity for a "sparring accident." I'm not so sure that's the case any longer.

One of things living in the Underworld has taught me is to be honest, even if it's only to myself.

The honest truth is that I desire Malone with a fervor I've never felt before. She's a fire in my blood, and I used to be able to convince myself that it's purely rage, but now I have to admit that it's more nuanced than that. I hate her. I want her. A small, unforgivable part of me even admires her for the sheer strength and ruthlessness she exhibits.

I put my shoes and socks back on and drag myself into the other room. Under normal circumstances, I like running. It soothes me in a similar way that a good scene does—an exercise for both body and mind. Right now, I'm too frazzled to do more than a few miles. I keep circling back to the fight.

She's better than I am. She might even be better than Allecto. I don't know why part of me thought she'd let herself go over the years. I've looked into the place she came from, and though news out of Sabine Valley is scarce, Alaric originally comes from the same city. His information is years out of date because of how things went down with his cousins, but he gave me the basic rundown. About how the Amazons are one-third of the big movers of that city. About how they, more than the other two, straddle the line of shadows and light. They are CEOs and COOs and the upper tier in all of the companies in their territory. Just like Malone runs her corporation *and* rules the illegal industries in her territory with an iron fist.

She still moves like a warrior that might have to step onto a battlefield at any moment. She's so fucking *strong*, too. Stronger than someone with her lean frame has right to be.

I touch my knuckles. They ache a little from the punch I landed on her face. I'm lucky she didn't take it as a true attack, just an extension of our sparring.

I... I don't know if I can beat her in an all-out fight.

I stop the treadmill and go through the motions of stretching. My thoughts whirl in increasingly frantic circles, a tornado of thorns that slice me with every rotation. I don't know if I can beat her. The whole point of agreeing to these two weeks was finally getting revenge for what she did to my mother, to put Malone in the ground.

The plan felt rock solid when I decided on it. Not even Allecto's arguments could get through my wall of stubbornness. But two days in, and I'm not sure I can pull it off.

I head back up to the penthouse in a daze. It's empty, so Malone either didn't come back here or has already come and gone. It's just as well. I don't know what my face is doing right now, and I have no faith that I can keep myself locked down enough to be in her presence.

The cat hisses at me as I walk past, and I hiss right back. "Mind your business and I'll mind mine."

A long shower does nothing to settle me. I walk out of the bathroom to find the demon cat sitting in the center of my bed. I eye the door. I must not have shut it all the way. The cat and I stare at each other. What did Malone say its name was? I glare. "Don't get too comfortable. That's my bed you're sleeping on." At least for the next ten days.

I consider my options for dinner. I'm still a little shocked at how Malone went all out with these clothes. It's more than the money she must have dropped on it. It's a cohesive wardrobe with enough options to almost fully replace the one I already own. And they're all top-of-the-line and in my size.

She must have had an assistant handle that. I have to believe that, because the thought of her handpicking each item with me in mind is too much for me. It makes me feel strange, like my skin is too tight. I don't like it.

Especially because there isn't a white garment in the entire closet.

I finally land on a short, red cocktail dress. It's long-sleeved and covered in sequins that will turn me into a walking disco ball. It's also short enough to almost be indecent and backless. It's extra as hell, but I'm instantly in love.

I style my hair down and vamp up my eyes a bit, finishing the look with red lipstick a shade brighter than the dress. The dress and makeup, combined with my indigo hair, make me look like a girly fantasy. I love it.

I find some nail polish—seriously, did she think of *everything?*—and paint my toes to match my lips. A silly little detail, but I like to go for the complete look, whether I'm running an errand for Allecto or spending a night working in the Underworld. Even if the details don't matter to other people, they matter to me. That's reason enough to do it.

Five minutes before seven, I slip on a pair of strappy silver heels and eye the cat. As much as I don't want to leave him in this room, I really don't want to go to dinner with claw marks all over my arms. I glare. "Your time is limited, my friend."

He starts cleaning his paws, completely ignoring me. Because of course. Not only am I in over my head with Malone, but her fucking *cat* is more dominant than I am. Great.

I leave the door cracked open and head for the elevator. The foyer is empty, and I'm still considering what I should do when I hear footsteps behind me.

I turn, and the breath whooshes out of my body. She's wearing suspenders again. Gods, why does that do it for me so hard? Malone is dressed in pinstriped tailored pants, tall black heels, and a slightly loose, light-gray button-down that she's left half unbuttoned. It's similar to what she wore the other day, but no less arresting for it.

Malone has a particular style, but when she wears stylized menswear, it's my favorite. The contrast with her achingly delicate features and the power she exudes hits me in places I have barely registered exist. It's everything I can do to hold still and not hit my knees as she approaches.

She takes me in and finally nods. "You look good, Aurora."

I wait for the cut that no doubt will go with the compliment, but it doesn't come. What's going on? I clear my throat. "Thank you."

"Let's go." She turns to the elevator and pauses.

It takes me longer than I'd like to admit to realize she wants me to take her arm. I edge closer to her, feeling skittish, and lightly place my fingers in the crook of her arm. We step into the elevator, and I start to drop my hand, but she covers it with her own. "What changed?"

"I don't know what you're talking about."

She gives me a long look. "You've gone from breathing fire to timid in the space of an afternoon. Surely you're not still sore about my pinning you."

Yes, but not for the reasons she'd expect. I try for a tight smile. "Why should I be sore about it? I came. You didn't."

One of her perfect brows arches, and her lips quirk up a little. She's wearing a nude-toned lipstick, and her makeup is understated, but somehow that only seems to accent her beauty. Gods, it almost hurts to look at her. She looks away as the elevator doors open, spitting us into the parking garage. I expect to see Sara, but it's the curvy Black woman from before waiting for us.

Malone motions an elegant hand at her. "This is Luna. She'll be our security for the night."

Luna falls into step behind us, and the skin at the back of my neck prickles. I'm not *really* expecting a knife in the ribs, but my instincts sense a predator, and it's hard not to turn so I can keep an eye on her.

We take the same vehicle from the other night. I can't help tensing as Malone settles in next to me. I can't anticipate what tonight will bring. It makes me nervous, but even I can't tell if it's the sickening nerves or the ones that spark right before a truly amazing scene. Fear is a spice like any other emotion, and when directed by a skilled Dominant, it can enhance a scene to go from great to outstanding. It's such a bladed edge to traverse, though. Push too far and it ruins everything. Don't push far enough and you don't drive your submissive to the desired heights.

Malone must know that, because she doesn't speak the entire fifteen-minute drive. It's only when we pull up in front of a building with a name I recognize that I realize our destination. Spindle, one of the most talked about restaurants in Carver City. I've never been, partly because the waiting list to make a reservation is over a year long, partly because of where it's located—right in the middle of Malone's territory.

She slides out of the backseat and offers me her hand. I don't really need it to climb out, but the motion is a demand, even if it's a nonverbal one. I slip my hand into hers, trying not to notice how soft her skin is, and allow her to assist me out of the car.

We walk through the front door, and the hostess practically falls all over herself to usher us back to a private dining room. She's a thin white woman with brunette hair and the kind of near-alien beauty found on the runway, and she's looking at Malone like she'd love nothing more than to kneel before her.

Something pricks me, an uncomfortable sensation beneath my skin. This woman looks at Malone like she *knows* her taste. It's there in the way she can't quite take her eyes off Malone, in the way she lingers in the private room for several beats too long before disappointment bows her frail shoulders and she leaves, closing the door behind her.

I take my hand from Malone's arm and eye her. "Is she an ex?"

Malone's mouth tightens. "She's an indiscretion. I usually have better taste than to blur the lines between business and pleasure, but I didn't realize she worked here when we met."

Met. She means fucked.

The pricking sensation inside me gets worse. "So why not fire her?"

"Fire her because of *my* mistake?" She gives me a look like she's disappointed in me. "Maybe that's how Hades operates, but it's not how I do things."

I start to defend Hades, but the truth is that I'm speaking without thinking, and Hades isn't who I want to discuss. "Did you even *talk* to her? Or do you just ice her out like you ice everyone out?"

Malone blinks. "There's nothing to say. It was only for one night, and she knew that going into it."

I don't know if that makes it better or worse. I have no right to the jealousy—yes, jealousy—I'm feeling, but I can empathize with the woman despite that. "So you fucked her, and now you come to her place of work and ignore her instead of talking? You are such an unbelievable asshole."

13

I stare at Aurora, trying to figure out where she's going with this. She looks...furious. A different kind of anger than she's brought to scenes in the past, but no less authentic. "Why do you care so much about some woman you've never met?"

"Because it's not right. You move through life, taking what you want and not caring about the consequences. It's *cruel*."

Now, I'm truly confused, but I manage to keep my cold expression in place. "Aurora."

But she's not listening. "Just because you're the most powerful one in the room doesn't give you the right to stomp on people weaker than you. Doing so doesn't make you strong. It makes you a monster."

A monster.

Is that really what she thinks of me? She's not exactly wrong, but it stings nonetheless. "You seem to think you know a lot about me. Please, do continue to tell me more about myself."

She opens her mouth and seems to sense the trap before she manages to blunder right into it. I give her a moment to sit in that knowledge and lean in. "I would never dream of policing you about how you interact with your exes and fuck buddies and clients. And you say *I'm* the cruel one."

"That's not fair." She drops her gaze and clasps her hands in front of her. "This is a two-week assignation."

"Yes, it is. Which also falls under my point."

Aurora wrings her fingers in a way that makes me want to grab her hands before she does herself harm. I manage to resist the impulse, but only for a moment. I take her hands and extract them from each other. "Use your words instead of doing this."

"I hate you."

"Yes, you keep saying that." It might even be true. She certainly looks at me with loathing from time to time. I'm more than aware of how a person can hold two feelings simultaneously. It's complicated and messy, but that's humanity. "That's not why you're doing this to your hands."

Aurora keeps staring down, as if she can divine meaning from the wood floor beneath our feet. I study her, trying to understand what the hell is going on. She's never had a problem speaking her mind to this point. I go back over the last few minutes since arriving at the restaurant, how Aurora tensed up, her harsh words... It all started around Genevieve. I blink. "Are you jealous?"

"No, of course not. Don't be absurd." The words rush out of her, tumbling over each other. *Lying* to me.

She's jealous.

I don't know why that knowledge shocks me. Aurora is a free spirit in every sense of the word. I'm nearly one hundred percent certain that even if she ends up in a relationship, she'll remain polyamorous. Trying to confine her to a monogamous relationship would be like trying to box in the wind. Impossible.

I lift her hand and drag my thumb over her knuckles. The same knuckles responsible for the way my jaw still aches. "Is it Genevieve in particular or the thought of sharing that bothers you?"

"None of it bothers me because I'm not jealous. I simply don't like the way you treat people."

"Mmhmm." I tug her toward the low table. Spindle uses cushions instead of chairs, and I urge Aurora down onto one before taking the seat next to her. She's tense enough to shatter, her long legs curled beneath her. The position makes her dress ride up to truly indecent heights, but I push away the lust that rises in response. There will be plenty of time for that later.

I don't know why I can't let it go. This assignation is about fucking, and she's only mine for another twelve days. But that's the stumbling block in my head. Temporary or not, she *is* mine for this duration. I can't deny the instincts demanding I take care of what's mine. Even this prickly woman bristling next to me. *Especially* her.

I prop myself back on my hands and watch her. "I have no problem sharing, but I'm not particularly free with my charms when I'm with someone."

Aurora very carefully doesn't look at me. "What are you saying?"

"I may invite someone to scene with us and play with you, but for the duration of this, I won't be with anyone else." It's not a reassurance I've ever had to make before. Oh, I've dated here and there over the years, but my position of power complicates things to the point where it's barely worth it. Either people look at me and assume they can use their proximity to me to boost their own power, or if they answer to me in some way, there's too much power imbalance for a true relationship to thrive. I may be a Domme, but I have no desire to do it all the time.

People don't worry about these types of negotiations overmuch when it comes to a single scene, but I find myself wanting to reassure Aurora. "Unless you don't want to be shared."

She manages a faint smile. "I think you've watched me enough to know I really like being shared."

"Yes." Against my better judgement, I can't help wondering what it would look like if she were mine in truth. I'm possessive, but I'm not jealous. A strange distinction, maybe, but an important one. If she wanted to stay on in the Underworld, I'd hardly stand in her way...

What am I thinking?

Keeping Aurora?

Absurd. This woman isn't for keeping, not for me. She doesn't even like me. I may admire her in a strange sort of way, but she's more of a handful than I want to take on when I'm already dealing with so much on any given day.

Aurora stares at the table for a few seconds. "You're the one who organized this contract. If you want to bang your way through Carver City during it, that's your right."

But she wouldn't like it. For someone normally so skilled at hiding her true self, she's shit at it right now. I resist the urge to take her hands, but only barely. "Like I said, I prefer to take my partners on a singular basis." It's how I've always been. Group play is one thing, and fun for spice, but I'm not polyamorous. It's just not how I operate. "I won't be with anyone else while you're here."

She exhales slowly. "I really dislike how I feel around you."

"Are you surprised by that?" This conversation feels strange and almost stilted, but I'm reluctant to move on. Aurora is still off, but I can't tell if it's because she doesn't believe me or for some other reason. I'm not like Ursa, able to use kindness and a soft touch to coax even the most stubborn person into doing whatever she wants. I am a blade, sharp and cold and just as likely to kill as to protect. "Though I didn't expect you to be jealous."

"I'm not jealous."

I give her the look that statement deserves. "No lies, Aurora."

She huffs and crosses her arms over her chest. "Look, I don't get it, either. I'm not normally the jealous type. I really, really resent it when other people get jealous when they're with me, too, so this feels really hypocritical and I don't want to talk about it anymore."

"You know better." She can't just drop a line like that and expect me to move on without comment. I idly nudge a knife that was slightly out of place until it lines up perfectly with the spoon beside it. I know she's dated over the years. Rumors fly in Carver City, especially when one spends time in the Underworld. Which is how I know that, in a fit of jealous rage, Aurora's last boyfriend tried to barge his way into the club one night when she was working. "One would think that anyone who dates you knows what they're signing up for." Not being her exclusive partner.

"One would think." She keeps her eyes on a spot on the floor. "But unfortunately you were right the other night when you said that the very thing that draws them to me is the thing they can't deal with once we're in a relationship. Oliver liked the novelty of having a professional submissive as his girlfriend, until he realized I wasn't going to take sex off the table with my clients. Hazel said she didn't care about my job at all, but the longer we dated, the more she demanded to know how she stacked up against the other people I was sleeping with. And Finn..." She sighs. "Well, Finn was a mistake."

The ache in her voice ignites one in my chest. Aurora is one hell of a prize, yes, but she deserves so much better than to be treated like she has. "You have terrible taste in partners."

At that, she finally looks at me, her eyes lighting up with anger. "Shall we start throwing stones? Because you haven't dated anyone seriously since you've been a territory leader."

"We're not talking about me." But it feels strange to pull forth an ugly truth from her without answering in kind. "The answer to that is in the statement. I am territory leader. I can't afford to pick the wrong partner, and after spending twenty years solidifying my base and building up a foundation for the people here, it's easier to just...not date. I get my needs met in other ways." In the Underworld, mostly, though I occasionally do indulge outside the club.

Aurora lifts her chin. "I've come to the same conclusion for similar reasons."

I don't ask her if it gets lonely. I already know the answer, don't I? Sex is wonderful, kink is equally wonderful, but there's a gap there that sometimes I suspect will stay forever. That kind of intimacy that comes with trust and caring like my parents had. I tell myself it's simply not in the cards for me, but the truth is that some days I wish it was.

We lapse into silence as the door opens and the server appears. He's a nice-looking Hispanic man with close-cropped hair and, if I'm not mistaken, some artfully subtle eyeliner. "Thank you for joining us tonight. We operate the private rooms a little differently than the open seating. I'll take your drink orders now, and when I come back, I'll take your food orders. After that, there's a button in the center of your table that you can push if you need anything, but otherwise I won't interrupt you." He gives us an easy smile. "What can I get you to drink?"

I originally had no intention of pulling a ridiculous move like ordering for Aurora, but I don't like this uncertain ground we're standing on. Better to go back to her bratty submissive role than to continue on with this awkward conversation.

I speak before she has a chance to. "We'll have merlot; the one I usually order. Bring water as well."

"Of course." The server leaves as quickly as he arrived.

"I didn't want wine."

I almost smile at the prickliness in her voice. *There you are*. "Yes, you did. You'll like this blend."

"It's incredibly creepy that you think you know so much about me." She glares. "What? Do you have a file on me somewhere with all my favorite things?"

"No need. I pay attention." I allow myself to look at her. Gods, Aurora really is magnificent. She's got a flawless kind of beauty that draws predators and protectors alike, but it's the core of pure flame that makes my mouth water. "But people who live in glass houses shouldn't throw stones when it comes to keeping files on potential enemies."

She holds my gaze, and I like that she doesn't get flustered in response. "If you were Hades, you'd do the same thing."

I already *do* the same thing. The first task I took on when arriving in Carver City was evaluating the territory leaders and the territories themselves for risk and potential. The city is mostly stable at this point, but I still keep an eye on things. No matter what others might think of me, war is only profitable to weapons dealers and leaders with weak holds on their people. I am neither.

I lean forward and enjoy the way her gaze skates down the exposed V of my shirt. "And what does my file say?"

"You're a good leader." She says it like it pisses her off. "Your people both aboveboard and below are happy and taken care of. You're also particularly vicious with your enemies and prone to making examples."

I honestly can't remember the last time I've had to make an example of anyone, but that's the point. I came into power brutally, but now those measures are the exception rather than the rule. I shrug. "It's how I was raised."

"An Amazon."

"Yes."

"Why didn't you stay in Sabine Valley?"

"I wanted to rule." My tone is off, but I can't seem to help it. I have never once questioned that my sister would take on the role of leader when our mother stepped down. I never *once* doubted her ability to lead. Until now. They say hindsight is twenty-twenty, but I can't see what alternate path would have been better. Should I have staged a coup and destabilized the community generations have fought and worked to bring to power and keep safe? Turned my back on my sister, whom I love?

No. There are no easy answers. I know that, even if I'm having trouble accepting it.

"But you couldn't lead in Sabine Valley because of your sister, right?" Aurora, savvy as always, narrows her eyes. "I heard the Amazons have had a bit of trouble."

"A bit of trouble." I sound bitter. I should keep my thoughts to myself, but the truth is that I can't speak to any of my people about this. No matter if we're in Carver City or

Sabine Valley, we're Amazons. We owe allegiance to our queen, flawed though she may be. We aren't a people who expect blind obedience, but unless I'm willing to wade in and try to fix things, I have no place to talk in a way that might undermine my sister's power further.

I shouldn't talk to Aurora about it, either. No matter that she stands outside the hierarchy, she is still Hades's creature. But... What does Hades care for other empires? He's a spider in a web of his own making. If he keeps his finger on the pulse of neighboring cities, it's only to serve the purpose of keeping *our* city stable.

I'm simply looking for an excuse. I open my mouth, but the server appears before I have a chance to decide if I want to shut down this conversation or indulge in it. Aurora cuts in and orders a salad before I have a chance to order for both of us, and amusement curls through me at her continued pushback. It's what I want, after all. She delivers in spades. I order and wait for him to leave the room before I turn to her.

Apparently I *do* want to talk about things.

"My sister underestimated her enemy." I still don't understand why. The Paine family created one-third of the power structure that kept Sabine Valley running smoothly. There were conflicts, of course there were conflicts, but that's what the quarterly feasts were designed to combat. They served that function perfectly when I was still in the city. Had things changed that much in the following decade that the Amazons and Mystics were willing to work together to oust the Paine family? I don't know. My information is incomplete, and Aisling isn't talking. "I don't know what convinced her not to send people to hunt them to the ends of the earth, but they survived the coup eight years ago.

During Lammas, the seven sons of our old enemy arrived and demanded to participate in the ritual combat."

Aurora takes a sip of her wine. "Why not just kill them then and be done with it?"

"It's forbidden. The laws of feast days *are* laws, if unwritten. No one can ignore them or they risk complete ruin. Every single person in Sabine Valley will turn against them."

Aurora's watching me closely, a strange look on her face. "It sounds like those guys have reason to want their revenge. Like they're justified."

"Undoubtedly." I stare into my wine. "And they've earned it through the ritual combat. They took on seven of the best warriors the three leaders had to offer and won. It's not the revenge that bothers me, it's the method."

"That seems rather nitpicky."

"There are rules, Aurora. You take your revenge with the people responsible. You don't go after those who had nothing to do with it." My hand shakes, and I can't tell if it's anger or sorrow. I carefully set the glass back on the table. "Two nieces and my baby brother. *They* are the ones paying the price for my sister's mistake. That is what I can't forgive."

She laughs awkwardly. "It's really weird to think about you with family. You're such a lone figure."

That surprises me enough to look at her. "Did you never stop to think that there's a purpose to that? When it comes to enemies, I am the only one with a target painted on my chest. No one will look at my people, at my friends, at my distant family, when they only have eyes for me." I can see from her face that she never considered it, and why would she? I have spent so long being the ice bitch queen, it shouldn't surprise me when that's all people see. It's the sole purpose of that role; though, after all this time, it hardly feels like a role any more. It's simply me.

But it's not all of me.

The sheer vulnerability that I just shared with her makes my skin crawl. I take a drink of wine and clear my throat. "That's enough of that. Pull up your dress. I'm ready for an appetizer."

14

AURORA

I almost welcome the sexual distraction. It's easier to deal with than this new angle of Malone. I have watched this woman for *years*, waiting for the right opportunity. In all that time, I've never once seen her as anything other than a woman who worships at the altar of ambition and little else. Yes, she takes care of her people, but that doesn't negate the damage she's done or the people she hurts. It doesn't change the fact that she took away one of the most important people in my life when I was far too young to withstand the loss.

I don't know why it never occurred to me that Malone would have family, friends, people she cared about beyond Ursa. She was just an ambitious monster who wasn't content with second place in Sabine Valley, so she came here to rule. Of course she didn't care about the people she left behind.

I realize now that I've been making a lot of assumptions.

It doesn't change what Malone did to my mother, but it also isn't the sum of who she is. The knowledge shouldn't change anything. There is a perfectly good steak knife sitting on the table between us. She's relaxed and distracted.

All I have to do is grab it and plunge it into her chest, bearing her down to the ground and cover her mouth so she can't scream. I can almost picture it in my head. Almost. All I have to do is move, is attack, is act out the revenge that I was so sure I wanted when I agreed to this.

I will my hand to move. I will myself to ignore the barely shielded pain in her voice when she spoke about her nieces and brother. I shouldn't want to comfort her. She's my *enemy*. I close my eyes for a long moment, but the fire that encased me when I formed this plan flickers just out of reach. All I feel is a drenching sadness. I unclench my fist and open my eyes. It doesn't have to be tonight. I can get my revenge later. "Is there anything you can do to help them?"

I half expect her to push the command, but she sighs. "No. The victor of the match sets the reward, and the reward they demanded for the loss in combat is handfasting. It was agreed upon by all parties. The ceremony was completed that night. There's nothing we can do."

I stare. I know Sabine Valley is a completely different environment, of course, but surely I didn't misread Malone *that* badly. "Since when have rules ever stopped you from taking what you want?"

"Rules are there for a reason. The more you flout them, the more ammunition you give the people who work against you. A ruler is only in place through will of the people, whatever their motivation, be it fear or love or loyalty. The moment you start breaking your own rules is the first step toward the end. All the Brides agreed to the handfasting. If my sister attempts to kill the Paine brothers now, the entire city will build a pyre with her name on it and scramble over each other to light the first match."

I shudder. Handfasting is a year-long marriage-type relationship. A year can be an eternity or a blink of an eye, but I can't imagine being strong-armed into that situation with the enemy will be anything but torture. "Still. Isn't there something to be done?"

She gives a faint smile. "My nieces and brother are made of sterner stuff than can be broken by this experience, and it's not in the Paine brothers' best interest to truly torture them. Every single person picked wasn't part of the decision-making process that resulted in them being run out of town. That was no doubt intentional." Her smile fades. "But it doesn't change the fact that my sister made a misstep. She'll have lost the trust of some of our people, and *that* is worrisome, especially when her heir is currently little more than a captive to Broderick Paine. It reeks of weakness for both of them, and that's something the Amazons will never accept. If something happens..." She gives herself a shake. "It won't. I don't know why I'm musing on this."

Because she's got the mind of a general predicting the waves of a war. I lean forward, curious despite myself. "What will happen if the Amazons lose faith in your sister and her heir?"

"We're a matriarchal society. They'll either skip to Aisling's second daughter, Thea, or they'll skip Aisling's tree entirely."

Understanding washes over me. "You're second in line."

"I am fourth in line," she says tightly.

"But if they skip your nieces, you're second."

Malone looks away. "I don't want the throne. There was a time when I did; it's the reason I left, because I love my sister too much to unseat her. But I don't want it now."

She left Sabine Valley because she loved her sister too much to stage a coup. I don't know why the thought rocks me. Everything about this conversation is turning my assumptions on their heads. It doesn't change the core of who Malone is, but...

I need time to process this new information. That's the only excuse I have for leaning in and kissing her. I can't say that she commanded me and I'm obeying. It's pure instinct. I can't even pretend it's entirely to distract—either me or her —because a small, traitorous part of me wants to chase away the lost look in her green eyes.

She goes still for the space of a heartbeat, as if I've surprised her, and then her hands are in my hair and she's taking control of the kiss. I find my hands on her shoulders and, when she doesn't stop me, I skate them down the slice of skin barred by her shirt. Her skin is so soft. I can't believe I'm allowed to touch her.

I should be grabbing the knife perched at the perfect angle on the table, should be looking for a way to use this vulnerability against her. I just...can't.

I have time. There will be other opportunities. I tell myself a thousand lies as I slip my hand into her shirt and cup her bare breast. She's built small and perfect, and she inhales sharply against my mouth when I stroke my thumb over her nipple. Malone lifts her head a little. "So bold."

"What? I'm not allowed to touch you?"

She shakes her head slowly. "Why did you say yes, Aurora? I know Hades gave you a choice about this assignation. You hate me. Why agree?"

I kiss her again instead of answering. I have a feeling she'll see through whatever lie I can come up with, and I'm sure as hell not telling her the truth. No matter how carefully she touches me when we're not in a scene, this woman is a brutal warrior. If she thinks I'm a threat, she'll slit my throat and deal with the fallout later. And she *can* deal with the fallout. Hades might be furious, but he's balanced too precariously to go to war over a single person, no matter how much he cares about me. He's not the type to let his emotions get the best of him. There will be consequences, yes, but nothing Malone can't survive.

She allows the kiss for a few long moments and then moves, shoving me back against the cushions on the floor and pushing up my dress to bare me from the waist down. Malone brackets my throat with one elegant hand and shoves two fingers into me with her other. "You don't want to answer that."

"No," I gasp.

"Just like you don't want to talk about your exes." She strokes me slowly. "Do your other partners realize how much you keep back, Aurora? How you use sex to deflect from subjects you don't want to discuss? It's rather clever."

I've had sex in front of other people more times than I can count. It's a common occurrence in the Underworld. I've acted out fantasies upon fantasies over the years, dredged every single one of mine from the darkness and thrust them into the light. I've never done anything like this. We're outside the kink community, outside the club, outside a personal residence. If someone walks in, they're not going to expect to find Malone finger fucking me before dinner. It feels almost wrong, but in the most delicious way possible.

Part of that is pure Malone. She's staring down at me with something wild in those green eyes, something fierce that calls to a part of me I'm still not entirely comfortable with. Her fingers flex at my throat, not cutting off my air at all, but making me feel chained in place. Held down. Captive. She slides her thumb over my clit. "Did you agree to this assignation to punish me?"

Too close to the truth.

I swallow hard, the movement pressing my throat more

firmly against her palm. "Why would I want to punish you?" She doesn't know who I really am. There's no way she'd interact with me the way she does if she realized the woman she took *everything* from twenty years ago had a daughter. A daughter Malone is sliding a third finger into right now.

"Could be any number of reasons." Her cheeks have gone a little pink and her lips are swollen from our kisses, her lipstick a little smeared. She strokes her middle finger against my G-spot, something like pure satisfaction flickering over her expression when I moan. "Maybe because I've been ignoring you for so many years."

I laugh a little, though it comes out as a gasp. "I don't know if you've noticed, but I haven't been hard up for company in the intervening time."

"No, you haven't." She circles my clit again. "Pretty, popular Aurora. You're everyone's favorite, and yet you're always left in the dust when they find their people to settle down with. They don't see you, and the ones who *do* want to change you. They don't appreciate you for the gift you are."

I'm suddenly terrified that Malone truly *does* see me. I try to keep my mouth shut, try to just enjoy this without digging myself deeper into a hole I'm not sure I can climb out of. "Do you?"

"Fierce Aurora. Protective Aurora." She picks up her pace between my thighs, driving me toward orgasm as if we've done this a thousand times before, as if she knows my body as well as I do. "*Deadly* Aurora." Her smile is just as fierce as her eyes. "Yes, I see you."

I orgasm. It's just a physical thing, just a tiny death, but it feels like something's shifting inside me. Like something is changing that I can't afford to change, not if I want to keep my feet on the path I've trod for more than half my life.

It feels like forgetting.

I shouldn't want to forget. I shouldn't betray the memory of my mother, my grandmother. I am simply *so tired*. Tired of fighting, of plotting, of *hope*. That must be why I'm craving this woman's touch. No one has ever undone me in the same way that she does. I've never craved that undoing the way I am now.

Malone gentles her touch, bringing me back down with the same expertise she ramped me up. She holds my gaze as she lifts her fingers to her lips and sucks them deep. Tasting me. My entire body clenches at the sight. It doesn't matter that I just came, that she's my enemy; I want her. "Malone—"

She ignores me and pulls my dress back down, smoothing it into place, her touch lingering on the sequins for a moment before she sits back. "I'm famished."

"Malone."

"Aurora." The snap is back in her voice, the coldness I recognize... Though it's different now. It feels brittle, like it might crack beneath my feet at any moment. Not like the deep permafrost it used to be. Or maybe that's all in my head. I honestly can't be sure.

It shouldn't matter. It *can't* matter.

I carefully sit up and move to a kneeling position. "Yes, Mistress."

"Don't do that."

"Don't do what?" I stare hard at the bright red of the cushion in front of me. "You want me to stop talking and stop pushing, right? Here I am, being obedient." Why am I so angry? I should be happy that she's reestablishing the proper boundaries between us, reminding us of our respective roles. I didn't expect to need that reminder as much as she apparently does. That must be why I'm furious. It's certainly not because she's shutting me out.

She presses a single finger to my chin and guides my face up until I meet her gaze. "We're not through talking." Without looking away from me, she reaches to the middle of the table and presses the button to summon the server.

He arrives a few minutes later, bringing in our food, replacing our pitcher of water, and disappearing just as quickly. I pick up my fork, but I've lost anything resembling an appetite. It's so tempting to put the utensil down and just drink some more wine, but I can practically hear Allecto's voice in the back of my head.

You want to defeat a warrior, Aurora? You have to train like one; and that includes eating.

A rousing pep talk when I was twenty-two. Now she just shoves extra protein on my plate any time she catches me during a meal. It's annoying and endearing in equal measure, and with that in mind, I start working on the chicken scattered throughout the salad. "If we're not finished talking, what are we talking about?"

"I would have thought it was obvious." Malone cuts her chicken like she does everything else—with precise violence. "We're going to talk about you."

15

MALONE

urora is no rabbit, but she certainly impersonates one when she's backed into a corner. She freezes, and her eyes go wide. "Me? What could you possibly want to know about me that you don't already?"

I eat a bite of chicken slowly before speaking again. "We've established that the innocent act doesn't work on me. Try again." It shouldn't irritate me that she keeps throwing up shields, treating me like every other one of her patrons. Maybe it wouldn't have before I forgot myself and told her too much about Sabine Valley and my family, though I doubt it. Aurora gets under my skin like no one else I've ever met, and I crave the truth of her.

She eats for several long moments, and I can practically see her considering and discarding strategies to react in a way that will get her what she wants. Which is obviously not to talk about herself.

If I weren't already determined to find out more about this woman, her resistance would only pique my curiosity further. I focus on my meal but watch her out of the corner of my eye. I have thousands of questions about this woman, but best to start with a relatively simple one. "You've been in the Underworld for nine years."

"Yes." The word is clipped and icy.

"Hades always did like to rob the cradle." Not that twenty-one is all that young. By twenty-one, I'd already left Sabine Valley behind and come here with the intent to take a piece of territory for myself. But Aurora is not like me, and we've more than established that.

She goes tense beside me. "It's not like that."

"Isn't it?" I'm provoking her, but asking in a direct way will guarantee she shuts me down. I have to rile her a bit. "Twenty-one and fresh-faced. It's no wonder he made a deal with you."

"If he was really what you seem to be suggesting, he would have had me working there when I originally made the deal eight years earlier."

Shock stills me. She went to Hades when she was *thirteen?* I don't know why that surprises me. At thirteen, I was hardly an innocent. Amazons don't shelter their children in the same way civilians tend to, but that doesn't change the fact that she was a child when Hades accepted that bargain.

Something barbed and dangerous slithers through my chest. "Did he touch you?"

"Of course not." She sounds so horrified, I believe her. "He gave me what I asked for, patted me on the head, and told me to come back when I was twenty-one."

There are few lines I won't cross, but grooming a child to work in the Underworld is unacceptable. "Did you see Hades during those eight years?"

"No." She glares. "I finished school, paid my way through most of a bachelor's degree, and was devastatingly normal." Something in her expression falters a little. "I waited a month after I turned twenty-one, but he never called the bargain due. *I* had to go to *him*."

Relief nearly makes me woozy. I hadn't thought the old man would cross that line, but if he had... I don't know what I would do. Going up against someone who is arguably the most powerful person in Carver City over something he did over a decade ago would have been a terrible decision. There's nothing to gain and far too much to lose.

That doesn't change the fact that my hand is itching to wrap around his throat at the thought of him taking advantage of a scared and vulnerable thirteen-year-old Aurora. "How did you even find him at that age?"

"You know better. Some people don't get a childhood, Malone. I've known who Hades was and what he is to this city since I was a kid."

"You *were* a kid when you made that bargain." Which just leads me right back to where we started. "What would drive a teenager to seek out Hades in the Underworld to make a deal?" What would cause Hades to accept it? But then, Hades might cover it up well enough, but he has a bleeding heart. For every ruthless bargain he makes, there is another one or two behind the scenes that help some unfortunate individual who has nothing to offer. Obviously, Aurora was one of those, but that still doesn't explain how she found her way to him.

She looks away. "I needed money to keep someone I care about safe."

Impossible to look at that situation and not feel like Hades took advantage. "So he gave a teenager a bunch of money in exchange for nine years of your life. Hardly seems like a fair deal."

"Yes, well, not all of us have such a privilege that we can

walk in and take what we want without an issue." She spears
a grape tomato and eats it.

This is getting me nowhere. If anything, it's making me
feel worse instead of better. Why do I care about the terms
of Aurora's deal? She made it. She's obviously not broken
beyond repair as a result. I know enough of how the background of the Underworld works to know that Hades
doesn't require anyone to engage in the sex work. He simply
offers the option if they want it. Most do, and why not?

It still bothers me.

"Surely your parents weren't willing to let you make that
sacrifice on your own?" Amazons might not shelter our children from the ugliness of the world, but we certainly don't
sit back and let them make deals with the devil.

"My father died when I was a baby." She picks at her
salad. "My mother also died. I lived with my grandmother,
and she wasn't aware of the deal."

"It sounds like she should have kept better track of you."

Aurora cuts me a look. "She did the best she could. She
never expected to be saddled with a grandchild, let alone for
it to be a permanent thing. She tried her best, but our
resources were limited."

Their resources were limited. I study her. There are all
sorts of reasons people make deals with Hades. Protection.
Ambition. Escape. Money. What could a thirteen-year-old
Aurora want so desperately that she was willing to walk into
the Underworld and bargain with Hades himself? It can't be
the former three. He wouldn't have sent her back into her
grandmother's home for eight years if that was the case.
"How much money could one child possibly need that
would inspire you to go to that lengths?"

Aurora finally meets and holds my gaze. "It's none of
your business, Malone. The terms of my deal are between

me and Hades and we've both fulfilled our ends of the bargain. It's finished. There are no dragons to fight and even if there were, do you really think that I would ask *you* for help?"

That stings far more than it has right to. She has no reason to trust me, and every reason not to. Despite my feelings about her bargain, it's obvious she hasn't come out the worse for it. "Was it worth the price?"

"Of course. Or at least I think so." Finally she drops her gaze, her expression closing down. "But ask me again in a year. I lost someone recently, and I'm not handling it well. I'm not sure of anything anymore."

The sorrow in her tone speaks of the truth, just like it warns me off pursuing this conversation further. It doesn't make me want to stop pressing her, but I understand all too well how far a person will go to escape the claws of grief. "I'm sorry for your loss."

She flinches as if I've struck her.

I know she won't accept comfort from me. I'm not even sure how I'd go about offering it. Instead, I blurt out the first thing that crosses my mind. "Will you continue on at the club after your bargain's time runs out?"

"Yes." She says it with such surety, some of the pain fades from her voice. "I like my job, I like the perks and that each night is a little different. I like working as Meg's second-in-command."

For a moment, I let myself follow the temptation of thinking of a future that's not for me. A future where Aurora becomes mine in truth. It's all fantasy, though. Aurora is not for keeping, not for me, and I have no intention of settling down into anything resembling domesticity. I like my life, like the balance I've achieved. Throwing a wrench into my perfectly operating machine is a mistake I'd like to avoid.

Aurora's watching me closely. "Why ask that?"

"Curiosity." I shrug. "It's as simple as that."

"I'm beginning to think there's nothing simple about you at all, Malone."

Something buzzes beneath my skin, an increasing desire to put my mark on this woman while I still can. I push to my feet. "Let's go."

"No dessert?" Her lips curve as if she knows exactly where my head's at, knows exactly how she affects me.

"You can order in." I hold out my hand before I can think better of it, and the feeling of her palm sliding against mine is so damn *right*, it rocks me to my core.

Aurora isn't for keeping. I have to remember that, have to hold that truth close. I'm not a woman who wastes time wishing on stars. I know the lay of the land with Aurora the same way I did as the second daughter of the Amazon queen. Some things can be changed and shifted and rearranged. Some things are simply truth.

I would never be queen, so I left to create my own queendom.

Aurora will never be mine, so I shall enjoy the time we have left and then move on with my life when she walks away at the end of these two weeks.

Simple. Easy. Tidy.

Unfortunately, I feel anything but simple, easy, and tidy as I all but drag Aurora out of the room. She digs in her heels before we get three steps. "The bill."

"Is already taken care of." No doubt I already have an invoice waiting for me. "Now, keep up, or I'm going to carry you."

"If you carry me, I'm going to flash every single person we walk past."

"Yes." I resume walking, and this time she keeps up

without effort. She's a few inches shorter than I am, but Aurora has a lot of practice matching the longer strides of her taller clients. It's fascinating how she manages to do so without seeming like she's working hard.

Luna waits for us next to the car. From the satisfied smile on her face, someone ran her down food while we ate. I make a mental note to double the tip. The service at Spindle, as always, is beyond reproach. Luna opens the door, and we slip into the backseat.

I keep hold of Aurora's hand. She tugs once, but when she realizes I have no intention of letting her go, she huffs out a sigh and sits back. For my part, I stare out the window and count down the minutes until we return to my building in an effort to keep from mauling her in the backseat.

I want to make her come again. More than that, though. I want to break Aurora into a thousand pieces and put her back together again, to be both creation and destruction, pain and pleasure. She a safe I don't quite know the combination to, and I can't shake the feeling that the only way to touch her is through dominance and submission. It's the only way she'll *allow* me to touch her.

It strikes me that I've never had someone hold out on me the way Aurora does. No matter what I do, she's always managed to maintain a distance between us, and it couldn't be clearer that she has no interest in crossing it.

Perversely, that makes me want to bridge the gap even more intensely. The feeling is disconcerting in the extreme. I pride myself on never losing control, but I'm dancing on the brink. I can't shake the impression that Aurora is a fortress, all locked away with doors barred and a thorny barrier outside. It calls to the warrior inside me, who's never met a barrier I didn't want to climb over or burst through. Surely that's all it is, my instincts demanding I break through to the very interior of her.

We ride the elevator up to my penthouse in silence. I'm too twisted up, too conflicted. The turmoil doesn't make for a good scene, and I almost don't care. Almost. I stop in the hallway and stare at the door to the playroom. If I walk through it right now, I can't guarantee I'll be in the right mind to take care of both of us. I'm too rattled, too raw.

I take a deep breath and then another and force myself to release Aurora's hand. "Go to bed."

"What?" I can feel her gaze boring into the side of my face. "That's it?"

"Yes." The first step away from her is the hardest, but then momentum carries me the rest of the way down the hall to my room. I don't look back.

But even with the door closed, I can *feel* her presence. In the few short days Aurora has been in my home, she's imprinted herself on the entire space. She's too close, and yet nowhere near close enough. It's frustrating and makes me want to tear my hair out. I've never been one to allow outward signs of frustration, but I'm in danger of breaking my own rule.

So I do the only thing I can think of.

I call Ursa.

Despite the late hour, she answers almost immediately. "Problem in paradise, darling?" The sweet venom in her tone is welcome, and I close my eyes and take my first full inhale in what feels like hours.

When I finally speak, I've managed to pull in my normal cool tones. "Gloating doesn't become you."

"Can you blame me for enjoying this moment?" She laughs, low and melodious. Everything Ursa does is melodious. She's the sharp blade hidden in a jeweled case. Glittery and smooth and dangerous in a way unsuspecting people never see coming.

"In fact, I can." Even if I got a perverse sort of joy watching her unravel not too long ago when her pair of submissives had her tangled in knots. It's different with Aurora. Ursa and Alaric were already in a relationship when they tricked Zurielle into auctioning off her virginity. Aurora isn't some sweet innocent thing with hearts in her eyes every time she looks at me. I'm reasonably sure she hates me as much as she says she does, though the emotion seems deeper than it should be for the simple act of not fucking her.

I sit heavily on the edge of my bed. "This isn't what I thought it'd be."

The amusement filters out of her tone. "You're not just off-center. Something's wrong."

That's just it. I'm not sure anything *is* wrong. There are a thousand little pricks of irritation and worry, starting from what's going on in Sabine Valley and ending with Aurora, but nothing is actually wrong. Not in any quantifiable way. "She really hates me."

"So seduce her into loving you if that's what you want." She says it so easily, as if there's no question it's possible. "That girl's been turning your head since the moment you saw her."

"Turning everyone's head, including yours."

A pause. "I didn't think that bothered you."

It didn't. It doesn't. I don't mind Aurora's history, even if it includes my best friend. Ursa only scened with Aurora occasionally to irritate me, but not enough to ever affect our friendship—a delicate balance she never landed on the wrong side of. "It doesn't."

She takes me as my word, a testament to the length and

strength of our friendship. "In that case, remove her feelings from the issue and tell me what *you* want."

"I want her." A simple and complicated as that.

"Then take her."

"Ursa."

"Malone." She mimics my tone. "Darling, don't try to tell me that you're not capable of seducing her properly. You have never hesitated to take what you want; it's something we've always had in common. You want Aurora? Take her."

"I have been taking her," I say drily. "Several times a day for the last few days."

"That's not what I mean, and you know it." Something rustles in the background, and I have the sudden image of Ursa in bed with her two submissives pressed against her on either side. A strange sensation hollows out the pit of my stomach, and I press my fist there. It almost feels like...longing.

"It's not like you to act this uncertain."

"No, it's not." I sigh. "It's more than her. The situation back home is devolving, and it's distracting me." I'm foolish to expect a call from my sister. I know how Sabine Valley operates. She'll figure her way out of this without my assistance. I have to believe that. I *do* believe that, despite the sliver of doubt that poisons every thought concerning my family.

"There's very little you can do about that situation."

"I know." And I do. It doesn't change the urge to *try*. Gods, I can't decide if I'm going soft or if I'm truly that arrogant. Possibly a deadly combination of both. "Your advice leaves something to be desired."

"I seem to remember a time when our situations were reversed and you laughed in my face, you bitch." She says it fondly. "Allow me this moment of amusement at your expense."

I snort. "Uh-huh. Is the moment over yet?"

"Yes." Ursa laughs. "Honestly, though. Make her yours, Malone. Aurora is a treasure, and no one will take better care of her than you will. I know you enjoy your solitary life, but if she's affecting you this much after a few days, isn't it worth considering? I'd hate for you to let her go and spend the next few years moping and snapping at everyone around you. It's tedious, darling."

Typical Ursa. Kind and cruel, all wrapped up in a smooth package. I force myself to pause my instinctive denial and actually think about what she's saying. Keep Aurora. Make her mine in truth. Haven't I already been dancing around this idea? She's right; it's not like me to hesitate when it comes to claiming the things I want. The people I want. Aurora is the exception to the rule, but maybe it's high time I get over myself. "I would hate to be tedious."

"An unforgivable sin, truly." I can hear the smile in her voice.

"Thank you, Ursa. Apparently I needed that shove."

"Easy to have perspective from the outside." The briefest pause. "If you *do* decide to do something about Sabine Valley, know that you have my support."

For a moment, it truly tempts me. Between the two of us, we hold the majority of Carver City. We could bring enough manpower and force to snuff out the Paine brothers once and for all. But the cost of such a move is too high. We couldn't guarantee the safety of my family members within their control. More, we'd effectively undermine the Amazons to the point where we would do more harm than good. "I truly appreciate the offer, but it's unnecessary."

"If you decide to change your mind, let me know," she

says breezily. "I always thought it'd be fun to go to war at your side."

I smile. "You never do declarations of friendship half-way, do you, Ursa?"

"Why bother to do something if you're not going to do it right?"

"Thank you. For everything." I glance at my door. "I'll consider your advice."

"Good night, Malone."

"'Night." I hang up.

I'm too off-center to sleep yet, especially with Ursa's advice circling my mind. She's right; outside perspective *is* helpful at times. I didn't need permission to decide this, but she has a way of cutting through the bullshit, right to the heart of things.

Deciding to make Aurora mine feels like a risk, and it's been a very long time since I've braved a risk on that level. Maybe it should worry me, but all I feel is energized.

I want Aurora.

So I'm going to take her.

"You goddamn *demon spawn*."

I stare at the ruined mess of a bed and curse harder. Apparently instead of leaving this room after we went to dinner, the cat decided to mark his territory by shredding the bedspread—and a pillow, if the feathers everywhere are any indication—*and* pissing all over everything.

I hold a hand to my nose. "What the actual fuck, you little shit?" I can't sleep here. I can barely stand in the room without my eyes watering from the smell of cat urine.

He's nowhere to be found, of course. Why stick around to deal with the consequences of his actions? Not that I'd *really* throw a cat out a high-rise window, but I want to at least threaten him with the possibility.

Maybe I can strip the sheets and the smell won't be too bad?

I take a step toward the bed...and gag. Nope, that's not going to work. If the smell is this bad, then he soaked the bedding and probably the mattress, too. "Of course Malone would have a demon cat that destroys everything and then pisses on it for good measure. It's the animal version of her, but at least *she* has some control."

"So glad you think so."

I close my eyes and spend a full five seconds wishing the floor would open up and swallow me whole. "Your cat is a monster," I say without turning around.

"Rogue is particular." She clears her throat. "Let's continue this conversation in the hall."

I don't know why it makes her seem a little more human that the smell seems to bother her as much as it bothers me, but it does. I back slowly out of the room, and Malone shuts the door. We both take slow breaths. I rub my nose. "You say *particular*, but I'm hearing sadistic."

"I don't have guests often." She contemplates my closed door. "Apparently he's feeling threatened."

"Or he's just a dick."

Her lips curve. "Or he's just a dick."

I look around. "Where is the little monster? He and I are going to have a chat."

"Rogue knows how to make himself scarce after he destroys something."

The way she says it so easily... I stare. "Does your cat often destroy furniture?"

"At least quarterly." She shrugs and heads down the hallway in the opposite direction from the bedrooms. "As I said, he's particular."

Malone keeps a cat that actively destroys furniture. I haven't seen any evidence of it in the house, which means she must replace the pieces after he fucks them up. The fact that she keeps the cat, even seems to love him despite it... It doesn't fit in with the picture of Malone I've crafted over the years. Very little tonight has fit in with that picture, and I don't know how to adjust.

It doesn't change what she did. Nothing can change that.

But she's more complicated than I first imagined. It was easy enough to imagine killing her when I thought her a cold monster. Now, I don't know what to feel. Her actions are unforgivable, but she's got layers that I can't help but sympathize with. It doesn't make me hate her less...except the deep rage I've had in my chest for so long feels strangely blunted.

I'm tired, that's all. A simple explanation that I'm over-thinking.

I follow Malone into the kitchen and watch as she pours two glasses of wine. She raises her brows at me as if daring me to challenge her. I decide to pick my battles and take the offered glass without complaint. It's an expensive vintage, and I relish the flavor profiles sliding over my tongue. "This is very good."

"I know." Malone props a hip against the counter and studies me the same way she studied the guest bedroom door. "Do you have any family beyond your grandmother, Aurora?"

"No. She's all I have." Rage has me weaving on my feet. I almost thank her for the reminder, for unearthing my reason for hating her so intensely. "Or all I used to have." I know Malone will assume the person I'm grieving is my grandmother, and I'm only too happy to let her make that mistake. The truth is that my grandmother passed six years ago in her sleep. It was a peaceful way to go, the way she said she always wanted, and though I grieved her, there was a strange sort of peace mixed in because she was finally at rest.

There's no peace when it comes to my mother.

"Ah." She sips her wine, still watching me closely. I can't shake the feeling that she's picked up more in those three words than I meant her to. "I'll have the mattress and bedding replaced tomorrow. The couch is chic but freakishly uncomfortable. You'll sleep with me tonight."

I blink. "What?"

"I did mention that I'm not in the habit of repeating myself."

She did, but I still can't wrap my head around how quickly this happened. Malone is letting me into her inner sanctum. No matter how intense she is, eventually she'll have to sleep. This could end tonight.

The knowledge is a stone in my stomach, weighing me down. I sip my wine through numb lips. When I originally set myself down this path, there wasn't a shred of doubt in my heart. Now? Now, down is up and up is down. I don't know what I'm feeling. I should want to end this woman, to make her pay for the pain she's caused me, the mother she took from me. For the memories that grow hazier every year, ones that I can never replace. The woman who birthed me is gone, body and soul. She's never going to wake up. Never going to smile. Never going to hug me again.

Because of Malone.

I close my eyes and wait to embrace the rage that lingers in me at all times. It's still there, still a roiling mess of darkness, but it doesn't surge the way I expect.

I am so fucking *tired*.

"Aurora."

I open my eyes as Malone plucks the wine glass from my hand and moves to the sink. She washes both glasses with quick, efficient movements and then sets them on a small drying rack I hadn't noticed before now. Malone turns, and it almost seems like she hesitates, though it's so brief a pause, I'm half sure I imagined it.

I swallow hard. "This is a mistake."

"Which part?" Her lips curve, but the smile doesn't reach her eyes. "I'm well aware of the pitfalls. Come along." She turns and walks out of the kitchen, leaving me to trail after her.

Except she's *not* aware of the pitfalls. No matter how formidable she is, she's not even on the same playing field because the possibility of me actually attacking her doesn't even register. I don't know why that bothers me so much. It *should* be an asset. My end goal is easier if she's caught unawares.

But somehow I'm opening my mouth, and words spring free. "Do you often invite people into your bed?"

"No. Never."

That makes me feel even worse. I rub the heel of my hand against my chest. The sequins are little pokes of pain that do nothing to calm me. "Then put me up on the couch."

Malone pauses in her doorway. Shadows hide her expression from me, but I can tell she's displeased by the tense line of her shoulders. "Tell me your safe word."

I stop short. "You are *not* turning me sleeping beside you into a scene."

"Aurora, we've been in a scene from the moment you arrived here. Tell me your safe word."

"Thorn."

She doesn't move. "Do you want to use it?"

Conflicting desires rise in me, tangling themselves up until I don't know what I want anymore. Against all reason, my throat goes tight. I am...so incredibly tired. I hang my head. "No, I don't want to use it."

She opens her bedroom door and steps back. "Go in and strip. I'll be there presently."

The numbness from before spreads, coating my cheeks, sliding down my neck, curling around my heart. I slide past her and pull off my dress. I followed the earlier instructions, so I'm naked beneath it, but I take the time to fold it and set it on the chair next to the stylized desk across from the bed. By the time I finish, Malone has reappeared with my toothbrush and hair wrap in hand.

She passes it over. "Is there anything else you need from the room tonight?"

"No."

"Get ready."

I'm almost relieved when she doesn't follow me into the bathroom. This is strange enough without brushing my teeth next to this woman in a parody of domesticity that can never exist. My numbness doesn't decrease as I go through the familiar motions of getting ready for bed. I can almost pretend that I'm not about to sleep next to my enemy. Almost.

Right up until I stand in the doorway and stare at her large bed. I'm still coming to terms with the thought of lying next to her, close enough to touch, to kiss, to taste. Close enough to strike.

Then she walks out of the closet without a single piece of clothing on, and it's everything I can do not to hit my knees right then and there. Malone is magnificent. There's no other word for it. Her hair is a little less than perfect, sticking up in places like she's been running her fingers through it, and her body is all lean, strong lines, save for the softness of the curve of her hips, her small breasts each tipped with a rosy-pink nipple.

She stops short, and we stare at each other. She's seen me naked more times than I can count by virtue of the Underworld, but right now she's looking at me like this is the first time. Like it means something that I'm standing here without a single physical barrier between us.

It doesn't.

It *can't*.

"You put me in a nightgown before because you keep this place so cold." It doesn't feel cold right now. It feels like I'm burning alive.

She barely glances at me. "My bedding and body heat are more than enough to keep you warm tonight."

"Malone—"

"Bed." She snaps her fingers and points to the left side, farthest from the door. Her expression is strange, as if she tries to pull on the icy expression but can't quite manage it.

I hesitate but finally obey. There's no other option. I'm too tired, too wired, to push her right now. I don't know what would happen if I did. Better to just submit to this tonight and land on solid ground tomorrow when she replaces the things her demon cat destroyed.

The bed is so comfortable, the sheets so soft, I actually moan a little as I settle in. The guest bed was nice, but this is on another level. I could... But no, I can't. I can't do shit, because I'm supposed to be figuring out how to end Malone instead of wiggling around in her bed like a puppy.

She stalks to the other side of the bed and flicks on the lamp there before moving to turn off the lights in the room.

I pull the covers up higher over me and watch her climb into bed. Am I supposed to say good night? Do we kiss? Do we fuck? I don't know, and panic over not having a game plan sends my brain swirling in frantic circles.

Malone cuts me a look. "Sleep." She turns off the light, bathing the room in inky darkness. With the curtains closed, we might as well be in a cave for all I can see. I've never been someone who needs a light to sleep, but there's something about the feeling of the mattress shifting beneath me as Malone gets comfortable that has me desperately wanting to see.

I close my eyes and focus on inhaling slowly and exhaling equally slowly. There was a time when sleep was difficult for me, and so I've acquired dozens of meditation techniques designed to help me drift off.

Not that any of them work now, when I desperately need them to. Time turns to taffy, the seconds ticking by in an endless loop. I keep my breathing steady. It's the one thing I can control, and so that's what I do.

Malone must think I've actually gone to sleep. She shifts, and then I feel a nearly phantom touch against my temple. Her fingers linger for a few moments, and then she withdraws, taking her touch with her.

I don't understand what's happening.

Things were fine as long as we didn't speak beyond kink, but now I can't stop seeing facets of this woman. How tired she is. How much she bears. How her people seem to respect and even love her.

Did my mother's people love her?

I don't...

I don't know. I don't remember much of her because she kept me so separate from the world she moved in. I lived with my grandmother even before the fight that put my mother into a coma. My grandmother was a hard woman, beaten down by the world. She's the one who taught me how to be strong, how to blend in so people would continually underestimate me. Always focused on survival at all costs. From the way she spoke, she thought my mother was the worst kind of fool for grabbing at power beyond her reach. Almost as if she believed my mother got what she deserved because of it.

I exhale slowly. It doesn't matter. No one deserves what

happened to my mother. Malone could have stopped the attack at any time. From the reports I've unearthed in the Underworld, she delivered one last kick to ensure my mother stayed down. The doctors can't conclusively say that last blow is responsible for the coma, but if not that, then what?

Next to me, Malone's breathing has evened out, her body relaxed in sleep. Now's the time to move, to climb on top of her and pin a pillow to her face. To do *something* except lie here and count every breath she takes.

I just need to move, to put myself into motion.

To...

17

I wake up with Aurora sprawled on top of me. I'm not sure which of us moved in our sleep, but it's disconcerting in the extreme to have her body weighing me down. Disconcerting, and also kind of nice. She smells good, a subtle vanilla scent from her lotion. Her breasts press against my side, and her breathing ghosts over my collarbone. She shifts a little, her leg sliding between mine as if she's trying to close the last minuscule bit of distance between us.

It's so *easy* to imagine waking up like this every morning. We're a long way off from that place, with so many fucking barriers between us, but the promise of something more remains.

I'm not sure what happened last night that put us even more at odds, just like I'm not sure how to retake the distance lost. I tend to go after every problem like it's a battle to be won, but that approach won't work with Aurora. She's just as stubborn as I am, and she'll dig in her heels and fight me until her last breath if I try to bully her.

No, this will require some finesse. Some...seduction.

Or maybe that's just an excuse as I trail my fingers lightly over the arm she has thrown across my stomach. Her skin is so unbelievably soft. Everything about Aurora seems designed to entice, from her carefully curated exterior to the flames she hides within. Those flames draw me as much, if not more, than the package that contains them. This woman would be right at home with the Amazons.

I always was attracted to strength.

It's the reason why I prefer my submissives to be sweet and biddable. It makes them safer, ensures that I'll never forget myself and become too attached. Only a fool who can't see beneath the surface would call *Aurora* sweet and biddable.

She rubs her nose against my chest and shivers. "Let's pretend this never happened."

"In a moment." How quick she is to put distance between us. Last night, I had intended to play out a scene that started in the restaurant and continued back here at the penthouse, but our talk derailed my intentions. For the first time, I can actually feel the seconds of this assignation slipping through my fingers. Not enough time. The distance between us is too gaping to cross with timid steps. If I want her, I have to take her.

Talking won't work. Not yet. First I have to bridge the space in another way.

I clasp the back of her neck and draw her up to take her mouth. She resists for the barest moment, but it doesn't last past the first nip of my teeth against her bottom lip. Aurora makes a sound almost like she's in pain, and then her hands are in my hair, and she's arching into me as if she can't get close enough.

Two sides to the same coin. She wants me, but she doesn't want to want me. I smile against her mouth. *Too bad.*

You've given me the key, and I'm more than happy to use it to get what I want. I release her neck and stroke my hand down the smooth line of her back to grab her ass, pulling her up a few inches so I can reach her mouth easier. Our legs get tangled up, and her thigh presses to my pussy. The shock of contact almost derails me, but I have plans this morning, and I fully intend to follow through on them.

In a moment.

Right now, I'm enjoying the way she kisses me too much to stop. Again, that voice deep inside me shivers awake. *It could be like this all the time.* But only if I play my cards right.

I roll Aurora onto her back and press her down into the mattress. She moans against my mouth, trying to pull me closer. I nip her bottom lip. "Hands against the headboard."

"Malone—"

"That was a command."

She sighs dramatically and obeys. I'd believe the brat act if she weren't shivering against me, the very picture of need coiled into a pretty package. I shift back to kneel between her thighs and just look at her. "It strikes me that I haven't explored you properly.'"

"Pretty sure you did that the first night."

I flick her thigh, making her jump. "I've been lax on the rules, but we're reinstating them for the duration of this scene. Be silent unless it's to answer a question or request permission to come."

Rebellion flares in Aurora's dark eyes, but she manages to resist it. At least for the moment. I smile and run my hands lightly up her thighs and over her hips. "Do you want children, Aurora?"

She blinks at me, her mouth dropping open. "What?"

I can't believe I just asked her that. For all my intentions to keep my planning careful, the words just sprang into existence. "We've talked about how little I like to repeat myself."

"Ah." She gives herself a shake. "I don't know. Maybe. I keep waiting for the urge to show up or my ovaries to twinge when Tink talks about babies, but maybe I just haven't met the right person to do the whole relationship and procreation with." She looks away. "Do *you* want kids?"

"I think so." It's one of those things I don't spend much time thinking about. I like children. My sister is nearly ten years older than me, so I spent most of my teenage years watching my nieces be born and grow into little people. Amazons value children, and I'm no exception. I could have gone forward and had my own without a partner; I have all the resources to make it happen. But something's held me back until now.

Maybe I was waiting for the right person to show up, too.

"Why are you asking me about babies?"

I'm not ready to answer that question. Deciding that I want to keep Aurora and actually managing to do it are two very different things. There are so many elements that must line up for any relationship to work, and we're already starting at a disadvantage. I know this woman's kinks inside and out, I know what turns her on and what gets her off. I know that she's a fierce friend who burns a little too brightly compared to those around her. But beyond that? Even with the little pieces of information she's allowed to slip through over the last couple days, so much of her is a mystery to me. "Spread your thighs wider."

She hesitates but finally obeys. I coast my hands over the dip in her waist and up to cup her breasts. I trace her brown nipples and the shiny silver piercings that intersect them with my thumb, enjoying the way she gasps. "Do they still hurt?"

"Sometimes." She meets my gaze. "I like it."

"I'm not surprised." I lean down and take one nipple into my mouth. She bucks under me but manages to keep her hands on the headboard. I take my time, teasing and licking my way over the curve of her right breast to her left. I have a meeting later this morning, but I can't quite bring myself to rush this.

I lightly rake my nails over her ribs, watching her stomach hollow as she gasps. She's squirming under my gaze, her hips restless on the mattress. I drag a single finger up the center of her pussy, nearly moaning when I find her soaked, and stop just above her clit. "If you were mine, I'd command you to pierce this, too."

Her eyes go wide, but I don't give her a chance to respond. I slide down her body and kiss her pussy. Gods, this woman's taste. It drives me crazy. I can't get enough of her, something that would worry me if I hadn't already decided to find a way to keep her. I dip my tongue into her and then move up to tease her clit.

Aurora makes a keening sound. "I'm close, Mistress."

I lift my head. "Already?"

She glares at the ceiling, when I know she wants to glare at me. "I'm very horny in the morning, Mistress."

"Brat," I murmur. I exhale over her clit, making goose bumps rise in a wave over her skin. "If that's so, I can always stop and wait for you to spontaneously orgasm from this morning's horniness."

She clenches her jaw, and for a moment, I think she might actually agree out of spite. Finally, Aurora shakes her head. "Please keep going."

"So polite when you want something."

"Isn't everyone?"

"No." I go back to what I was doing. I should wait, should tease this out, but she's too damn sweet. "You have permission to orgasm." I want her to come, and I want to be the cause. I want... Fuck, I just *want*. There are so many sins one could lay at my feet, if I believed in that sort of thing. Lust. Pride. Greed drowns them all. It's what drove me from Sabine Valley when I could no longer contain my desire to rule. It's what built me an empire within Carver City, what made me arguably the most powerful territory leader, short of Hades. I don't know that I've ever looked at a person and had that same greed flicker to life, the all-consuming urge to possess them in every way possible.

Not until Aurora.

Her whole body goes tense as pleasure takes her, pleasure that *I've* dealt. I draw wave after wave out of her, teasing her to new heights, until she collapses back to the mattress, a fine sheen of sweat coating her skin.

I lick my lips and sit up. Yes, I could get used to a sated and spent Aurora in my bed. It's just as pleasing a sight as the warm and cuddly version I received upon waking.

She blinks up at me. "Malone?"

"Yes?"

Gods, the way she looks at me when she forgets herself. As if she wants to taste every part of me, as if she wants me exactly as much as I want her. She's too drunk on lust to keep her impressive walls in place, and I luxuriate in the knowledge that I'm the one who got her there.

Finally, Aurora says, "I would very much like you to sit on my face. Right now."

I don't point out that she's edging far too close to a command. Not when I want this as much as she apparently does. Not when *her* wanting it makes it that much hotter.

Instead, I climb up her body and carefully arrange myself astride her face. The grin she gives me feels like a kick in the ribs. And then there's no more space for thinking because she grips my hips and lifts her head to lick my pussy.

I brace my hands on the wall and stare down my body at her. She's got her eyes closed, as lost in this moment as I'm in danger of being. Gods, it feels good. She explores me with her mouth, intent on devouring every bit of the desire spawned from when *I* tasted *her*.

Belatedly, I realize that I've relinquished control. I start to lean back, to say something to bring the situation to heel again, but Aurora sucks hard on my clit, and a moan springs free from my lips. I rock against her mouth, enjoying the slick slide of her tongue, the pleasure coursing through me.

She skates her hands up my sides and cups my breasts, her clever fingers toying with my nipples. And then the little asshole bites me. Not hard enough to do damage; no, she sets her teeth against the spot right over my clit just hard enough to send a spike of pain, quickly followed by the pleasure of her tongue. It surprises me so much, I orgasm on the spot. I grind down on her mouth, moaning and cursing, until the last wave crests.

Only then do I slump to the side and stretch out next to her. "That was a nasty little move."

Aurora swipes her thumb over her bottom lip, making a show of gathering up the evidence of my orgasm, and sucks it clean. "I didn't hear you complaining."

I kiss her. There's no artifice behind it, no ulterior motive. I just want to kiss that bratty mouth, and so I do. She meets me in the middle, half pulling me back on top of her. And then there's no more time for thinking. We're off again, my hand dipping between her thighs, her hand cupping my pussy and pushing two fingers into me. It's messy and rushed and damn near a frenzy as we kiss and stroke each other toward the peak again. And again. And again.

By the time we surface, my phone is buzzing on the fifth call from someone, and the clock tells me I'm going to be late. Fuck.

"I have to go." I press my forehead to Aurora's.

"Are you sure you have to go?" She kisses my neck and skates her hands down either side of my spine, urging me to keep rocking against her. "Doesn't this feel good?"

"You're nothing but trouble." I kiss her and disengage before I can reconsider. As good as this fucking has been, it's too easy to forget that I'm trying to scale her walls and simply revel in the pleasure of it all. I can't shake the feeling that she's well aware of that, too. That maybe she's using it as a distraction to keep me at a distance.

That won't do. It won't do at all.

"Stay there." I stalk out of the bedroom and down the hall to the playroom. It takes ten seconds to find the toy I'm looking for and return to find Aurora exactly where I left her. I toss it onto the mattress next to her. "Six times."

She blinks. "What?"

"Use that to make yourself come six times after I leave. After every one, you will say, 'Thank you, Mistress,' before you begin again."

She props herself up on her elbows and eyes the vibrator. It's a relatively new piece of technology designed by a genius of a woman to deliver blended orgasms. I've used it on myself, but never with a partner. Not until now. Aurora makes a show of frowning. "What's to stop me from lying?"

I toss her phone, which I had pocketed, next to her. "You'll record it. I've already put my number into your phone."

"If you wanted a sex tape, you could have just asked."

I allow myself a smile. "No, Aurora. I don't want a video of your pussy as you come. I want one of your face." I watch the understanding dawn in her expression as she realizes the vulnerability I'm demanding of her. It's one thing to orgasm with another person—or several—in the heat of the moment. It's entirely another to do it alone with the knowledge that it will be viewed later. I point at the phone. "Six orgasms, six videos. Text each to me as you finish."

She presses her lips together. "And if I don't?"

I shrug, because I knew this was coming. Aurora wouldn't be Aurora if she didn't push back with every step forward we make. "Then you won't orgasm for the remainder of this assignation. It's your choice." I turn and walk away, allowing myself a smile as her curses follow me into the bathroom.

Some days, it's good to be queen.

18

AURORA

As soon as Malone leaves the room to go to work, I flop down on the bed and curse hard. I am a fucking failure. Not only did I not take advantage of the opportunity being in Malone's bed offered, but I woke up humping her like a horny teenager. Worse, for those few hours with her mouth on my skin and my hands on her body, I forgot I hated her at all. There was no room for anything but sheer need.

"What the hell am I *doing?*" I pick up the phone and stare at it. I already know I'm going to obey her command. No matter what questions I asked, there was never a drop of doubt that I'd be recording myself orgasming and sending the videos to her.

Maybe that's why I start dialing. I've been here less than a week, and I've already lost sight of the ultimate goal. I need the reminder, the slap in the face to get my head on straight. There's only one person capable of doing it, only one I've trusted enough to tell the full truth.

I call Allecto.

Despite the relatively early hour, she answers quickly. "Do you need out?"

Guilt swarms. Of course she would assume that's why I'm calling—that I've killed Malone and need an escape. "No, I'm fine."

Allecto blows out a long breath. "You are hell on my blood pressure, you know that?"

"I'm sorry." And I am. I never really thought I'd end up with a family of sorts in the Underworld, but that's exactly what's happened. Their presence in my life doesn't negate what I lost, but I can't deny that they have enriched my life and given me more love than I thought possible. Allecto will always be there when I need her, and as much as I need her right now, I really don't relish the coming "I told you so" she'll no doubt deliver. "I, uh, need some advice."

"End the assignation early and come back to the Underworld today. There, see how easy that was?"

Against all reason, I laugh. "Shouldn't you wait to hear the situation before you start offering advice?"

"No, because I know you. This ends one of two ways. Either you kill her and have to leave the city to avoid her people strapping you to a pyre and setting you on fire, or you can't go through with it and you end up mired in misplaced guilt and bullshit self-loathing." She softens her tone. "I know you're grieving your mother, but this isn't the way to do it, Aurora."

I close my eyes. It would be so much easier if the only reason I was calling was to request an exit. She's right; it's the smartest course of action. But I've never been smart when it comes to Malone, and I only seem to get more foolish as time goes on. "I can handle this."

"Is that why you're on the phone with me right now? Because you're handling it so well?

I glare at the ceiling. "She deserves to die."

Allecto makes the jump with me without hesitation. "We've all done shit that could be argued we deserve to die for. You know my past isn't free of sins. No one in the Underworld is—including you."

"It was *one* tiny fire."

"Aurora, the only reason that asshole isn't dead is because his brother hauled him out a window. He still suffered two broken legs from the fall."

I can't help my satisfied smile. "Maybe he shouldn't have fucked with Tink, then." Not that she knew what I'd done. No one but Allecto did, and only because I needed her security clearance to get the relevant information on the man who'd tried to rough up Tink in one of the private rooms. He hadn't gotten far before security stepped in, but Hades chose not to do anything beyond banish him from the neutral territory. That wasn't enough of a punishment for me.

"My *point*," Allecto continues, "is that Malone was perfectly within her rights as challenger to do what she did. It doesn't make it less shitty, and it doesn't make you less hurt by it, but no one in that territory sees things the way you do."

"We've gone over this before." My voice catches. "My mother is dead because of her."

"Yes. And I'm sorry for that, but it doesn't make a damn bit of sense to throw away your life for something that happened twenty years ago." She pauses. "I know it doesn't feel like twenty years ago, not with what happened last week, but that just confirms that you need to be here, with your people, not off on a reckless path of revenge."

"If I wanted a lecture, I would have called Hades."

"Great idea. Let's loop Hades into this." Her tone goes

dangerous. "Hades who does *not* know about the decision you made regarding your mother."

Guilt flares. "If he knew, he would have said no."

"Yeah, he would have." She huffs out a breath. "What happened? Obviously, something changed, or you wouldn't be calling me right now."

Now that I have her on the phone, I'm not sure I can verbalize it. It feels like too much a betrayal to my mother. I swallow hard. "She's not what I expected."

"Considering you expected her to be a fire-breathing dragon, I'm not surprised."

"I've read her file."

"We all have. Stop stalling, and spit it out."

"She's just so human at times; not like a monster at all. It's messing with my head."

Allecto's silent for a long time. Long enough that I have to bite my bottom lip to keep myself from babbling. Finally, she says, "It almost sounds as if you like her."

"Don't be absurd."

"That's not a no."

"It's also not a yes."

She waits a beat. "*That* isn't a no, either."

I drag my hand over my face. "Liking her would be unforgivable. You know that. After everything she did, I need to hate her. I *do* hate her. She took everything from me, and she deserves to see consequences because of that."

"Are you trying to convince me...or yourself?" She doesn't wait for me to answer. "Aurora, you're human. So is Malone. Is it really that surprising that she's got nuance and that there might be stuff about her that you actually like?"

"Weren't you ready to take her out so I wouldn't have to?"

"Yeah," she answers easily. "But that was to protect you, not because she's a monster."

"Whose side are you on?"

"Yours. Obviously." She sighs. "But cut yourself a break. No matter what your history, you've been drawn to Malone from the start. It's not exactly surprising that there might be something more there."

"There is *not* anything more there." Even as I say it, I feel like a liar.

Another of those sighs, like I've disappointed her. "If you can't kill her and aren't going to change your mind, you might as well call off the assignation now. Hades will be overjoyed. He's been stalking around here, looking half a breath from ripping people's heads off. Everyone's so scared of him, they're on their best behavior, and it's making my job too easy. You know how I hate being bored."

She's right. I know she's right. If I can't follow through on my plan, I need to get the hell out of here. I have no reason to stay without that driving me. And yet... "I'll stay through the end."

"Mmhmm."

"Don't you dare make that sound at me, Allecto."

"Mm*hmm*." She snorts. "Tell her that if she mistreats you, I'll gut her myself, golden queen or no. But as long as she's on the same page, I look forward to an invite to the wedding."

"You are *such* an asshole."

"Just because I'm an asshole doesn't mean I'm wrong, and you know it."

Except she is wrong this time. Ribbing me or no, there is no version of Malone and my relationship that ends in happily ever after. Even if I can get past what she did to my mother, the hurdles to surmount are impossibly high.

Better to just end things now. I close my eyes and try to steel myself to do exactly that. There is absolutely no reason for me to ride out this assignation. Not a single one that makes sense.

I still can't bring myself to make that call. Not yet.

"Aurora." Her tone has changed, some of the amusement falling away. "Do you need *me* to make the call and get you out?"

A small, cowardly part of me that I've worked so hard to exorcise wants to beg her to do exactly that. If someone else makes the call, then I'm not responsible for how things fall out. I don't have to figure out my confusing feelings for Malone. I can just run. Allecto won't hold it against me, either. She's got no problem wading into a situation and hauling her people out, regardless of wrong or right. She just does what she feels is necessary.

I clear my throat. "No. I have it under control."

"You sure as hell don't." She sighs. "I'm trusting you to call if you need me."

"I will. I swear I will." I even mean it. Except... Some things you have to do on your own. This is one of those things for me. If I can't follow through on my original intention—and I'm still not sure if that's true—then I need to get myself out of this mess with my own willpower and strength. Allecto would call me seven kinds of a fool for feeling that way instead of using the plentiful resources I have at hand with my friends, but Allecto has already fought all her personal demons and won.

I glance at the clock by the bedside. "I have to go."

"Stay safe."

"You, too." I hang up and flop back onto the bed. What a mess. I don't know if I really thought calling Allecto would result in the heavens opening up and the answers falling into my lap, but obviously that didn't happen. No way forward but through this.

I prop myself up on my elbows and look at the vibrator Malone left. Part of me wants to ignore her command out of spite, but she's not bluffing about not letting me orgasm for the rest of the assignation if I do. More than that...I *want* to send her the videos. Thinking about her watching them down in her undoubtedly fancy office makes my toes curl. And if they distract her a bit from that laser focus she has? All the better.

The vibrator is a little different than the ones I've used before. I mess around with it for a few minutes, finding it extremely bendy. The internal portion has a movement that, when lined up correctly, should stroke my G-spot, and the clitoral stimulator motion mimics oral sex. Damn, this thing is cool.

It takes a little time to get the fit right, but before too long, I'm rushing toward my first orgasm. I barely remember to grab the phone in time. Knowing she's going to watch this video only makes it hotter. I don't bother to try to hold out, not when I have five more where this came from. I come with a cry and bite my lip hard enough that delicious little pricks of pain heighten my pleasure.

I stare at the phone and grin. "One." Then I end the video and send it to the number she programed in there before she left.

I almost keep going, but if I'm going to obey, I'm going to do it my way. It takes a little doing to get the setup right, but when I'm finally happy with it, I lie back down and start up the vibrator again. This time, I *do* go slower, edging myself up to a truly impressive orgasm. And, yeah, I play it up a bit as I give myself over to the pleasure. I always did like putting on a show.

By the time I let myself come, I'm shaking and moaning, and I'm pretty sure the top of my head is in danger of exploding. I ease the vibrator out of me and reach down for the phone, unable to help my satisfied smirk. "Two." A few seconds later, the video is winging its way to Malone.

Now that I have the challenge in place, I decide to keep things interesting. She thought she'd use this command to make *me* vulnerable, but I'm going to turn it around on her.

You want to watch me come, Mistress? Enjoy the fucking show.

19

By the time I get out of my first meeting of the day, I have two videos waiting for me. I'd wondered if Aurora would dig in her heels, but apparently she's decided to play by the rules for once. I head for my office and shut my door, pausing to flip the lock, and take a seat behind my desk. It would be wiser to hold off watching the videos until I'm almost done for the day, but they're a temptation I can't quite ignore.

The first is exactly what I asked for, a close-up of Aurora's face as she works herself to orgasm. She's got her eyes screwed shut, but it doesn't matter. She can't hide from me, not like this, not this close. The sound she makes when she comes has my whole body flushing hot. I've never met another person quite as perfectly blended between sweet and tart, and the tart only makes the sweet more addicting.

Then I open the second video.

"Motherfucker," I breathe.

She's brought in the mirror from her closet and arranged it behind her head at the top of the bed. The video is still of her face, but there's no way to miss the fact I can see her entire body as she arches and shakes and plays with her tits while the vibrator hums between her thighs. It's a one-woman show, and it's all for me. This time, she doesn't shut her eyes. She challenges me with her gaze, with every moan past those pretty lips.

Goddamn it.

My phone beeps as another text comes in.

Aurora: You alone?

Oh, this is a trap if I ever recognized one. That doesn't stop me from typing out an affirmative and sending it. A few seconds later, a request for a video call comes through.

I glance at my door and accept the call. "I only have a few minutes before my next meeting."

"This won't take long."

I look at my phone, and a rushing sound rattles through my ears. Aurora is in my bathtub, her hair carefully piled on top of her head, her skin dewy with condensation. The water is low enough that her nipples breach the surface with every inhale. She looks good enough to eat. It takes more effort than it should to keep my tone dry. "If you drop that phone in the water and ruin it, you'll have no proof of the remaining orgasms."

"Give me a little credit." Something's changed since I left her this morning. I'm not sure what it is, but she's giving me a wicked grin that almost seems real. Aurora leans back a little, baring her breasts further. "Are you alone?"

"Does it matter?" I'm honestly curious. Aurora likes an audience, but I don't know if that extends outside the Underworld.

"Not to me." Another of those smiles. "But if no one is in the room, no one will see it if you give in to the temptation to slip your hand in your pants and finger yourself while you watch me come."

Aurora is more dangerous than a grenade with the pin pulled out. "That would be highly inappropriate during the workday."

"I know." She laughs, and the sound trails off into a breathy moan. "Gods, Malone, this toy is something else. I'm surprised you didn't invest in it the moment you heard about its existence."

"What makes you think I didn't?" As much as I keep a stranglehold on the underbelly of my territory, I like to keep my interests varied everywhere else. Investing in that particular toy has brought me a significant amount of profit. Most of my investments do.

"Of course you did." She adjusts the phone, and I realize she's propped it up on a chair next to the tub so she has both hands free. The angle gives a little more of her body, the image vaguely blurred by the water teasing at revealing her. I can't see below her hips, and for the first time, I regret the command to only see her face.

But, fuck, what a face.

She's perfectly relaxed as she builds her pleasure. I can see evidence of it in her quickening breaths, in the way her lips part as if begging for my mouth, in her eyes fighting not to slide shut when it gets too much.

I don't make a conscious decision to do as she asked, but I unbutton my pants to slip my hand between my thighs. It's as if it was a foregone conclusion the second I accepted this call. I'm drenched, and I drag the wetness up to circle my clit. My body is already tense and ready. Gods, Aurora is like a fever in my blood. I can't think straight, my normal coolness slipping through my fingers. "I should make you come down here and lick me clean after I'm done."

She lifts her chin. "Do it."

The temptation rises again, to throw all my careful plans

for the day to the wind and just fuck Aurora until we exhaust this sizzling connection. Except I don't think there *is* any exhausting it now, do I?

That means there need to be boundaries. I've worked too hard for this life to let a single person derail me. Those words used to feel firmer, more like a statement and less like a question.

"Orgasm. Say my name when you do."

I keep stroking myself, my harsh breathing creating a symphony with hers. All at once, she arches her back and cries out. And, gods help me, she moans my name as she gasps her way through her orgasm. I don't even try to hold out, not when I've been dancing on the edge and waiting for her to join me. I press my lips together as I come, shoving down any foolish desire to give her the same treatment. We're not there yet. We've only just begun to make progress, and if I move too quickly, Aurora will spook. I doubt she'll give me a second chance if I fuck this one up.

I ease my hand out of my pants and lean forward. "Well done."

"I try." Her smirk holds only a fraction of her usual brat-tiness. "Three." Aurora hangs up before I can respond, which is just as well.

I take my time cleaning myself up. The temptation to go to her is almost too much to resist, but I've a long habit of resisting the things I want most. I can last a few more hours until we spar again this afternoon.

Then I'm going to fuck her on the mat.

The plan makes me smile, and the knowledge of what's to come buoys me through two meetings that could have been emails before Sara arrives in my office to update me on the status of the territory. We touch base on them every couple of days, barring some kind of disaster, and today is more of the same.

Sara sits back. "Everything's fine. Shipments are on time. Suppliers are happy. Buyers are happy. The people are happy." They sound vaguely disgusted. "There's one that's running a little late, but it will be here by noon, so it's hardly worth noting."

"War is bad for business," I remind them.

"I know. I'm just..." They make a vague motion with their hand. "If things were going wrong, it'd give me something to focus on."

Something besides what's going on back home. I can't say I feel any differently. I frown. "Did something else happen?"

"No. No new developments. The Brides are all safe, best I can tell; or as safe as they can be given the circumstances."

Handfasted to the Paine brothers. Gods, that sounds like a nightmare if I ever heard one. If those men are anything like their father, their Brides are in for a hellish year. That man was brutal enough to give even *me* pause. The thought of seven of them, three of whom are now handfasted to my family members... It has my muscles tensing in preparation for a strike. "My sister will figure it out," I say carefully.

Sara doesn't blink. "And if she doesn't?"

"She will." I can't afford to think anything else. "And if she doesn't, Monroe will." My eldest niece, the one named in my honor. She's as ambitious, brutal, and cunning as her mother and myself combined. If Aisling falters, Monroe will ensure the Amazons land on their feet, her being handfasted to Broderick Paine or no.

Finally, Sara nods. "You're right. I know you're right."

I understand where they're coming from. It's difficult *not* to worry, but I won't be responsible for buckling the trust

our people have in Aisling, even from a distance. The
Amazons on my staff are still Amazons first.

I won't be a traitor.

I let the realization wash over me, let it settle down deep.
I won't be a traitor. I left Sabine Valley to prevent my ambition from harming my sister and my people. Nothing's
changed, no matter what the current situation back there is.
They will find their way through, and if Aisling needs my
assistance, she'll call me. Trying to muscle my way back in
because I don't like how she's handled the situation will
only cause further rift and undermine her authority. That's
bad for everyone.

Restless energy fizzles in my blood, and I push to my
feet. Cancelling my last few meetings is out of the question,
but the temptation is there all the same. I turn to look out
the window, at the visual reminder of everything at stake. I
have my own kingdom to look after now. I am the best
person to run this territory, and no matter my loyalty to my
family, there are more lives than simply my nieces' and
brother's at stake.

And yet...

I smooth my hands down my pants. "Would it make you
feel better if I check in with her?"

"Would it make *you* feel better?"

I give Sara a long look. "Yes." I reach for my phone and
dial my sister's number from memory. I stare out at Carver
City while the line rings. My home in a very different way
than Sabine Valley is—a place that's mine and mine alone.

My elder sister's voice comes over the line. "Hello,
Malone." I don't know why I expected her to sound different
after everything that has happened. Our mother's training
runs too deep. She's just as coolly collected as I am.

Except I don't feel cool and collected right now. I feel

frazzled right down to my nerve endings. "When were you going to tell me about Lammas?"

"When it became something you should concern yourself with; so likely never. It's under control."

This is why I haven't called since hearing the news. I love my sister. I have always loved my sister, even when I put serious consideration into dethroning her. But it takes a grand total of thirty seconds for her to work her way under my skin. She's one of the few people in existence who's capable of it.

Aurora is another.

I push that thought away. "You underestimated the Paine family."

"If I wanted someone to tell me things I already know, I'd talk to Jasper."

Irritation rises. "Yes, well, that's out of the question now since he's handfasted to Ezekiel fucking Paine." No use thinking about how painful that must be for him, given their history. "You really fucked this up."

"It's under control."

"What part of this situation is under control, Aisling? What happens if Monroe or Winry gets pregnant? Then—"

"Stop underestimating your nieces. You left, Malone. You built your kingdom elsewhere and I've never begrudged you that. Trust that I've raised my daughters as capably as Mother raised us."

I wish I could. I wish I had anything but doubt and worry worming through me. "Monroe may be fine, but Winry is too soft. He'll break her."

"*Malone.*" She all but snarls my name. "Did you call for a particular reason or just to clutch your pearls and whine about things that have already happened?" I already know what she's going to say before she continues in a slightly more moderate tone. "Lammas caught us off-guard, but it's being handled. Have faith in your family." A meaningful pause. "Have faith in your queen."

You're not my queen.

I bite the sentence back before it can emerge. I needed this reminder, I realize. Needed to have the reason I left Sabine Valley shoved in my face. I love my sister, yes. But both our personalities are too strong to occupy the same space without tearing into each other. I close my eyes and strive for a calm tone. "Give me the courtesy of keeping me updated."

"Why, when you already have plenty of contacts still within our territory?"

I have to fight not to grind my teeth. "That's not the same thing, and you know it."

Aisling finally sighs. "Yes, I'll keep you updated." The barest pause. "They'll be fine. They're made of tougher stuff than you realize. Even Winry. They're Amazons, after all."

At the end of the day, there's nothing to argue with. I haven't been home for more than a few days at a time in twenty years. I have more contact with my younger brother than I do with Aisling, but even that is just the odd phone call here and there. I don't really know my nieces beyond surface-level facts. Monroe was seven when I left Sabine Valley, barely more than a baby. Aisling is right. If she's raised them half as capably as Mother raised us, they'll survive this.

They might even come out on top.

I have to believe that. Still... "Is there any way I can be of assistance?"

"I will call if I need you." Her tone says the exact opposite, and even though I shouldn't hold it against her, I can't help but do exactly that. If I were in her position, I'd be doing the same thing in regard to warning off a person with the potential to further destabilize our territory. Aisling hangs up before I can formulate a response, which is just as well.

Sara raises their brows. "That went well."

"A necessary reminder." I take a few slow breaths, working to pull my icy calm around me once more. Normally, it happens naturally, but it takes a considerable bit of effort after that call. "They have things under control."

"Good to hear," they say carefully.

I head for the door. "Please ensure Aurora is in the gym by the time I'm finished with my meetings for the morning."

"Will do."

"Thank you." I find myself with a lot of energy to dispel.

Aurora's just the person to act as conduit.

20

I knock out my final three orgasms quickly, and I wish I could say that I pulled on some of my many memories with others to get me there. It's not the truth. No, it's Malone's ragged breathing in my ear that pushes me over the edge. The knowledge that she slipped her hand down her pants and fingered herself while on the phone with me. I shouldn't have initiated that call, but there are a lot of things I shouldn't have done in the last few days.

She doesn't respond to my videos again.

I want to be smug about that, to believe that I rattled her. I'm not sure it's the truth. Maybe she just tired of the game.

That would be preferable. If Malone tires of me, it's the best outcome for everyone, especially since I'm coming to terms with the fact that I won't be following through on my plans for vengeance. If I'm not here to kill Malone, then I have no reason to be here.

Except... I don't really want to leave.

Not yet.

The second I return to the Underworld, I have to deal with reality. The end of my contract. My plans for the future.

My grief. It all hovers at the edge of my mind, ready to ambush me the second I cease being distracted.

I push the thoughts aside and pull on a pair of shorts and a sports bra. It's time to go another round with Malone. I want to win today, to be the one to demand some kind of payment. Really, I just want to beat her. She's too good, wins at everything, is too deadly. I want to prove that I'm able to stand on equal footing.

A child's dream, foolish in the extreme.

A training accident would be a clever way to cover up her death...

A hiss stops me short. I look around the room, and catch sight of Rogue crouched beneath the couch, glaring at me with his eerie cat eyes. I glare right back. "I was only *thinking* about it. I'm not really going to do it." I scrub my hands over my face. I should have listened to Allecto, just this once, when she told me not everyone is cut out for murder. Fires are different. Even fighting is different. It's violence in the heat of the moment, the first lick of flame that translates into a pure bolt of power.

Even then, without some kind of outward motivation, I hesitate.

I pull my hair back and fasten it up away from my face. My mother should be motivation enough. She was in a coma for twenty years. *Twenty years.* I barely remember her from before that, only have flashes of images that I'm still not certain are real. She was never around, and my grandmother was so withdrawn, I used to comfort myself with imaging all the things my mother and I would do once I was old enough to join her. And then all those possible futures were gone in the space of a single fight, my fantasy of my mother boiled down to a harsh reality. There was no comfort in standing over her bed and watching a machine breathe for her. The spark that made her who she was gone long before I made the decision I did last week.

I'm still not sure if knowing that makes it better or worse.

I pull on a pair of shoes and stride to the door. Can you fail a person you barely remember? I don't know if I'd be hesitating if Malone hurt one of my friends—Allecto or Tink or Meg. The fact that I'm *not* sure makes me feel worse. I'm a terrible daughter, and I've only gotten worse with each passing year.

Sara meets me at the elevator, and they've got a strange expression on their face. We step inside and go down two floors to the gym, and only then do they speak. "She's on edge."

"I don't care." It tastes like a lie on my tongue.

Sara snorts. "Sure, kid. Just be careful in there." They step back into the elevator, and the doors close before I can formulate a response. What is there to say? Malone's on edge. I am, too.

It'll be a party.

The room looks the same as it did yesterday, the thick mat for sparring and the lights up bright. It's also empty. After the slightest hesitation, I stride onto the mat and begin to warm up. Ten minutes later, I'm wondering where the hell Malone is. Not showing up would be a power play, but I can't imagine she'd have Sara deliver dire warnings if she didn't intend to be here.

My question is answered almost as soon as I consider it when the doors swing open and Malone stalks through. She's changed out of her work clothes and into a pair of pants and a tank top. She snaps her fingers at me. "Let's do this."

"You don't want to warm up?"

"No." She's on me before I can respond. Gods, she's fast. And strong. I deflect a punch and the impact rattles me right down to my bones. It's everything I can do to keep ahead of her, to keep some space between us while I frantically look for an opening.

It's startlingly clear that the only reason I landed any blows yesterday was because I surprised her. She wasn't expecting me to be as good as I am. Now, she's not holding back. I suppose that's a compliment, but it doesn't feel like one when she lands a punch to my stomach that drives my breath from my lungs. "Fuck," I wheeze.

One second I'm trying to get oxygen, the next I'm on my back with Malone sitting on my chest, her legs pinning my arms to my sides. "Fuck," I repeat.

"You're distracted." She glares. "You put up more of a fight yesterday."

It takes several long moments before I can breathe well enough to answer. "You're extra motivated this time." Even though part of me demands I let it go, I can't quite seem to help myself. "Rough day?"

"Something like that." Malone shifts back so that she's perched on my hips and plants her hands on either side of my head. "I win."

I should leave it at that, let us chase the heat flaring in her green eyes. I can't quite manage it. "We can talk about it, if you want." Why am I offering this? Why am I craving knowing what's going on inside her head? I don't even know anymore.

She studies my expression. "Maybe later." Malone dips her fingers beneath the straps of my sports bra and pulls them over my shoulders and down to free my breasts. She leaves it there, further trapping my arms. I could get out of it easily enough, but that's not the point. It *feels* like intense bondage.

She palms my breasts, expression intense. "You'll be naked for the rest of the day."

"Okay," I manage.

Malone pinches my nipple. "Try that again with a little more respect."

I nibble my bottom lip. "Yes, Mistress."

"Better." She circles my nipples with her thumbs. Pleasure tightens my stomach, and I have to fight not to moan. Malone traces my breasts as if memorizing them. It's too much and not enough and, gods, being studied by this woman is its own kind of foreplay. She leans down and drags her tongue along the curve of my breast.

I'm still trying to settle into the touch when she moves. She shifts off me and flips me onto my stomach. With my arms trapped at my side, I can't catch myself and end up with my face pressed to the mat. She urges my ass into the air and yanks my shorts down my thighs to just below my knees. The position is far too vulnerable, but she places a hand on the back of my neck, keeping me still.

Malone strokes her free hand over my ass and down to squeeze my thighs, urging them wide. The move tightens my shorts around my shins, once again creating the feeling of bondage without actually being bound.

"I'm going to beat you tonight. Welt this pert little ass." She squeezes my ass. "But first..." Malone palms my pussy and spears two fingers into me. I can *hear* how wet I am, and my skin heats, though I can't begin to say if it's in embarrassment or desire.

She strokes me idly, as if she doesn't have me pinned to the mat in the middle of a brightly lit gym. As if she has all the time in the world and intends to make use of it.

The door opens, and I tense, but Malone doesn't stop the slow slide of her fingers in and out of my pussy. From my position, I can see Sara nearly miss a step before they continue into the room. They glance at me, and I can't help picturing how I must look right now. My face and bare breasts pressed against the mat, my ass in the air, Malone's fingers buried inside me. A little slut, that's all I am, because I swear I get wetter knowing we have an audience.

Sara clears their throat and focuses on the woman currently finger fucking me. "There's a small issue with one of our shipments. The one that was late."

"How small?" She sounds perfectly normal, as if she's sitting behind her desk instead of down on the floor with me. How often does she fuck in front of her people? This isn't the first time; despite Sara's initial surprise, they don't seem the least bit uncomfortable with this situation.

"I can handle it. But I figured you'd like to know. We were missing about ten percent of the promised goods."

I might as well not even be here for all they're paying attention to me. Humiliation heats my skin, desire chasing on its heels. Malone only makes it worse when she wedges a third finger into me and uses her thumb to stroke my clit. I bite my lips hard to keep from moaning. Gods, if they don't end this conversation soon, I'm going to come all over her hand in front of Sara while they give their report.

I want to.

Fuck, I want to.

"Ten percent," Malone muses. "That's bold of them to think we wouldn't notice."

"I expect they *did* realize we'd notice and hoped to provoke a reaction."

"Agreed." She doesn't pick up her pace, just keeps idly fucking me. "Very well. Make an example. Nothing deadly;

it's not worth the headache. But ensure they know we won't allow this 'mistake' again."

I'm shaking. I can't seem to stop. I bite my lip so hard, I taste blood, but I can't stop the whimper that slips free. Sara glances down at me again, expression still unreadable. "Will you be available if things get messy?"

"Of course." Malone picks up her pace the slightest bit, edging me closer and closer to coming. "If that's all?"

"It is." Sara ducks their head and moves to the door. They pause before leaving. "Want me to lock this behind me?"

"No."

Then Sara is gone. The door barely swings shut behind them when Malone withdraws her fingers and gives my pussy a slap harsh enough to jolt me. "You're holding out."

"No, Mistress," I grind out.

"Liar." She rubs my clit, and I can't help sobbing out my exhale. "This pussy is mine for the duration. If I want you to come in front of Sara, then you come in front of Sara. Do you understand?"

"Yes, Mistress," I whisper. The rebuke, the humiliation, only makes this hotter. I arch my back a little, a subtle offering that she notices immediately. She picks up her pace, hurtling toward an orgasm that's already curling my toes. I moan. "Mistress, please let me come."

"I shouldn't." She still sounds like she's musing even as she works my body. "I should leave you hanging on the edge after that little bit of defiance. You think you're in charge, Aurora, but you are most assuredly not."

"*Please.*"

"Oh, very well."

My orgasm crests, washing away everything but this woman. How does she do this every time? How does she manage to break me into minuscule pieces? We're not even doing anything particularly intense when it comes to kink, at least not on the surface, but *everything* is intense with Malone involved. She breathes intensity, and I crave the taste.

She eases me onto my back. My shorts are tangled around my ankles and my legs splayed, and the look she gives my pussy... I lick my lips. "Malone."

"You're terrible at following rules. Absolutely horrid." She parts my pussy with her thumbs, resuming that idle touch that is somehow even hotter than when she's driving me to orgasm. She touches me like she owns me, and in this moment, I'm not sure she's wrong.

She considers me. "I would like a picture of this."

It takes me several long beats to realize she's asking permission. I should say no. The videos are bad enough; giving her yet more ammunition is a mistake. But I'm already nodding. "Yes." A small, fierce part of me gets off on the knowledge that Malone will be undoubtedly fucking herself while she looks at this picture sometime in the future, after this assignation has long since passed.

If that's not power, what is?

She already lives rent-free in my head. Forgive the fuck out of me if I want to return the favor, even in this small way.

Malone pulls her phone out of a pocket tucked into the leg of her pants and lifts it. "Gods, Aurora. You're sin personified."

"I don't believe in sin."

"Neither do I." She clicks a few pictures and then leans forward and pushes two fingers into me. Another click of a picture. Malone licks her lips. "Yes, this will do." She hooks my pants and pulls them the rest of the way off me and then does the same with my bra. "Come along."

I expect her to head for the exit, but she moves to a door on the other side of the room. It leads to a hallway that looks like one in every other high-end gym in existence. Malone bypasses the locker rooms and walks to a door with a narrow window.

The sauna.

Malone points to the door. "Wait for me in there."

I obey. I don't even consider arguing, not when the idea of letting heat work its way into my tired body sounds like a little slice of heaven right now. I know that's not all that's on the menu, and it only makes my anticipation grow. The sauna is a square room with a wooden bench seat in a U-shape against three of the walls.

A few minutes later, Malone returns, wrapped in a white towel. She perches on the bench next to me and lets out a long sigh. She closes her eyes and rests her head against the wall. "Relax."

Relax. Is that supposed to be a joke? How am I supposed to *relax* when a mostly naked Malone is sitting six inches away?

I shift to face her. Now is the time to put some distance between us, to accept the boon of silence she's obviously intent on offering me. Except... I don't want to. "Malone."

"You are outstandingly terrible at following orders."

She's not wrong. And yet, I can't seem to stop myself from reaching out and running my finger along her sharp collarbones. Her skin is already dewy with sweat, just like mine, and I find the sight intoxicating.

"Aurora."

I ignore the warning in her tone and skate my fingers down to the spot where her towel is tucked into a fastening over her chest. The tiniest of tugs, and it slithers free.

"Aurora." She opens her eyes. "What are you doing?"

"I don't know." I shift to my knees in front of her and part the towel, pushing it aside to bare her body. Malone isn't flawless, for all that she's so gorgeous, it actually hurts to look at her. There's a small scattering of scars on her torso and one on her thigh that looks like it might have been a bullet wound. But, gods, the strength poised in her narrow frame. I place my hands on her thighs and coast them up her hips and sides, inching closer.

"You don't know." She arches a brow, but I don't miss the way she parts her legs a little more to make room for me.

"No." I lean forward and rub my face over her breasts. Even after coming so much today, I'm practically shaking with need from being this close to her. "I just...need you right now."

21

MALONE

E very time I think I understand Aurora, that I can anticipate her moves, she throws me a curveball. Another time, I might luxuriate in the surprise to have her kneeling between my legs, running her soft hands over my body. Another time, I might play this out beat by beat, twining the pleasure around us until we're both shaking with need.

Another time.

Now, I simply sit and let her touch me. Let her trace patterns over my skin and follow them with her heated gaze. For once, there's no conflict in her dark eyes when she looks at me. Simply desire. This woman looks at me like she's not sure if she wants to start at the top or the bottom, but she's most certainly going to get to every inch, given enough time.

She leans down and presses a line of kisses from my sternum to my lower stomach. Soft. Sweet, and yet not sweet at all. "Do your shipments often come up short?"

I exhale. "Mining for information?"

"Not really." She drags her tongue over my hipbone. "Just seems like something you'd want to handle yourself."

As tempting as it is to shut down this line of conversation, I have the strangest desire to make her understand. "When you run a territory, you can't drop a nuclear bomb for every little transgression."

She pauses and looks up at me. "*You're* the nuclear bomb?"

"Yes." I give in to the urge to stroke my fingers over her temple. "Sara and their team are more than capable of handling things like this, and it allows the threat of me to be maintained." I should leave it there, but I find myself continuing. "They don't deserve my personal attention; it wouldn't do for them to get ideas."

"Bringing a shotgun to a knife fight."

I give a tight smile. "Yes, something like that."

She's still watching me closely. "But why not do that? It'd stop any dissent in its tracks. People would fall all over themselves to prove their loyalty."

While she's not wrong, it exhausts me just thinking about it. "I am feared, Aurora. With good reason, and by design, but it doesn't change the fact that it wears on a person to see terror in the eyes of every person they come across."

"But your people love you." She sits back, trailing her fingers down my thighs. "Your employees for both businesses worship the ground you walk on."

"They still fear me."

She opens her mouth, stops to reconsider, and finally shrugs. "Power has a price."

"Yes." Suddenly, I'm tired of talking. What does it matter if I'm feared by nearly everyone I encounter? What does it matter if my mother didn't rule the same way? Oh, our people respected the threat she could bring to them if they crossed her, but they loved her in way that couldn't be feigned. The times I've been home since leaving Sabine Valley, I've found my sister inspires that same kind of feeling. An intrinsic difference between us, yet another reason I would have been ill-suited to be heir. I don't have the gift of setting people at ease while still commanding their loyalty.

I am only the way I am.

I lean back and give Aurora a long look. "Put your mouth to good use, Aurora."

She doesn't hesitate. She simply lowers her mouth and presses delicate, soft kisses to my hips, my thighs, before finally working her way to my pussy. I like the look of her mouth on me. I like the look on her face even more. She's as blissed out by giving this as I am at receiving it. For fuck's sake, she moans at the first taste of me.

How am I supposed to remain unaffected after witnessing that?

I fist her hair in my hands and spread my thighs wider. It's tempting to ride her face, to hold her in place as I chase my own pleasure, but I want to see what she'll do given a little freedom.

She doesn't disappoint. Aurora parts my pussy with her thumbs and traces her tongue over every inch of me. Like she'll never get another chance and she wants to memorize every second of this. She spears me with her tongue and then moves up to focus on my clit. Again with those teasing little licks, pushing my desire until I'm shaking in an effort to hold still. That's when she pushes two fingers into me and twists her wrist to find my G-spot. She strokes it lightly as she picks up her pace on my clit, quickly finding the rhythm that has my thighs shaking.

She winds me higher and higher, until my control snaps. "I need—" I tighten my grip on her hair and roll my hips, fucking her mouth. She makes a happy sound, and I belatedly realize this was her goal all along. To push me until I took what I wanted.

Gods, this woman is a gift.

I drag Aurora up my body and kiss her. It's tempting to keep going, to lose myself in her until we're both wrung out, but we have to get out of the sauna. I carefully nudge her back. "Let's go."

We grab robes from the locker room and head back up to my penthouse. We take our time in the shower and appreciate this moment of peace after everything that's happened. It's not enough to truly put my concerns out of my head, not with my ever-present worry about Sabine Valley, not when I'm all too aware of the clock ticking down on the assignation with Aurora.

I take the time to call Sara and check in, but as expected, they've handled the situation. The supplier magically found the missing ten percent within five minutes of Sara showing up. I don't ask what kind of example they made. They've been my right hand for long enough that I trust they did what was necessary without crossing over into being too much. A delicate balance, but one at which Sara exceeds.

And there's nothing else on my plate.

Aurora's watching me, her expression contemplative. I raise my brows. "Yes?"

"I don't understand you."

"Do you need to?" I find myself holding my breath while I wait for her answer. I don't know what the right one is; I don't know which one I crave.

Finally, she looks away. "I'd like to."

"Why do you sound so put out by that?"

"Because it's irritating as hell." She makes a face. "It was easier to hate you."

"Hate takes as much effort as any other emotion; more

than some." It's much preferable to apathy, honestly, but I'm not about to say as much. If Aurora no longer hates me— No, no use following that rabbit hole into a spiraling game of what-if. "If it makes you feel better, there are large swathes of you that I don't understand, either."

"*Me?*"

I give her the look that faux innocence deserves. "The bratty submissive. The fierce friend. The princess of the Underworld. You're all that, but it's only the tip of the iceberg. You must have a life outside of Hades."

She tucks her hair behind her ear. "Is there a question in there?"

"Surely you're not content to be the pampered princess forever? There's a fire in you that needs to be fed. You can only rise so far in Hades's territory." Hades will be ruling for some time yet, and he's got both Megaera and Hercules beneath him. Should he decide to retire, surely those two will take over running operations. And Hercules is several years younger than Aurora. She'll never run the Underworld, no matter how many years she works there.

Aurora finally shrugs. "I don't really know what I want. I had this guiding light for a really long time, but now that the bargain with Hades is coming to an end, that light's faded. I have a master's in business administration, but I mostly got that because it seemed like the logical next step and I had money to pay for it."

"Have you done anything beyond the Underworld and school in the last nine years?"

"Stop it." She looks away. "You say that like it's a bad thing, but what else could I possibly want? I've dated outside the Underworld, and you already know how well *that's* worked out. Carver City might be run by territory leaders, but most of the people who live here are normal. I don't fit in. I don't *want* to fit in. That's a choice I made for myself, so stop looking at me like you pity me."

"I don't pity you." It's the truth. But I can't help feeling that Aurora could do so much more if she ever had the fire of ambition lit inside her. One only has to look at how she blossomed as Megaera's second-in-command to see that she only needs the space and she'll continue to expand. But she won't thank me for saying as much. I turn away. "Come along."

"Where are we going?"

"Tonight? Nowhere. I have plans for you." I walk into my closet and pull on a pair of lounge pants and a fitted shirt. Then I lead the way into the spare bedroom. It smells of lemon and pine, and the mattress has been removed—Rogue was too effective in marking his territory, and it's well beyond ruined. "You're lucky the closet was shut or Rogue would have done a number on your shoes."

"*Your* shoes." She pauses in the doorway as I peruse the selection. "You're the one who bought all of this."

"And you'll take it with you when this is over. Consider it a tip." I finally land on a black, oversized knit sweater that's long enough to be considered a dress—barely. I pull it off the shelf and toss it to Aurora.

"A tip, huh?" Her lips curve the tiniest bit. "It wouldn't be a way for you to mark your territory the same way your demon cat does?"

Truth be told, I *do* like the idea of Aurora wearing clothing that I personally picked out. It satisfies something deep and dark inside me that I mostly refuse to acknowledge. "Stop calling Rogue a demon. You'll hurt his feelings."

"That creature doesn't have feelings. All he has is spite."

I arch an eyebrow. "He simply sees you as an intruder and took the steps to rectify the situation."

"Uh-huh." Aurora makes a face. "How many pieces of furniture have you replaced because that animal destroyed them?"

"In the last year or since I've had him?"

She blinks. "How old is that cat?"

"Ten. He was among a litter left in a box by my building. The kittens were so young, not all of them made it, but Luna has his sister." I frown. "*That* cat is a demon."

"I'm going to ignore that statement, since you are obviously biased." She shakes her head. "How many pieces of furniture has he destroyed in the last year? I'm afraid of the lifetime answer."

I do a quick count, realizing halfway through that I'm going to lose this particular argument. "Eight, not including the mattress." When she stares, I cross my arms over my chest. "As I said, the mattress was a territory dispute and so is completely justified."

Aurora looks at me like she's never seen me before. "You love that cat."

My face heats under her intense gaze, and even as I try to muscle down the reaction, I have a feeling that a tinge of pink colors my cheeks. "We have a mutual understanding."

"Right. Sure. A pair made in heaven."

"I'm taking that as a compliment, rather than the insult you intended. Rogue is particular with people." I turn away before she can keep pressing. The truth is that the cat barely tolerates me, let alone anyone else, but I like that about him. Some days he feels like my own personal dragon, guarding our castle of a penthouse. A fanciful thought, but Rogue has the tendency to attack unwanted guests at his whim. The fact that he hasn't touched Aurora, marking his territory aside, is moderately shocking.

"As I said, a pair made in heaven."

I lead the way into the kitchen and head to the fridge. As promised, there's an entire meal waiting with a note about reheating instructions on the top. I double-check them and then preheat the oven. When I turn around, Aurora has an expression on her face like she's trying not to laugh. "What?"

"When I saw how stocked your fridge is, I thought you cooked. But you don't, do you?"

"No." I'm capable of putting together a simple meal in a pinch, but when a person is as busy as I am, they learn to delegate. I can't do that with many of my business responsibilities, so I farm out as much personally as possible. "I have a chef who usually preps a week's worth of meals on Sundays."

Aurora moves closer into the fridge. "That's not a week's worth of meals."

"No, I had her do something special tonight." I realize how that sounds, but I don't take the words back. They're the truth. "She'll come around this Sunday and get back into the swing of things, but this week was irregular."

"I see." Aurora peers at the food containers. "Interesting."

"Are you allergic to anything?" Something I should have asked before, but I didn't even think of it.

She shakes her head. "No."

I bring out a bottle of wine and pour us each a glass. We drink in what's almost a comfortable silence as we wait for the oven to preheat. It dings its readiness, and I put the container into the oven and set the timer. Then I motion for her to follow. "We'll wait in here." I lead the way into the living room and sink onto the couch.

After the briefest of hesitations, Aurora sinks down next to me. Does she realize that, even a few days ago, she would have chosen another seat, would have put as much distance between us as possible? I don't comment on it, though. A patient hunter gives the prey plenty of time to settle in before making their move. It doesn't matter that this woman makes me feel frenzied and out of control.

I *will* have patience.

I sip my wine and study her. She looks good here in my home, dressed in the clothes I purchased her. A feeling almost like possession rises up in me, but I stifle it. This isn't the time or place for such messy emotions. Not yet. I need her to want me first. Crave me. Desire me like a fire in her blood that she never wants to douse.

Then, and only then, will she be mine.

22

"I would like to know what drove a thirteen-year-old to make a deal with Hades."

I flinch. I thought we were done talking about that. I really should have known better. The rage on Malone's face when she found out my age at the beginning of the deal was a fearsome thing. "It's irrelevant."

"It hardly feels irrelevant. If the rest of the territory leaders knew what he'd done, they'd string him up, leader of neutral territory or no. Especially Ursa. There are lines, even for the likes of us. What he did crosses them."

She's working herself up again, and while part of me almost enjoys this moment of Malone feeling protective of me, I refuse to indulge this line of talking. "We've already been over this."

"I remain unsatisfied."

I reach out and give her arm a squeeze. "I chose this. There's nothing more untoward going on than there usually is in the Underworld, in this city. It's not worth going in there and fighting with Hades. The worst he's done since I moved into the Underworld is be overly over-protective of me. That's it."

"He's not the only one." She murmurs it so quietly, I'm almost convinced I misheard her. She picks up her glass and takes a long drink. "What could possibly drive a thirteen-year-old to show up in the Underworld, let alone make a bargain like that?" A question she's asked several times now. One I'm no closer to answering.

I look away. I'm a coward in so many ways. If I can't enact my revenge, the least I can do is shove what she did in her face. If she's feeling protective of me, if she cares even the slightest bit, surely she'll feel guilty for the fact that *her* actions put me on this path?

The moment I break my silence, this thing between us ends.

That should make me happy. She's my enemy, after all. It doesn't matter how good it feels to fuck her, how high I fly when we scene. She is the *enemy*. But that word feels flimsy and untethered. I close my eyes and take a deep breath. "I don't want to talk about it."

Silence for a beat. Two. Finally, Malone says, "I don't suppose it's a happy story."

"It's not."

The soft stroke of her finger down the side of my face has me opening my eyes to find her searching my expression. I'm not sure what she finds there, because she nods almost to herself. "Growing up as an Amazon is very different from a lot of other places. We value our children above all else. All we do—the ambition, the hostile takeovers, the territory skirmishes—are to pave a better life forward for them. We spoil them and let them have free rein until they hit high school. Then they begin training in earnest."

I swallow hard. "Why are you telling me this?"

"Because it seems that something went sideways during your childhood, and I'm sorry for it."

She's not apologizing for what she did to my mother. She doesn't even know that the former leader of this territory *was* my mother. Still, the words echo through me. *I'm sorry for it.* I swallow past my suddenly dry throat. "You're better than Allecto on the mat. Surely you had to start training at thirteen to get that good."

"Aurora, I'm forty-one." She gives a small smile. "Even if I didn't see the inside of a studio before high school, I've still had more than enough years to become proficient at any number of things."

"That's not an answer."

"No, I suppose it isn't." She rises slowly to her feet and tugs me up with her. "We give our children free rein, yes, but they start combat training as soon as they can walk." My shock must show, because she shrugs. "Part of the way we settle disputes with the other factions in Sabine Valley is ritual combat during the feast of Lammas. It's important that every one of our people can hold their own, should it ever come to that."

I don't know much about the pagan feasts beyond roughly when they are in the year, but even I can connect the dots. Lammas is at the beginning of August, which means it passed not too long ago. "So if Lammas is the ritual combat feast, what are the other ones?."

"Lammas is more than ritual combat. That's just the part everyone talks about because it's flashy." She leads the way down the hall toward her playroom. "Samhain is a sober feast where we honor our dead and fallen throughout the year. Everyone gets drunk and poetic and forgets we're all enemies. Imbolc is usually when marriages and alliances and various agreements are forged. Everyone celebrates together." Her lips curve. "And Beltane is a night when there are no factions, no enemies, nothing to hold anyone back from pursuing the pleasure they crave with whomever they please."

It sounds like something out of a fantasy novel. I knew they followed strange paths in Sabine Valley, but I didn't realize *how* strange. She mentioned a bit last night, but it doesn't feel any less strange now. "Oh."

"Let's not talk about painful things anymore." She opens the door and heads for the large cabinet that contains her plethora of toys. "I'd rather focus on pleasure."

Malone opens the wardrobe and trails her fingers over her rainbow of strap-ons. They range from average size, if funky shapes, to downright ruinous. My gaze lands on the red one at the end—it's shaped like a fist and is damn close to life-sized. I shiver. "Do I get to pick?"

She snorts. "No."

I didn't think I would. I don't really want to. The lines have blurred, and the rules I was so sure were unable to bend no longer seem to be in effect. Better to experience the sharp edge of desire, to reestablish those careful boundary lines, than to give in to the strange emotions in my chest. The *soft* emotions in my chest.

The timer in the kitchen dings, and Malone strokes her hand down my spine. "Let's eat."

How can she show me this preview for the night and expect me to be able to concentrate on dinner? Except that's not what she expects, I realize as I follow her out of the room. This is the appetizer for what comes after the meal. For *dessert*.

The dining room is smaller than I expected, just large enough for a table capable of seating four. It's appointed as lavishly as the rest of the penthouse, but I get the feeling that it's rarely used. It's a little too pristine, though I don't know what gives me that impression when everything else is equally pristine. It's just a feeling.

Malone sets down her wine and motions for me to take a seat. "A moment."

It's not until I obey that I realize how *wrong* this feels. She shouldn't be waiting on me, though that's not what this is. It's her taking care of me.

That traitorous warmth springs to life again. It doesn't mean anything. It *can't* mean anything. No matter what else is true, I simply cannot fall for Malone. It's bad enough that my revenge slipped so easily through my fingers; half my life spent wanting to hurt her the way she's hurt me, and the moment I get a chance to put all that pain and sorrow into action, I flounder.

But falling for her?

It would be a failure on an entirely different level. It would paint me in the ugliest of tones, would turn me traitor to the mother who lost everything, to the grand-mother who sacrificed so much to ensure I was safe. Surely I can't be that weak, that horrible?

Malone sets my plate in front of me. It's lasagna, and the smell immediately has my mouth watering despite my tumultuous emotions. I take a bite, mostly to keep my hands busy and my thoughts internal, and moan as the taste explodes over my tongue. "You should give your chef a raise."

"She makes quite a pretty penny for her services." Malone sounds amused.

I realize I've closed my eyes to better savor the food and force them open, only to find her watching me with an expression I've never seen on her face. It takes several beats for recognition to filter through me. I've seen the exact same expression on Hades and Gaeton and Beast and Hook and Ursa. It's a fond sort of indulgence.

And she's looking at *me* like that.

The temptation to close my eyes is nearly overwhelming. Maybe if I pretend I didn't see it, I can ignore the way it makes me feel. As if she's wrapped me in a cozy blanket and held me close. As if she *cares*.

Oh, this is bad. This is very, very bad.

It's been less than a week, and she's already undermined everything I thought I believed in. What more can she do, given the rest of the assignation? Will I be panting after her like a love-struck fool when she sends me on my way?

Because she *will* send me on my way. This isn't forever. It can't be. Even without our history, I have no intention to stop working at the Underworld anytime soon. I love it there. Allecto and the others are the family I've chosen. The work is fulfilling and fun. There are plenty of people who frequent the place who wouldn't have an issue with that, but Malone doesn't strike me as a person who shares outside of the odd scene here and there. Choosing her means giving up all of that.

What am I even saying?

Bad enough that I can't follow through on my revenge, and I can't even pretend that I want to. Bad enough that I lust after my enemy. Bad enough that I now see her as a complicated person rather than the villain I've painted her.

Choosing her? Wanting to do more than fuck and scene, to actually spend time with her? How can I possibly want that?

Gods, I'm in danger of losing my mind. I feel like I'm standing in the middle of a storm pulling this way and that, threatening to tear me to pieces with the force of conflicting desires. It's too much. It's far too much.

My appetite disappears, and I spend the rest of the meal moving my food around on the plate. If Malone notices, she doesn't comment. I hate that I appreciate the mercy. What would I say, after all?

I'm upset because I should want to kill you, but all I want to do is sit at your feet and worship you for the next ten years or so.

I really am a traitorous daughter.

Something is wrong with Aurora. The meal started off well enough, but somewhere in the middle of it, she shut down. I watch her as I finish my food, but she hasn't taken a bite in nearly ten minutes. I already know that she won't answer honestly if I ask what's going through her head. That knowledge stings, though it has no right to. We've known each other a long time, but we've been opposed for most of that time. I can't honestly expect her to crack herself open for me simply because I desire it.

And I do desire it.

"You're staring."

"I like looking at you." It's the truth, but I've never wanted the ability to read minds as much as I do right now. "You said you agreed to this because you lost someone recently."

She tenses. "Yes."

I set that knowledge aside when she first mentioned it because she obviously had no intention of telling me who it was, and she just as obviously didn't want to talk about it. I can understand that. When my mother died, it was like someone punched a hole in my chest. I walked around in a daze for several weeks, and it's only the loyalty and stubbornness of Sara and the others in my immediate circle that kept this territory running during that time. They ensured I'd have a safe place when I finally came back to myself.

Aurora doesn't trust me. She might be using me to forget for a little while, but eventually she's going to have to deal with whatever put that shadow in her eyes. And there's a good chance I won't be there to stand guard over her while she does, no matter how much I increasingly want to be that person.

No, I can't be the safety net for her, not with our current relationship, but I can give her tonight. A scene to keep her firmly in her body and chase away the ghosts that linger around her.

Starting now.

I motion to her plate. "Are you finished?"

She frowns. "You're not going to press me for more information?"

I desperately want to, but even I know when to stop a frontal assault and flank my opponent. "Do you want to talk about it?"

"No."

I thought so. "There's your answer. Now, answer *my* question."

"I'm finished." She pushes the plate away.

"Come along." I gather the plates and head into the kitchen to deposit them in the sink. Then I lead the way down the hall to the playroom. "Close the door behind you."

She obeys without a word, which just reconfirms that she's nowhere near her normal state of mind. A sliver of worry stabs me, and I look at her again. I had intense plans for the night, but for the first time, I'm not sure if they're the right ones. I don't want to make her feel worse. I want to offer her the escape she so obviously craves. "What do you need?"

Aurora blinks. "What?"

"Aurora." I inject some censure into my tone.

"Right. You hate repeating yourself." Her lips pull up a little at the edges. "You've repeated *that* several times over the last couple days."

There she is. I cross my arms over my chest and raise a brow. Waiting.

Finally, she sighs. "I don't know what I need. I'm all tangled up inside, and everything seems complicated and wrong." When I don't immediately respond, she stares at the floor and seems to steel herself. "I can't... I can't cry. I haven't been able to since..." Her breath catches. "It feels like it's all bottled up inside me. I need to let it out."

I have the strangest desire to go to her and wrap my arms around her. I already know she won't accept comfort in that way, but I have more tools available to me. Aurora needs me to break down her defenses until all those feelings she's been avoiding come rushing through. To lance the wound.

I can do that.

"Take off your clothes."

She obeys instantly, fumbling in her haste to divest herself of the sweater dress. She seems to make herself pause and take the time to fold it and set it carefully on the floor by the door. Then she comes and stands before me, her hands clasped in front of her and her head bowed.

I feather my fingers over her temple. "I think the cane will work nicely tonight."

She shivers and wets her lips. "Thank you, Mistress."

For the first time possibly *ever* I want to tear away the veil of kink and just have a fucking conversation. I want to hold her and comfort her and let her cry it out. But that isn't what Aurora needs, and I'm the only one who can provide her with a way to purge her emotions.

"Go to the bench and bend over it."

She obeys instantly, crossing to the spanking bench and gracefully bending her body over it. I allow myself to look at her for a long moment, to see the way she's already shaking, just a little. It's all I need to get myself under control. I can't afford to be distracted right now, to let *my* emotions slip their leash. Tonight is about Aurora, and that's the way it needs to be.

I stride to the wardrobe and select a cane, a paddle about the width of my hand, and my favorite strap-on. It's orange and wickedly curved—one of my favorites because it specifically strokes the G-spot. After a quick internal debate, I take a few moments to step into it and get it situated around my hips. I doubt I'll want to pause to do it once I get going.

I take up a position behind Aurora and stroke my hand over her ass. "I'm not going to tie you down tonight. You've chosen this, and so you're going to be a good girl and stay perfectly still while I beat you." Her muscles tense beneath my hand, and I give her a light smack. "And then I'm going to fuck you. Understand?"

"Yes, Mistress."

"Good." I don't ask her safe word this time. We both know it, and I have no intention of pushing her anywhere near her limit. This is a delicate dance that I excel at, and I will thread the needle between too much pain and too much pleasure with Aurora tonight. Enough to shatter her, but not enough to break her.

I don't relish the challenge as much as I might have in the past. How can I when I'm actually worried about her? I want to be the one to give her whatever comfort she'll allow, but I'm achingly aware of how easily this could go wrong.

She's using me. She has been since the beginning. The knowledge didn't bother me before, and I'm not sure it bothers me now, but there's no escaping it either way. No matter what I want, I'm not certain we have a future. I don't think there's an answer to that question available until Aurora deals with her grief.

Tonight will begin that process.

I set the cane down and heft the paddle. I've spanked more submissives than I care to count over the years, have developed my skills until they're damn near art. I know what I'm doing.

So why are my palms sweating? My stomach twisting itself into knots? Why am I more nervous than I was during my first scene? I know the answer as soon as the question rises. It's because it's Aurora. Because it's never mattered overmuch before the way it does right now. *She* matters to me.

Damn it, I'm falling in love with this little asshole.

I swing the paddle, coming down squarely in the middle of her ass cheek. She jumps and lets loose a cute little whimper, but I don't give her much time to recover before I begin working my way over every square inch of her ass and the backs of her thighs. I'm warming her up right now, pushing her past the first initial resistance to pain, that moment where she doubts that this is what she really wants. Getting her ready for the deeper strikes of the cane that will have her struggling to sit down for days. The ones that will bruise her pretty little ass.

It's fine. I'll kiss it better later.

I beat her until she's shaking and her hips are rolling against the bench, though she can't rub against anything useful in her current position. Then I drop the paddle, letting it clatter on the floor. Aurora whimpers. She knows what comes next.

Instead of picking up the cane, I step to her back and press myself to her, sealing us together from knees to hips and letting her feel the strap-on pressed against her aching ass. She jumps and then moans, arching back against me. I bend down to press my chest to her back and move her hair off the back of her neck. "How do you feel?"

"I can take more." Her tone is a little dreamy, a little dazed.

I kiss the bared spot on her neck and smile against her skin. "I know. And you will." She truly is a delight. I drag my nails lightly over her skin as I shift back and squeeze her ass. She jumps again, whimpering in a way that makes my pussy pulse.

The cane feels good in my hand, and I take a slow breath and then bring it down on the top curve of her ass. There are times when I would move down the space her body provides in uneven strokes, but what Aurora needs is to be out of her mind with pain and then pleasure. So I stripe her, one strike after another, layering them so there isn't a centimeter of spared skin.

It takes time and concentration and effort, and by the time I reach the bottom of her thighs, I'm sweating lightly, and my arm aches. Aurora has gone totally limp, her breathing heavy and even. She's firmly in subspace, and now I just need to bring her home.

I toss the cane aside to join the paddle and move forward to squeeze her ass. She moans. "How do you feel?"

"You keep asking me that." She sounds almost drunk, her words slurring a little. "I feel fucking terrible and wonderful, all at once."

I carefully pull her up, keeping a hold on her when she weaves, and turn her around. "I'm going to fuck you now."

She looks down at my cock and gives me a happy smile. "Okay."

"Lie back, love." The endearment slips out, but she's too out of her mind to notice. I hope. I nudge her onto the spanking bench on her back and urge her legs wide. Her pussy is drenched, but I still take the time to press two and then three fingers into her, spreading her, readying her. The orange strap-on isn't as massive as the red, but it's large enough that I am concerned about hurting her if she's not ready for it.

She gasps as I fuck her slowly with my fingers, moaning and writhing around me. I could finish her like this. She's already primed for it. But that's not what she needs right now. Instead, I intentionally wind her tighter and tighter, edging her toward an orgasm...only to stop before shoving her over the edge.

Aurora makes a mewling sound and tries to follow my fingers as I withdraw them. "No! I'm so close."

"I know." I hold her steady with one hand on her hip and stroke up her stomach and play with her breasts. Allowing her time to recover while not letting her wind down completely.

When her breathing begins to even out, I start the process again, this time with my mouth. I have to be careful, so fucking careful, because all I want is lick her and suck her and nibble on her until she comes all over my face. But that's not what Aurora needs right now. *Shatter, not break.* She's close to the point she needs, but she's not there yet.

Her thighs tighten around my head, and I force myself to stop. I'm panting, my body shaking as my desire battles against my control. Aurora digs her hands into my hair, trying to force me back up to her clit. She's babbling now, her words tripping over themselves as she begs me to let her come. The longer I stay there, my forehead pressed to her lower stomach, resisting her increasingly frantic hands in my hair, the more the words compress down to two words.

"PleaseMalonepleasepleaseMalone*please*."

Finally, slowly, I lift my head and push to my feet. She's staring at me as if she's never seen me before, tear tracks down her face. It's not true crying, not the kind of soul-wrenching sobbing she needs to let out, but it's a start.

It's time.

I press a hand to her stomach and use my other to guide my cock to her entrance. I go slowly, working into her in short strokes as her body fights to take the girth of it. By the time we're sealed together, hips to ass, she's panting and shaking. I guide her legs up over my shoulders, a position that means I'll be pressing against her newly beaten ass and thighs with each stroke. Pain with her pleasure, pleasure with her pain. I search her face, her lips parted around each panting breath, her eyes too wide. "Good?"

"Please don't stop," she whispers.

"I won't. Not until you shatter." And then I begin to fuck her. Hard, fast strokes designed to unravel her completely. I press forward and down, bending her in half, spicing her pleasure with pain, and then it's the most natural thing in the world to kiss her. I claim her mouth even as I claim her body, and then her hands are in my hair and she's sobbing against my tongue as she orgasms.

And then she's just sobbing.

I ease out of her and yank on the harness, loosening it enough to allow me to step out of the strap-on, and then I gather her into my arms and carry her out of the playroom and down the hall to my bedroom. I don't think she sees me, for all that she's clinging to me, her tears soaking the fabric of my shirt.

"I've got you, love. Let it out." I carefully sit on the bed and pull the comforter up around us. And then I simply hold her, offering her a safe place to let go completely.

I have been warrior and queen and villain, but the only thing I want to be in this moment is exactly what Aurora needs. A strong partner who can withstand the force of her grief. She's always so damn careful never to let her walls down fully. It's no wonder she hasn't allowed herself to cry since her loss. I gather her closer and press a kiss to her temple as she sobs. There's no need for words right now. My strength is enough for both of us.

Time passes, but I don't bother to check the clock to see how long. It matters less than the way Aurora's sobs finally ease, devolving into little hiccupping breaths that break my fucking heart. I smooth a hand over her hair. "I'm here."

She releases a long exhale. "Thank you." Aurora lifts her face a little and winces. "I sobbed all over you."

"It's fine." It's more than fine. Fulfilling this need for her did something to my chest. Sometime in the last few hours, that possibility of love turned into reality. It's not something I can say to her, not something I can add to her list of things to deal with when she's obviously already got so much on her plate, and the knowledge sits ill with me.

I smooth my hands over her wet cheeks. "I'm happy I could be there for you." It's the truth, though not the truth I want to say. I have the sinking sensation that I won't ever be able to tell Aurora my truth. That I love her despite it being too soon, despite us spending a decade being on the opposite side of a line I only managed to cross a few short days ago.

I love her, and I'm going to lose her.

24

AURORA

I wake up encircled in Malone's arms, her body curled around my back as if determined to protect me, even in sleep. As if she sought to fight off my nightmares through her presence alone.

The irony is not lost on me.

The reason I'm grieving right now is because of actions she took twenty years ago. The reason we met in the first place is because I had nowhere else to turn and ended up in the Underworld out of sheer desperation. She's the very last person I should allow to comfort me.

And yet that's exactly what she did last night.

She broke me to pieces in a way that only she seems to be able to do, built my pain as beautifully as a cathedral, and then took a wrecking ball to it with pleasure.

Then she held me while I sobbed for hours.

My feelings are so tangled up inside. I didn't expect to find parts of Malone that I like, that I am drawn to. Not beyond the physical. But, now that we're several days into this, I am faced with the fact that she's more complicated than I imagined. Ruthless and ambitious, yes, but if she was really the monster I've believed all this time, she wouldn't have blinked at taking the throne from her sister back in Sabine Valley. She wouldn't care about her team the way she obviously does. She wouldn't carefully manipulate people who test her, rather than simply eliminating them and making a brutal example to foster fear so no one will challenge her. She's a master chess player.

The two versions of her do not overlap. Not really. She can be cruel, but there seems to be a method to it. There's a reason she chose my mother's territory to come after, a reason the people here seem to welcome her in a way that I *know* they didn't welcome my mother. My grandmother admitted as much a long time ago.

So what is true?

I can't ask Malone. I'm not ready to. The moment I rip the veil off what this is, it's over. Maybe I'm just as much a monster as I believed her to be, because I don't want to give up the few short days I have left with her. No matter my goals at the beginning of this, it was doomed from the start.

I can't kill her.

I sure as hell can't fall for her.

There is no happy medium where I release the past and fall into her arms. There is no future where she catches me. These two weeks were merely to satisfy her curiosity. When they're over, *this* is over.

Malone shifts at my back, pressing her hand to my stomach and bringing me back more firmly against her. "You're thinking very hard over there."

"Guilty," I whisper.

The barest hesitation. "Do you want to talk about it?"

I don't know if I'll ever be able to talk about it. "No." No, there are better options for us. Last night she made me forget. Hell, every time she touches me, she makes me forget. If I'm a traitorous daughter, I might as well embrace it until the bitter end.

I turn in her arms and am already moving down her body before she rolls onto her back. I kneel between her spread thighs and hesitate, waiting for her to stop me. But Malone just looks at me with green eyes gone almost soft from sleep. *She* looks soft right now. Soft and rumpled and too beautiful for words.

I'm a fool because I don't want to stop this. I want her to keep looking at me like that, as if she cares. As if I'm hers and she's mine.

Unforgivable thoughts, but I lean down and kiss her stomach before they can take root. They'll still be there when this is all over. They can wait for now.

I'm rationalizing and I know it. It's enough to say I want this, so I'll take it. There's time for recriminations and doubts later.

"Aurora."

I ignore the question in her voice just like I ignore the half a million doubts circling my brain. But Malone isn't the type to let something go once she's set her mind on it. She clasps my chin gently. "We should talk."

"Not yet." I feel my lower lip quivering despite my best efforts. "Please not yet."

She hesitates, and for once, her thoughts are written across her face for me to see. Conflict. Warring desires. My confused feelings reflected right back at me. Finally, she nods. "Before the end of this, then."

Relief makes me a little light-headed. "Yes, before the end of it." Cowardly. So fucking cowardly of me not to just deal with this now, to grab as much light and pleasure as I can handle before reality crashes back in. Before I have to answer for what I've done...and what I haven't.

Even if the only person I have to answer to is myself.

Malone releases me, and I keep kissing my way down her stomach. She lets me urge her thighs wider, lets me dip down and drag my tongue over her pussy. It strikes me all over again how she took care of me last night. My needs, my emotions, my comfort. She put all of it before her own. I don't understand it. I don't understand it at all.

But I want to make her feel good right now, to lose myself in the taste and feel of her until it washes away everything else.

She lets me lead. As I grip her thighs and suck on her clit, I distantly recognize that she's taking care of me even now, offering me an escape I desperately need. My heart gives a dull thud and then another. Gods, I can't fall for Malone. I *can't*. Everything else is forgivable, but not that.

I'm terrified that it's too late.

That maybe it was too late the moment I agreed to this assignation.

I push two fingers into her, chasing her pleasure the same way I chase forgetting. She arches her back, and I find myself captivated by the sight of her. The arch of her spine. The way her breasts shake with each ragged exhale. Most of all, the way she holds my gaze as I taste her. It's so tempting to close my eyes, to shut out this vulnerability. Except... I don't want to.

I pick up my pace, focusing on winding her pleasure tighter, on driving her higher. I want to see her come undone; I want to be the one to cause it.

I want her to remember these two weeks forever.

When Malone orgasms, it's as beautiful and powerful as she seems to do everything. She barely slumps back to the mattress before she's tugging me up her body and kissing me as if this is the last time. As if she cherishes me. As if she never wants this to end.

She pulls away a little. "Aurora."

"Please." I don't know what I'm begging for. I just know we can't follow the road where her tone leads. "Please not yet."

She exhales slowly and leans up to press her forehead to mine. The contact grounds me even as part of me continues to spiral out of control. Finally, she gives me another long kiss and eases back. "Let's run you a bath."

I blink. "What?"

"You're going to be extremely sore today. The bath will help." She gives a ghost of her normal cruel smile, though her eyes remain warm. "Otherwise you're going to be limping around for days, and neither one of us wants that."

Now that she mentions it, I *am* incredibly stiff and sore from the scene last night. I grimace. "You didn't miss an inch of skin, did you?"

"No." She carefully nudges me off her. "It's what you needed."

I can't argue that because it's the truth. It *is* what I needed. I sit up and look at her. It feels strange to say this but... "Thank you. For last night. You didn't have to do that, any of it."

"Aurora." She cups my face and presses a quick kiss to my lips. She's gone before I can sink into it, climbing to her feet and heading for the bathroom. "Don't you understand by now? It's my pleasure to take care of your needs. You're mine, after all."

Only for another week or so.

I don't say it aloud. We both are in this strange place and thrusting forth the reminder that this is nearly halfway over isn't what I want to do. I don't think it's what she wants, either, though I'm scared to try to guess. Instead, I let myself play her words over and over in my head as I listen to her get the water running in the bath.

You're mine, after all.

It feels right, which means it feels wrong. How can I simultaneously want to be Malone's but also acknowledge that she's the one who put my mother in a coma that she was destined to never wake up from? I don't know. I just don't know.

Malone returns a few minutes later and looks down at me. "Can you walk, or do you need me to carry you?"

I can walk. There's no doubt about it. I'll probably be limping just like she projected, but I am capable of it. I lick my lips, feeling suddenly unsure. "What if I want you to carry me?"

She gives a smile that's nothing like her usually icy expression. It's warm and soft and makes my chest give another of those dull thuds. "I'd like that, too." She carefully scoops me up and gives a sympathetic look when I hiss at the touch of her arm against the back of my thighs. "I know it hurts. It will feel better in a little bit."

She carries me into the bathroom and sets me into the tub with the utmost care. Malone grabs a hair tie and gently pulls my hair back and fastens it out of the way, allowing me to sink into the warmth of the water. She presses her fingers lightly to my temples and starts a slow massage that has me melting even further.

We sit like that for a long time, Malone carefully massaging my head and neck and the water doing the rest of the work. I feel ridiculously pampered and cared for, and it only makes my chest ache more. I love this. Last night and this morning. The kink and the sex and the comfort. Truth be told, I even love our conversations. Sometimes it's verbally sparring and sometimes it's simply getting a glimpse at how her brain works. She's magnificent. A part of my soul recognizes something in hers that feels like kinship, even if I can't fully describe why. "Malone?"

"Mmm?"

But words fail me. I really am a coward, after all. I don't want to say or do anything to break moment of calm, of peace. I'm greedy for as many moments as I can have, because eventually it will end.

The balance will tip, the sky will fall, and reality will come rushing in.

Aurora and I settle into a smooth rhythm over the next week, interrupted only by the check-in that Hades insisted on. It goes off quickly and without an issue, but it's still strange to have Allecto prowling around my house as if she expects to find evidence of nefarious activities. She and Aurora disappear into the spare bedroom for twenty minutes, and when they come back out again, Allecto announces herself satisfied and Aurora has shadows in her eyes. She doesn't want to talk about it.

She never wants to talk about it.

I leave her in my bed each morning and head down to work for a few hours. We meet in the gym and spar. She wins a few matches; I win more. Then we end up back in my penthouse, fucking until we're too exhausted to move. She's still a little brat, but the edge of hatred is gone, leaving something warm and almost soft in its place.

It should be perfect.

This is what I want, after all. A slow and steady build into something more. A chance to pave the way for this to extend beyond our deadline.

But after ten days, there's no escaping the truth.

Aurora is holding something back.

I have no business demanding more of her, especially so soon, but sometimes she looks at me and gets this strange expression in her dark eyes. It's not grief. I've seen her grieving, and the night I beat her with a cane and then shattered her with pleasure seems to have blunted the edge of her sorrow. No, this is something else.

I've never met a mystery I was able to leave alone, and this is no exception. The stakes are too high. I want her. Whatever she's hiding is preventing me from having her entirely.

It comes to a head three nights before the end of the assignation. I can feel the seconds slipping through my fingers with each tick of the clock, and it puts me in a foul mood. "Aurora."

"Hmmm?" She looks over from where she's been contemplating the fire crackling in the fireplace.

Maybe I've been going about this wrong. Wanting her to give herself to me without being vulnerable in turn isn't going to work. I should have known that from the start. I take a slow breath. "I care about you."

She tenses as if she's going to jump off the couch and flee the room. "Don't say that."

My patience threatens to snap, but I hold it together through sheer force of will. "I realize that things are complicated between us, but I'm not misreading things when I say we've both had a lot of fun since you've been here."

She won't quite meet my gaze. "Yes, we've had fun."

"More than fun." A small part of me tries to put on the brakes before I push us into something we can't take back, but I've never been good at sitting still when the prize I want is before me. "You've enjoyed your time with me."

"Malone, please." There it is, that expression I can't define. "Let's just enjoy the next three days."

I should let it go. I already know I won't. I lean forward and try to get her to meet my gaze. "What if this extended past the next three days?"

Aurora clears her throat. "Why did you leave Sabine Valley?"

This is what's bothering her? What she's been chewing on for the last week? No, it doesn't make any sense. We've talked about this already, or at least touched on it enough that it's not a mystery.

This is just the lead-in question to circle whatever is bothering her. With that in mind, I answer honestly and without hesitation. "Because if I didn't, I might have ended up fighting my sister for the Amazon throne." I catch her look and shrug. "I was never going to be content with second place, but I love my sister and I love my people, so I chose to leave to spare us all that."

"Couldn't you have just *not* tried to stage a coup?"

"I am ambitious. I always have been." She's still looking at me like I'm speaking Latin, so I try to elaborate. "My mother was the most powerful person I've ever known. Sabine Valley has fail-safes in place to ensure the territories don't go to war, but there are a thousand things that could happen to spell the end of an heir's life that have nothing to do with violence. She wanted to ensure our people would be cared for regardless, which meant she raised us both to rule. But my sister was healthy and strong. There was no need for the spare."

"She raised you to be a queen and then gave you second place."

"Yes." I don't begrudge her that. Her plans made sense from a tactical point of view, and they ensured the

Amazons would remain under a strong leader. If I got the raw end of the deal, I've never held it against her. I would have done the same in her position. "I stayed in Sabine Valley until Aisling had her third daughter, Winry, but the second-in-command position chafed. And my sister might love me as much as I love her, but she doesn't trust me entirely."

"Can you blame her?"

I arch an eyebrow. "Of course not. I wouldn't sleep well with someone like me as next in line for the throne, either." I sit back and pick up my wine glass. "It was better for everyone that I leave."

"Why Carver City?" She's still not looking directly at me, still edging this conversation in such a way that I'm not sure of our destination.

Oh well. I resign myself to being along for the ride. If she needs to talk this out, it's the very least I can do to indulge her. "Of the two cities closest to Sabine Valley, Olympus is too entrenched in its leadership. There's no way I could come in as an outsider and end up as one of the Thirteen." And no way that I would be content as one of the bit players beneath Zeus. "Carver City offered more opportunities."

Aurora pulls her knees up to her chest and wraps her arms around them. "Why this territory?"

There's no harm in telling her. The news is two decades old, after all. "It had the most potential for growth—and the weakest leader. The people were unhappy; they needed someone strong to give them a path forward."

She inhales sharply. "I suppose that makes sense."

It does, but what doesn't make sense is her reaction to this mundane information. I frown. "Aurora, what does this have to do with continuing this thing between us past the end of the contracted assignation?"

"I..." Aurora takes a deep breath. "I heard that you almost killed her when you took over."

It feels like there's a question within her statement, but I can't figure out the flavor of it. I debate for a moment but decide to answer instead of pushing her. This time. But I want an explanation, and I want it soon. "I dislike coups that come in the form of a blade in the back. It's cleaner to have a fight for it out in the open. I declared my intentions to take over, and Amelia chose not to take me seriously. She could have left, and I wouldn't have touched her, but she didn't. We fought. I won. It's as simple and complicated as that."

"You almost killed her."

I study her. "Where is all this concern for something that happened twenty years ago coming from?"

"You had her down and beaten, and you still chose to keep going." She's still not looking at me, her voice low and fierce.

"An Amazon doesn't leave an enemy at their back," I say softly, my mind racing. Why is she so worried about the former leader of this territory? It's no coincidence. Aurora's anger is too personal to be on behalf of some faceless stranger. No, there's something else going on here. But what? Aurora was maybe ten or so when that fight happened. There were no children involved; neither Amelia nor her inner circle had kids. I would have known.

"I see," she whispers.

I cup her face and gently guide her to look at me. Part of me wants to let this go, to kiss her and distract us both until whatever lurks beneath the surface of this conversation stays locked away. I can't shake the feeling that this revelation will crush the fragile bloom of possibility we've nurtured the last week.

It's not in my nature to shy away from an ugly truth, let

alone a fight. I search Aurora's pretty face, looking for answers she's determined to hide from me. Finally, I ask the question I know, deep down in my poisoned heart, that will break us. "Who was she to you?"

The silence stretches thin between us. Aurora shudders out a sigh. "My mother."

Shock has me dropping my hand. "Impossible."

"It's really not."

I'm already shaking my head. "She had no family. It was the first thing I looked into when I got into the territory."

Aurora goes back to staring at the fire, her expression curiously blank. "I lived with my grandmother. She didn't want the dangerous elements of her life to touch me. At least not when I was a child. I doubt the same would have held true if she were still ruling when I turned eighteen."

I'm still trying to wrap my mind around this revelation. Twenty years is a long time. I barely remember what Amelia looked like, let alone down to the kind of details that I could hold up to Aurora as a comparison. I remember she was a slim Black woman, but that's it. Her features have blurred over time, and I never spent any effort into solidifying them. Why would I bother?

Now, I wish I had.

"I didn't know," I find myself saying faintly.

"Would it have mattered if you did?"

A comforting lie might work in my favor right now, but I don't make a habit of untruthfulness. Not with the people I care about. "No." The die was already cast the moment I chose this territory to make my own. Amelia was a shitty leader, sloppy and far too willing to give in to excess and power. Even if I hadn't been the one to take her out, someone else would have stepped in before too long. She was an opportunity just waiting to be plucked.

I can't say that to Aurora. Not now, knowing the woman was her mother.

Aurora lets out a painful laugh. "Yeah, I didn't think so."

Several things become clear all at once. "That's why you made the deal with Hades. For her." When Amelia was put in the hospital in a coma, no one thought she'd wake up. She's been medically brain dead since about a week after our fight. I know. I checked. For Aurora to have made a deal that desperate, there could only be one cause. "You're the one who moved her to a private clinic."

"Yes."

I look at her closely, my chest getting strangely heavy. "Is she still alive, Aurora?" If one can call her existence life. It's been argued either way by medical professionals, but I land on the negative. I went to visit her once before she was moved from the hospital, and the spark that made her Amelia had been extinguished. Only the shell remained.

But Aurora came to me grieving someone close to her.

"No. Not anymore. I made the call before I agreed to this assignation."

Fuck.

She kept her mother alive for twenty years, sold herself to Hades to do it, and all for nothing. The woman never woke up. She was never going to. Gods, this situation is so fucked. "I'm sorry my actions hurt you."

At that, she flares to life. "That is the shittiest of apologies. You're not sorry you hurt *her*."

I won't lie to her, not even in this. "No, I'm not. She was a weak leader, petty and cruel, and if I didn't take control, someone else would have staged a coup. Everyone looked at her and saw an opportunity."

"Stop it."

I lean forward, knowing that she'll hate me after this but

unable to stop. "Why do you think she sent you away, Aurora? Because she knew she wasn't strong enough to keep you safe. I was in this territory for a month to observe her, and during that time, there wasn't a vice she met that she didn't embrace fully. Even her generals were sharpening their knives and eyeing her back. She wouldn't have lasted the year."

"Stop it!" She swipes a hand across her face. "It doesn't excuse what you did, what you took from me."

"No, I suppose it doesn't." I clench my hands to keep from reaching for her. With this new information, it's easy enough to understand why Aurora said yes to this assignation. The one mystery I could never quite answer, not to my satisfaction. Lust isn't enough of a driver for her, not when she can fulfill that desire filled with anyone she crooks a finger at in the Underworld. "How were you going to do it?"

She blinks. "What?"

"You came here to get revenge, correct? An eye for an eye is very biblical of you, but I can't fault the logic. You were going to kill me. Or at least attempt it." It feels like something is stuck in my throat, something sharp and jagged and far too large. "How were you going to do it?" She hadn't brought in any weapons; I would have known.

"I hadn't decided."

I have no right to feel anger. Her desire for revenge is an honest one, even if it's against me. In her place, I would have done the same thing, albeit on a faster timeline. Feeling hurt because she got close enough to strike me is ridiculous. Feeling betrayed when this was only ever supposed to be sex...

I am a fool.

I laugh hoarsely. "You have been sleeping next to me for over a week. I have been as helpless as I am capable of being every single night for hours at a time. Why haven't I woken up with one of my butcher knives embedded in my chest?"

"Stop."

"No, you answer me. You came here for revenge." I motion at me, at the room around us. "You have had opportunity after opportunity to strike. Why haven't you?"

She shoots to her feet, fists clenched. "I hate you!" She stares down at me, turmoil in her big dark eyes. "But I don't only hate you. It's more complicated than I expected."

I don't only hate you.

Hardly a declaration of caring, let alone something like love. Hardly anything at all. I laugh again. I can't stop speaking, can't stop twisting the knife. This was never going to work. I shouldn't have allowed myself to hope. "Sounds like you lost your nerve."

"That's not it." She shakes her head, still looking furious. "You aren't what I expected, and it's got my head all screwed up. Forgive the fuck out of me if I'm not as easily inclined to murder as you are."

I push to my feet. I don't crowd her, though. No matter how much I want to. "Yes, Aurora. Paint yourself as the helpless damsel instead of the ruthless hunter. Others might believe that lie, but it doesn't work on me."

"I am not a ruthless hunter."

"Lies." Gods, this hurts. I didn't expect it to hurt so much. "You spent ten days fucking me, letting me hold you, talking with me, coaxing me to let you in. All the while, you were thinking of ways to kill me." I shake my head. "You've accomplished your goal."

"What are you talking about?"

"You might not have wielded a literal blade, but you've broken my fucking heart." I turn away. "Get out. Sara will take you back to the Underworld."

"Wait."

But I can't wait. I have to get her out of here before I crumple. I glance over my shoulder. Aurora looks lost, and every instinct I have demands I go to her. I make myself hold her gaze for a long moment. "Do not, under any circumstances, tell anyone outside the Underworld what you had planned. My people rarely disobey me, but they are protective in the extreme. They will kill you to keep me safe."

She stares. "Why protect me? After all this, shouldn't you want to tie up the loose end I represent?"

Yes, that's exactly what I should do. Hades might not believe me if Aurora died of an accident, but unless he could prove I was directly responsible, there wouldn't be a damn thing he could do. Maybe Aurora held herself back this time, but there's nothing to say she won't try to come for me in the future.

I can't do it.

Even if it's a logistical mistake, I can't stand the thought of the world without her in it.

"Goodbye, Aurora. I truly am sorry for the pain I've caused you." I turn around and walk away.

I don't know how it happens. One moment, I'm watching myself drop a bomb on the careful happiness Malone and I have created. The next, I'm being ushered into the back of a car by Sara. It happened *so fast*.

I didn't expect it to hurt this much.

I didn't expect to care.

To...fall for Malone.

It was never supposed to be real. I press my hands to my chest as if that can hold in my tears. The wetness leaking out of my eyes almost makes me laugh. It took Malone beating me and fucking me into oblivion to allow me to grieve for my mother, but she breaks up with me and I'm in danger of sobbing like a lost child. Except you can't break up with someone you never dated. The last two weeks wasn't dating, wasn't a relationship, it was an *assignation*.

Somehow we both forgot that.

Another blink and we're idling at the curb outside the Underworld. I look out the window, and the horrible feeling in my chest gets worse when I see Allecto step through the doors. She stalks to the car and yanks open the door. "Are you okay?"

"She's fine," Sara says from the front seat. "Now get out of my car." Gone are the easy grins and amusement. They sound like they want nothing more than to rip my head off my shoulders with their bare hands.

I can't even blame them. I did something I thought impossible. I hurt Malone. As I take Allecto's hand and let her haul me out of the car and hustle me into the building, all I see is the stricken look on Malone's face before she turned and walked away from me. I *hurt* her.

I should be happy. It's what I wanted, after all. If I couldn't end her life, at least I dealt her a wound that will take time to recover from. I should be fucking elated.

All I feel is empty.

Allecto doesn't speak until we're in the elevator. "Tell me the truth." Her voice is low and fierce. "I convinced Hades that there was nothing to worry about. Did she hurt you?"

Yes, of course she hurt me. A thousand delicate cuts over the course of eleven days. Pain and pleasure. Pleasure and pain. She delivered both in abundance, and I welcomed it with open arms. I stare at my reflection in the doors. I look as lost as I feel. "No." I swallow hard. "I hurt her."

Allecto inhales like she's about to start demanding more details and then hesitates. "Ah. I see."

"I told her the truth." I sound like I'm reading the weather report. This is wrong, wrong, wrong.

The doors open, and Allecto steps out, but she grabs my arm before I can take another step. "Hades wants to see you, but if you go in there with *that* look on your face, he's going to go tearing into Malone's territory and start some shit that we can't take back. So I'm going to need you to get your shit together."

I close my eyes and focus on breathing. I can't *think*, let alone dredge up a sunny smile to put him at ease. I don't even know what the truth is anymore. How am I supposed to feel? Guilt and sorrow and grief and, yes, love, have created a tangled mess in my chest.

Gods, I love Malone.

"What's wrong with me?" I give a broken laugh. "Why *her?*"

"Aurora." She hesitates, but it's too late. We're standing in front of Hades's office and there's no more time. Allecto gives my shoulder a squeeze. "Do you need me to stall?"

"No. I've got this." I don't sound the least bit convincing, but she doesn't call me on it. Allecto just gives me another squeeze. "Do you need the training room or a bottle of whiskey?"

"Both?"

The concern on her face deepens, but she nods. "Change after you're done with him, and we'll spar first. Then you can drink yourself goofy."

"Thanks." I try for a smile, but it feels more like a grimace. Then I push through the door into Hades's office before I can think too hard about it. Better to just rip off the bandage and get this over with.

Hades pushes up from his desk and rounds it before I make it halfway across the room. He stops in front of me, and for a moment, I'm sure he's going to take my shoulders, but he manages to restrain himself. He runs a critical eye over me. "You look terrible."

"Thanks."

He shakes his head slowly and points to the couch on the other side of the office. "Sit."

There's no disobeying that tone of voice, and I don't particularly want to. I manage to make it to the couch before my legs decide they're done carrying me. The horrible empty feeling in my chest doesn't fade now that I'm back in familiar territory. If anything, it gets worse.

It hurt to lose my mother, to finally release the hope that she'd ever wake up. The grief still clings to my skin, mixing with guilt. But losing Malone feels like someone pressed a shotgun to my chest and pulled the trigger. I have a gaping hole where my heart used to be, and I don't know how I'm supposed to keep walking around as if I'm a whole person. I'm not. I have the sneaking suspicion that I never will be again.

Hades comes and sits on the other side of the couch. That's when I notice that he's got two glasses and a bottle of his best whiskey. He sets the glasses on the table in front of us and pours a healthy splash into both. "Drink."

"I'm supposed to spar with Allecto after this."

"No, you aren't." He nudges the glass toward me. "You're going to drink this. We're going to talk about why you conveniently forgot to inform me that you chose to take your mother off life support right before accepting the assignation with Malone. After that, you're going to sleep."

I lift the glass, hating the way my hand shakes. "You're being bossy right now."

"Don't do that." His voice goes harsh. "You have been here nine years, Aurora. You know what I am, and you know where my lines are. So drink your fucking whiskey."

Realization rolls over me in slow waves as I sip the whiskey. Hades isn't angry. He's...worried. For me. Worried to the point of being scared. I blink at him, trying to reconcile the unflappable man I've known a full third of my life with the one sitting a few feet away, looking like he's about ready to start shredding his way through the office. "When did you find out?"

"A few days after you left. The facility called me to inform me that the payments would be cancelled going forward as they were no longer necessary."

Ah. That explains it. "I'm surprised you didn't send someone to collect me the moment you found out."

"Believe me, I tried." He glares at his whiskey. "Meg and Allecto refused to accept the order. Tisiphone supported them."

Even Hades can't ignore it when all three of his Furies unite to draw a line in the sand. I take another, larger, drink of whiskey. "Poor Hades. Sometimes it's a pain in the ass to be king."

"We're not talking about me." He searches my face, and I have no idea what I'm showing him. My shields lay in pieces at my feet. I can't rebuild them. I simply don't have the strength. His expression softens. "I'm sorry for your loss."

Against all reason, *that* is what has my throat closing and my eyes burning. I blink rapidly and drain the rest of my glass. I haven't eaten today, and the whiskey warms my stomach and is already giving me a delicious, floaty feeling. Maybe that's why I tell him something I've never told another soul. "I was starting to resent her. That's horrible, isn't it? I just wanted her to wake up, and the longer it went on, the more I started to hate the weight of carrying that hope."

"It's human." He states it without a shred of pity. "Is that why you went to Malone? Because it's easier to hate her than it is to hate yourself?"

I flinch. "She put my mother in a coma and took away any chance I ever had of knowing her."

Hades takes my hand. "Do you want the comforting lie, or are you finally ready for the hard truth?"

I don't want hard truths. I just want to wrap up in a

blanket and close my eyes and wait for the world to stop spinning in the wrong direction, wait for the hole in my chest to scar over. To check out from reality in a way I've never allowed myself to before. I set down the empty whiskey glass.

What I want is not what I need.

I have been a coward long enough.

I take a deep breath. "I probably won't thank you for the hard truth, but tell me anyway."

"Your mother wouldn't have lasted the year. If Malone didn't do it, someone else would have, and they would have done it in a far crueler fashion." He holds my gaze. "I understand your blaming her. I sympathize. But do you want to know what the territory was like under your mother's rule?" He continues before I have a chance to respond. "Crime was at an all-time high, and everyone suffered because she wouldn't make rules, let alone enforce them. Innocents were harmed because she was a weak leader."

Impossible not to compare that with the reports I've all but memorized about the territory now. Stable. Everyone kept in tight check by Malone and her inner circle. She's given everyone fucking *benefits*. The territory is flourishing under her rule, and even though I've tried to find fault with it, I can't.

I clear my throat. "Why didn't you tell me that before?"

"You weren't ready to hear it." He gives my hand a squeeze and sits back. "I'm not certain you're ready to hear it now, but your mother finally passing isn't what's put that look on your face, is it?"

He's being too gentle, too kind. This isn't the normal Hades, and I'm powerless to keep my pain bottled up in the presence of this version of him. I press my fingers to my temples. "What kind of monster am I if I care about the woman who did that to my mother?"

"Ah."

But I'm not finished. "She *is* a monster. She hurt my mother."

"Your mother went into a coma twenty years ago." He sounds almost idle. "And yet you didn't find your way to me until three years later."

I open my eyes, not sure when I closed them. "What's your point? They were going to take her off life support, and I had to do something."

"Do you know how long hospitals usually allow a patient to stay in a coma where there's no brain activity?"

Something slithers through me, something I can barely recognize. I let my hands drop to my lap. "Not three years."

"Not three years," he confirms.

It feels like the ground is opening up beneath me, but I'm helpless to do anything but stand here and let it swallow me whole. I simultaneously don't want to ask and desperately need to know. "Why was she on life support for so long?"

His expression goes sympathetic. "Because Malone paid for it."

I wait for the words to make sense. Wait for them to be anything but a lock I can't find the key to. "But *why?*"

"Do you know how many of the current territory leaders killed the person who came before them?"

This is a trap, but he's not going to let me avoid it. "More than one."

"Jasmine, though technically Jafar is the one who removed her father. Hook, though again, Tink killed Peter. Ursa. Malone. Me." He leans forward. "This is the world we move in, Aurora. The world *you* move in. It always has been."

I want to turn away from this knowledge, but I can't quite make myself. "It's different. They were monsters."

"You don't think those monsters had people who loved them?" He arches an eyebrow.

I want to scream that it's different, that she was my mother and that means something. I already know what he'll say. Everyone has loved ones, everyone has *someone* who will mourn them when they're gone. It suddenly strikes me that he's lumping my mother in with the monsters. "Was she really that bad?"

He doesn't pretend to misunderstand. "She loved you. She wouldn't have sent you away if she didn't. But she wasn't a good leader, and people were harmed while the territory was under her care."

I don't know if that makes me feel better or worse. I had built up this picture in my head of the woman my mother must have been, driven by the hole her absence left in my life. But even Grandmother had criticisms of my mother. I draw in a shaky breath. "I don't know if that changes anything."

He nods. "That's for you to figure out. Take your time."

"She won't wait for me." The words burst from my lips despite my having no intention of saying them.

He gives me a slow smile. "You might be surprised what Malone will do if given half a chance." He glances at the door. "The moment you walk out there, you're going to be set upon by Meg and Allecto. They've likely called in Tink as well."

My chest warms, but even knowing that my friends are closing ranks around me in my time of need isn't enough to do more than highlight the gaping hole where my heart should be. The feeling of missing something vital, something I need to go on. There's been too much new information today, too many revelations. I don't know what to think, can barely see the path in front of me.

But the thought of letting Malone go forever?

Can I do that?

I rub my chest and stare hard at the empty whiskey glass. "I've never felt the way I do when I'm with her. Not with anyone else. It's not comfortable."

"Love rarely is." Hades pushes to his feet and gathers the glasses and bottle. "It has a habit of showing up when you least expect it, with the people you least expect it from."

He's talking about Hercules. The son of his old enemy. The man he seduced out of a desire for revenge and ended up falling in love with.

I look up at him. "If we both fell for our enemies, what does that make us? Really smart? Or really foolish?"

"Ah, Aurora." Hades smiles. It's warm and soft and changes his entire face. "It makes us very, very lucky."

As he turns to walk to his desk, I pull out my phone. I stare at it a long time, my thumb hovering over the call button. In the end, I'm not quite as brave as I'd like to be, because I text her instead.

Me: I need time to think.

She doesn't make me wait long for a response. I watch the three dots appear and disappear for several long minutes before her reply appears.

Malone: I would think you made your feelings perfectly clear.

Me: Did you mean it? When you said you cared about me?

Again, those three dots. I stare hard at them, my entire body tight with a heady combination of fear and something like euphoria. It feels like a free fall, but I don't entirely hate it.

Malone: I meant it.

I exhale a shaky breath.

Me: Will you give me a chance to figure some things out?

Malone: I detest having these conversations on text. Come to me when you want to talk.

Me: Wait for me?

This reply takes longer, but when the message lights up, some of the weight I hadn't realized I've been carrying slips from my shoulders.

Malone: I will.

I know myself well enough to know that I have to sit with this knowledge for a while. To let go of my fantasy about how things were and reconcile msyelf with the truth. It hurts to think of my mother as a monster but... Am I really that surprised? Didn't part of me know all along? One doesn't claw their way to power in Carver City with kindness. They don't keep that power without strength.

I don't know what it says about me that, even after all this, the person I want to go to so I can talk and get my thoughts in order is Malone. I want to fall into her arms and pour out all the poison I've been carrying for so long. I want her to comfort me in the way only she's capable of, with pain and pleasure intertwined in an exquisite dance. I want to hold her while she whispers her fears to me in the darkness that puts us on equal footing.

I want Malone.

I suppose that makes me a monster, too, but I'm strangely okay with that.

27

MALONE

I know better than to wish on stars. To hope for the impossible. No matter what Aurora texted me two weeks ago, she's not coming back. She's not going to change her mind. She doesn't really care, and she'll realize that once the haze of lust passes. How can she really care for me when I'm the one who put her mother in a coma? When I tore down the vision she'd built of the woman her mother was?

I should have kept my mouth shut. Should have simply taken her hate as my due and let her walk out of my life. But I've always been a selfish creature when it comes to the things I want, the people I want.

Damn it.

I scrub my hands over my face and reread the report in front of me for the fourth time. The words blur and swim across the page, incomprehensible. I curse and toss it onto the desk. This is a waste of time. I can't concentrate. I haven't been able to since she walked out of my life and took my fool heart with her.

Really, she's accomplished her goals whether my pulse

still beats through my veins or not. I feel like I've suffered a mortal wound, and I don't know how to recover from this. I don't know what I'm supposed to do, how I'm supposed to act.

A knock has me lifting my head, desperate for whatever distraction the interruption can provide. "Come in."

Sara slips through the door and closes it behind them. They move to the chair across from the desk and sink into it. "You're a mess."

"Thanks, Sara, tell me how you really feel."

"If she can't see that you're priceless, then fuck her." Sara perks up. "Want me to toss her off a building?"

"*No.*" No matter how much Aurora hurt me, I can't condone harm against her. Even if she's not at my side, the thought of her moving through the world is comforting in a strange sort of way. She'll land on her feet. She's too stubborn and strong not to. "I don't want any unfortunate accidents, Sara. I mean it."

Sara sighs. "I can't control it if she's clumsy at the top of a set of stairs."

"*Sara.*"

They grin. "Kidding."

No, they weren't, but they also will respect my wishes in this. "Ensure that the rest of the team is aware of that. I want no accidents. No *jokes.*"

"Got it." Sara leans back, draping a long arm over the back of the chair next to them. "Though if you feel that way, why not chase her down and bring her back? She's obviously all tied up over you, whether she wants to admit it or not. I don't get why you just let her walk away."

I almost tell them to get out of my office, but we've been friends long enough that I feel like I owe them an answer. "If she chooses this, it has to be real. It can't be because I overwhelmed her." The thought had crossed my mind, but I don't want a fling with Aurora. I want forever. It feels like a sudden decision and, at the same time, one I've been working toward for nearly ten years, since that first time with her. "She has to choose me."

Sara studies me for several long moments. "You love her."

"Yes." No point in denying it. They would have figured it out eventually, even if Aurora never returns. I'm moping. I *never* mope.

They sigh. "Then I suppose I should tell you that she's waiting in the lobby."

I freeze. "What?"

"Aurora is waiting in the lobby," they repeat with exaggerated slowness.

"And you're just *now* telling me."

"Yep." They push to their feet. "If you didn't love her, I would have sent her away."

I plant my hands on the desk. "That's not your call to make."

"Wrong. I watch your back, Malone. That girl got to you, and she messed you up enough that I can't trust you to protect yourself when it comes to her." Sara pauses at the door. "I'll respect your wishes. For now."

"I do *not* want you sharpening a knife every time she and I have an argument." This might be jumping the gun a bit, but it needs to be said. "She doesn't present a danger to my body, and so you will not strike back simply because we argue."

"Of course not." Sara shrugs. "Your relationship is your relationship. I can respect that boundary, as long as she doesn't harm you."

A tiny line, a microscopic distinction, and yet I have a

feeling it's the best I'm going to get. "Fine."

"I'll let her up."

"Wait." I push to my feet. "Send her up to the penthouse. I'll meet her there."

"Got it." They turn and walk out of my office.

I force myself to count slowly to ten, long enough for them to reach the elevator, before I stride out of my office and make my way to the stairs. I don't run, but I certainly don't linger as I hurry up to the penthouse. Once I'm inside, I have half a thought to change, but that's ridiculous. Aurora has seen me in many modes already. It shouldn't matter if I'm wearing a suit or pajamas.

Still.

I take two seconds to fix my lipstick and run my fingers through my hair, guiding it back from my face. As I'm leaving the bedroom, I hear the front door open.

"Malone?"

Gods, her voice. I close my eyes and take a slow breath. Just because she's here doesn't mean this is going to go the way I desperately want it to. She might be here to tell me that my membership to the Underworld is revoked, or simply to say she never wants to see me again. Aurora's the type to do that sort of thing in person rather than through distant measures.

I can't dredge up my icy facade. It's melted to a puddle at my feet. I am only me as I walk out of the hallway to find her standing in my living room.

She looks good. Better than good. Her hair is back to the bright pink she favored a little over a year ago, and she's wearing black ankle boots, dark jeans that hug her legs, and a loose, gray knitted sweater. She's utterly gorgeous.

She tucks her hair behind her ears. "Hey."

"Hi," I say faintly. I don't know what I'm doing, what I'm

supposed to say. Once again, I'm reminded my mother always taught me to never step onto a battlefield unless I'm sure I can win, and I've already lost when it comes to Aurora. If I'm going to be honest, I lost the second I saw her all those years ago.

She looks around the room, eyeing the gray chair. "That's new."

"Rogue took exception to the last one."

Her lips curve. "That cat is a menace."

"Yes, he is. It happened the day after you left. I think he missed you." This is horrible. She's here and yet not here, and I don't know what I'm supposed to say. In the end, I can't keep up this meaningless small talk. "Aurora, why are you here?"

"I talked to Hades." She clasps her hands in front of her, still not quite meeting my gaze. "And I've talked to Allecto and Meg and Tink, and even Hercules."

Where is she going with this? "I would think they'd want you as far from me as possible."

"They want what's best for me." She gives a sad little laugh. "And they respect that I know myself well enough to know what's best for me."

I wait, but she's too busy wringing her fingers together to keep going. I clear my throat. "What are you saying?"

"Do you know who I wanted to talk to the most while I've been working through things for the last two weeks?" She finally releases the death grip she has on her fingers and tugs at the hem of her sweater. "I was so angry and confused and hurt and then angrier, and even though all my friends were around me, there was only one person I wanted."

I can't breathe. I'm half sure I've turned to stone. "Who?"

She gives a breathless little laugh. "*You.*"

It's what I want to hear, but I'm so afraid to trust it. "You hate me."

"I..." Aurora shakes her head. "I had to hate you to deal with how much I wanted you. It's easier to blame you than to blame my mother for her choices. She was gone, even before she died, and you were here and larger than life and constantly making me feel things I didn't want to feel."

"Aurora—"

"I realize that this seems too good to be true, but it's what I feel." She looks away and then back at me. "I'm a mess, Malone. I've been grieving my mother for twenty years, and there were times when I felt like there was no end to that feeling, but I'm ready to let her go. I'm sorry that I wanted to hurt you."

"Don't be." I want to reach for her, want to pull her into my arms, but I don't want to make a wrong move. "You're more than entitled to hate me."

"But that's just it. I don't hate you." She smiles suddenly. It's not her bright sunshine smile; it's a bittersweet little quirk of her lips that warms her dark eyes. "I love you."

Of all the things I expected her to say... "*What?*"

"I know. It surprised me, too. But that doesn't make it less true."

I can't stand this distance between us any longer. I hold out my hand. "Aurora, come here."

"In a moment. There's a few other things." She shifts from foot to foot. "I forgive you for what happened twenty years ago. I can't promise that it won't knock me for a loop periodically because grief is weird, and I'm still working through it, but I promise not to throw it in your face."

It's more than I could have imagined. "And the other?"

"I'm going to keep working in the Underworld, albeit I'm going to scale back to four nights a week. It makes me happy, and even though I love you, I'm not..." She shrugs. "I'm polyamorous. It's who I am."

"I know." I'm not remotely surprised. Haven't I considered that possibility from the moment I decided on her? Still, I have to ask questions instead of blindly agreeing. "What about Hades? He'll have a problem with you working there and then coming home to me."

"Hades trusts me enough to keep business and personal separate. The secrets of the Underworld stay there, just like whatever happens here stays between us. That is, if you agree."

"I agree."

She blinks. "You're not even going to think about it first?"

"Aurora, do you honestly think I hadn't considered this from all angles before I told you I wanted to continue things past the deadline of the assignation? You love working in the Underworld; of course you were going to continue there if that was an option. It makes you happy."

"It really does," she says quietly.

"I want you to be happy." I curl my fingers at her. "Come here."

Slowly, oh, so slowly, she places her hand in mine and allows me to tug her toward me until I can wrap my arms around her. The sigh she releases as she relaxes into me is the most beautiful sound I've ever heard. I inhale her subtle vanilla scent and something in my chest unclenches. "I only have one condition."

She tenses. "What condition?"

"Talk to me. Regardless of what you're feeling, if it's a day you hate me, talk to me. I can't read your mind, and I won't be able to provide what you need if I don't know where your head is at."

"Only that?" She laughs a little. "I'll try. I can't promise perfect communication, but I promise I'll try."

"That's enough." I allow myself to inhale deeply, pulling her vanilla scent into my lungs as I hug her tightly to me. "I missed you."

She buries her face in my neck. "I missed you, too. It was driving me crazy not being around you, even when I was furious, but I couldn't come back until I figured some of my shit out."

"I'm glad you came back at all. I would have waited longer if you needed it."

Aurora runs her hands up my arms and over my shoulders to cup my face. She looks up at me, and there are no shadows in her eyes, no shields in place. She just looks relieved and happy. "Forgive me?"

"You were already forgiven the second you walked out the door." I place my hands over hers. "I know what's it's like to want revenge for pain caused and loved ones lost. It hurt, but I can't pretend I didn't deserve it." This still seems almost too good to be true, but it doesn't matter, because she's here. Against all odds, she's chosen me, and I'm going to do my damnedest to make her happy and keep her at my side.

"Even if you forgive me..." Mischief alights in her dark eyes. "I would very much like to make it up to you. Starting right now."

"Oh?" I arch my brows as she goes for the front of my slacks, undoing them quickly and shoving them down my hips. My shirt is next, and Aurora doesn't even bother with the buttons. She just pulls it over my head and tosses it on the floor. I glance at it. "Messy."

"I'll fold them later. I've missed you too much. I need you now."

I don't think I'll ever get tired of her telling me that she misses me, that she loves me. "I love you." I run my fingers through her bright-pink hair and give it a sharp tug. "But if you want to make it up to me, I'm not going to stop you."

"Good." She nudges me back to the couch and topples me onto it. Then she's between my thighs, running her hands over my hips. She hesitates. "I mean it, Malone. I did miss you. I do love you."

"I love you, too." I give her hair another little tug. "Now, show me, and then I'm going to spend the rest of the day returning the favor."

Her grin is as bright as the sun. "Yes, Mistress."

THANK you so much for reading Queen Takes Rose! I've been teasing Aurora and Malone's story nearly since book one, and I hope you enjoyed finally getting to read it! If you did, please consider leaving a review.

NEED a little more Aurora and Malone in your life! Sign up for my newsletter to receive a bonus short!

CURIOUS ABOUT SABINE VALLEY and Malone's family? I have a brand new series starting that follows the Paine brothers as they come back to Sabine Valley. Their story begins with Abel, but we will see Monroe and Cohen (Beast's ex) as well!

KEEP READING for a sneak peek of Abel!

. . .

WE TIME OUR ARRIVAL PERFECTLY. The feast is more than halfway over. The early fights, the ones people froth at the mouth for, have come and gone. By the sound of voices low in conversation, people have begun to eat and enjoy themselves, relishing the fact that it's one of the few nights a year when Sabine Valley's three factions can mingle without repercussions.

We're about to ruin their night.

We're about to ruin their whole fucking life.

I glance back at my brothers. They have their emotions locked down tightly. This *will* go our way, but it's impossible to ignore the fact that last time we were in Sabine Valley, we were running for our lives. Eight years later and it's time to settle the score. "You with me?"

One by one, they nod.

I turn without another word and lead them across the rooftops to the edge of the grounds. From this vantage point, I can see everything. The deep curve of the natural amphitheater that marks the center of the island in the center of the city. The three factions have mingled a little, but the lines are still remarkably clear. Each of the leaders have a dais at the edge of the amphitheater, creating three parts of a large triangle.

In the center of the amphitheater, two fighters are in the middle of combat. From the look of them, they're an Amazon and a Mystic. The Amazon is Latina woman who's a good six inches taller and moves with the deadly efficiency her faction is known for. The Mystic is a thin Black man with flowing robes who looks like a stiff wind will blow him over.

"Mystic will take it," Cohen murmurs at my side.

"When they're finished, we go in. Don't let anyone stop you." As long as we can get down there and issue an official challenge, there's not a damn thing any of the factions can do except meet it. The laws of the feast days are there for a reason. To ignore them is to invite ruin. That shit *should* have been enough to keep peace, but the rules didn't help my father when these fuckers slit his throat, and they didn't help me and my brothers when we were forced to flee for our lives. Now I'm going to make them choke on their goddamned laws.

As we watch, the Mystic catches the Amazon's punch in his robe, twisting the fabric to trap her. He delivers a brutal jab to her throat and bears her to the ground, punching her in the face once, twice, a third time. Her hand slaps the ground. Just like that, the fight is over.

The Herald steps forward. She's an ancient Korean woman with her long white hair pulled back in a high knot at the top of her head. "Gerald wins. The Amazons will allot him the agreed upon amount."

A cheer goes up from the wedge of the amphitheater that's mostly Mystics. They're easy to pick out because they dress like fucking weirdos. Robes in a variety of colors as if they live in another time and place, wild hair stuffed with trinkets and ribbons, some of them like to renounce shoes because it makes them feel closer to the gods or some bullshit like that. They're also smart as hell and like to use others' perceptions of them to their advantage. They're not as strong and fierce as the Amazons, not as brutal as the third faction, but there's a reason they've held their wedge of the city since its inception. They are not to be underestimated.

"Now," I murmur.

One by one, we drop off the low roof to the street. I pause long enough to ensure all seven of us are on the ground and then lead the way through the crowd. It doesn't take long for people too start noticing us. Seven men in dark clothes with murder in their eyes. Even if they don't recognize us for who we are, they begin to part, pushing each other to make way for us.

We reach the lip of the amphitheater and start down the stairs. One of the Herald's guards moves to stop us from entering the sand, but she holds up a hand and he shifts back. This woman has been Herald since I was a child, a neutral party that oversees all the feasts and calls no faction home. She surveys me and finally nods. "Have you come to challenge?"

It's obvious to everyone present that it's exactly why I'm here, but Sabine Valley is nothing without its ridiculous rituals. I can't ignore them if I want this to work. "Yes, Herald."

Her dark eyes flick over my face and those of my brother's behind me. "What grievance have you brought to us, Abel Paine?"

"My brothers and I were wronged by the leaders of the factions present." The space naturally amplifies my voice, but even if it didn't, every person present would hear me. They've all gone silent. "Seven fights for the seven lives they've ruined."

She studies me for a long moment. The Herald has never stopped someone from engaging in ritual combat during Lammas, but she still has the authority to do it. "Who will be fighting?"

"I will."

"You'll stand in proxy for your brothers?"

"Yes, Herald." Things aren't traditionally done this way, but that's going to work in my favor tonight. Those fools will look at me and think that there's no way I can possibly win seven fights. They'll happily wager the things they can least afford to lose on that assumption. And then I'm going to shove their failure down their throats and make them choke on it.

The Herald tilts her head to the side. "And the stakes?"

"For every fight I win, one of my brothers chooses a Bride as restitution."

Her eyes widen ever so slightly. "A high price."

"So was exile."

At that, she nods and turns slowly to meet each of the faction leaders' gazes in turn. I've avoided looking at them until now, but I can't avoid it any longer. First up is Aisling, queen of the Amazons. She's a fierce bitch and looks every inch of it, a lean white woman with hard green eyes and pale blond hair braided back from her face. I once watched her gut a man and walk away without so much as a hitch in her stride.

She sent her warriors to set my childhood home on fire on the night my father died.

Now to Ciar, the Mystic's leader. He's a grizzled white man with a cloud of gray hair who looks like someone boiled him down, papery skin stretched tight over muscles and tendons. He likes to pretend the gods speak through him and uses it to rule his people with an iron fist. He's also got thirteen wives at last count and dozens of children.

It was his order that commanded his people to provide the drugs that sent our household to sleep, killing dozens in the fire.

And finally the person I've both dreaded and craved seeing. I stand there and stare up at the man who was once my friend. Eli Walsh. He's filled out since I saw him last, a white guy with long-ish blond hair swept to the side and black frame glasses. He always was too pretty, and now he looks fucking flawless. Someone who didn't know better would assume he's as useless as he's pretty, and he likes to play up those perceptions. In truth, he's nearly as deadly as I am.

His father slit my father's throat and would have killed every single one of my brothers if I didn't take them and run for our lives.

All while Eli stood by and did nothing.

The Herald raises her hands. "The rewards are fair. Send your warriors."

I turn to my brothers. Six faces that I know as well as my own, and none of them look happy. They've locked their shit down and they trust me to take care of this. I pull my shirt over my head and toss it to Broderick. "Wait on the stairs."

He shakes his head, a small smile pulling at his mouth. "Never could resist a chance to take off your shirt."

"They want a show. I'm going to give it to them."

"Uh huh." He nudges Gabriel, our youngest brother, with his shoulder. "Let's give him room to work." He gives me a long look. "Don't die."

"Please. As if these assholes could kill me." Technically, fights on Lammas *can* go to the death without repercussions, but that's not on the agenda tonight. If I slaughter my way through seven of their best people, it will turn the city against me. We're back and we're here to stay, which means playing by the rules. Even if it's only obeying the spirit of the feast, rather than the explicit rules.

The faction leaders spend ten minutes communicating and then seven people move out onto the sand. I study them the same way they're studying me. Three women—all Amazons—and four men. Two from Eli's people. Two Mystics. I only recognize two of them. This should be interesting.

The first steps forward. It's one of Eli's people, a Latino

man built like a prize fighter. He's light on his feet as he approaches me. I roll my shoulders and take a slow breathe.

Eight years of exile. Eight years of fighting and scraping and clawing for survival in a world that wants nothing more than to eliminate me and my brothers.

It ends tonight.

The Herald lifts her hand. "Begin."

My opponent rushes me. He's even faster than I expect and he moves like he knows what he's doing. I hold perfectly still as he closes the distance between us. He takes that as my being unprepared and strikes with an upper cut that would take off my head if it landed.

I shift back just enough that he misses. He sank too much into that punch and it leaves him wide open. I hammer a brutal punch into his ribs. Something cracks beneath my fist and he stumbles. I don't give him time to recover. I kick his knee, dislocating it, and then punch him in the face.

He hits the ground and doesn't get up.

One of the Herald's people comes over and crouches next to him. She presses two fingers to his neck. "He's alive."

The Herald nods. "Abel wins the first match. The prize?"

I glance at Gabriel. My youngest brother is pale and looks vaguely sick, but he steps forward and lifts his chin. "I claim Fallon of the Mystics as my Bride."

A murmur goes through the crowd in a wave. I hold my breath as I wait to see what they'll do. Ciar looks like he wants to kill us, but he finally waves a hand and a gorgeous redhead steps forward. She comes down the stairs quickly, moving with a grace that screams combat training. Her face shows nothing as she crosses to stand next to Gabriel.

One down, six to go.

The factions sent their best. I'm better. I defeat them one

by one. I'm not showy, choosing to conserve energy instead of being entertaining. One by one, my brothers claim their Brides. Sons and daughters, siblings, loved ones of the people responsible for our father's death, for our exile.

Until there's only one left.

He's a giant of a man, a huge white guy who has six inches on me and probably outweighs me by fifty pounds. I turn my head and spit blood—the last Amazon got in a couple good hits—and motion. "Let's get this over with."

The crowd doesn't cheer, doesn't speak, doesn't seem to breathe. Guess I'm being entertaining, after all.

The giant lumbers toward me. Too slow. This is their final fighter? I almost laugh at the absurdity of it. This time, I don't wait for him to reach me. I rush forward and hit my knees, driving my fist up into his balls with everything I have. He makes a high-pitched whistling sound and topples, curling in on himself like a dead bug.

I climb to my feet and look down. He's too busy clutching his balls to tap out, but it's clear he's not getting up anytime soon.

The Herald raises her eyebrows. "Abel wins the final match. The prize?"

Here it is. The thing I've been waiting for. I turn and find Eli. He's leaning forward, his elbows propped on his knees. His expression is smooth and free of worry, but that shit doesn't fool me.

I give him a bloody grin. "I choose Harlow Byrne."

Eli's woman.

ORDER ABEL NOW!

ACKNOWLEDGMENTS

Thank you to all the readers who have come on this journey with me. The Wicked Villains has been such a joy to write and your enthusiastic reception of it has inspired me in such a huge way. None of it would be possible without you. Thank you.

Biggest thanks to Jenny Nordbak and Sarah Hawley and the Wicked Wallflower Club Facebook group. Without all of you, this series never would have happened, and Hades wouldn't have a BDSM club named the Underworld.

Thank you to Asa Maria Bradley, Piper J. Drake, Nisha Sharma, and Andie J. Christopher for listening to me ramble on about ideas and plot holes and cover goodness and "Do you think it's too far if..." questions.

Last, but never least, thank you to Tim. This year has been... a lot, and you've been my rock through it all. Thank you for the support, for lending me some of your Self Assurance when I need it most, and for packing a couple hundred signed book packages. Love you, always and forever.

ABOUT THE AUTHOR

Katee Robert is a *New York Times* and USA Today bestselling author of contemporary romance and romantic suspense. *Entertainment Weekly* calls her writing "unspeakably hot." Her books have sold over a million copies. She lives in the Pacific Northwest with her husband, children, a cat who thinks he's a dog, and two Great Danes who think they're lap dogs.

www.kateerobert.com

Made in United States
Orlando, FL
29 November 2022

25195667R00161